The Novgorod Master

The Novgorod Master

Christopher Arthur

Pearl Press

The moral right of Christopher Arthur has been asserted
First published in Great Britain by Pearl Press Limited

ISBN 978-0-9565001-5-1

Printed by Good News, Ongar, Essex. England

First of all my warm thanks to Nilda Ginn for casting her highly discerning eye over the texts of these stories as they were written and for her critical appraisal.

My thanks also to Mervyn Burleigh for his shrewd observations - as well as for the contents of his bathroom shelf which provided the trigger for one of the stories!

Contents

The Novgorod Master

The first thing that struck Nicko when he saw Viktor across the restaurant was that he had put on weight. For a man only in his mid twenties he looked a bit too comfortable, though it went well enough with his stocky Russian build. Even before he reached his table, where he was standing to greet him, Nicko sensed that Viktor was doing well.

'Good to see you again, old boy', said Viktor in his pleasantly blended plummy English and Russian accents as he hugged him warmly.

England, it seemed, had retained its mark on his wardrobe as well. He was wearing his old school tie- silk of course - and his shirt might have been bought in Jermyn Street. His jacket was a rugged tweed, which Nicko, who favoured heavier, more traditional fabrics, noted with approval.

'Vera would have liked to be here to meet you, but she's at home doing her duty with the malchik,' Viktor explained. 'I say duty, but I can't tear her away from that child. How do you say it in English? Not with wild horses?'

'It'll do,' said Nicko. 'The same old Viktor, I see, still collecting English idioms. The leopard hasn't changed his spots.'

The two young men laughed.

'But she's dying to meet you and to introduce you to Nikoshka,' went on Viktor. 'After all, the malchik does bear your name.'

'Is that the reason you gave it to him? It hadn't occurred to me. Nikolas is a common enough Russian name, isn't it?'

'Pravda,' said Viktor, 'but that's no reason for not giving him the name of my dearest English friend, Nicholas Orloff is it? Or should I say my Russian friend?- my Old Russian- friend?'

His ponderous irony had not changed.

'You know something, Vik?' Nicko said.

'You're still full of shit.'

They both laughed and Viktor squeezed his friend's shoulder affectionately. 'What's it to be then- to kick off with I mean? Vodka?'

'I think I'd better go easy on the vodka,' said Nicko, 'especially in your company.'

'Oh dear, as bad as that, is it?' sighed Viktor. 'And talking of such things, how is - what is he called? Uncle Frank? You told me that his precious vase was glued together again and looks as good as new.'

'He's dead.'

'What? Uncle Frank dead? Poor old Uncle Frank! I hope his heart didn't break at the same time as his vase. Was he a very old man?'

'Not especially- somewhere in his seventies.'

'Old enough for a Russian, maybe, but these days you English are expected to live a bit longer than that. And his collection? Including the what-do-you-call-it?' He eyed Nicko thoughtfully.

'The krater - the wine bowl. All gone - packed off to the Ashmolean - in Oxford. Lock, stock and barrel.'

'Say that again, Nicko.'

'Piss off Vik. The whole bloody lot. Every single piece of it. I don't think he trusted his own godson to look after it, not after our symposium.'

Viktor laughed. 'Our 'Russian' symposium, you mean. And while we're on the subject, don't you think it's time we got- how do you say - stuck in?'

'What? Hold another Russian symposium, you mean? Right here, in the restaurant? Well, I suppose we could trash the place readily enough. And we are in Russia, after all. That chandelier would go for starters.'

Viktor laughed. 'Well, it's sad about Uncle Frank's collection all the same, to lose it like that, but it's water under the bridge by now, I expect. Is that right?'

'Viktor, fuck off, will you?' returned Nicko, giving him a playful punch.

Viktor ordered a bottle of vodka and a menu.

'I'm really looking forward to meeting Vera and Nikoshka,' his friend told him.

'And you? Nothing? How do you say? Nothing in the pipeline?'

'Nothing so far,' said Nicko, 'but, for Christ's sake, Viktor, give me a chance, won't you? When I'm thirty-five I'll start to worry about things like that. I need to make some money first. I don't have your knack. The stuff seems to stick to your fingers. I'm not exactly a New

Russian, you know.'

His old school friend said nothing, but raised his eyebrows and rocked his head from side to side, as if weighing up the merits of his statement.

It was a curious friendship that had grown up in an English public school between two products of Russia's turbulent twentieth century: Nicholas Orloff, the great-grandchild of an aristocratic exile from the Bolshevik Revolution and Viktor Nikishov, the scion of a Stalinist satrap, a man who had been master of life and death in the notorious Kolyma gold camps in the remote east. Viktor was a New Russian while Nicko was descended from the blue-blooded old kind. Both had been conscious of this distinction and a dash of snobbery lurked below the surface in Nicko's attitude towards his friend, but snobbery tinged with a romantic envy of the others more palpable Russianness. For Nicko's vision of the land of his Orloff ancestors had been largely coloured by reading nineteenth century Russian novels - in English translation, of course. He probably wouldn't have found a great deal to share with the brash New Russian if he hadn't cast him in his mind's eye as a character out of Gogol.

The event that had sealed the bond between them had been the disastrous so-called symposium that had taken place in the Chelsea flat of Nicko's godfather - Uncle Frank- when the pair of them had got hopelessly drunk together and smashed the krater, the centrepiece of his fine collection of fifth century B.C. Athenian red figure ware. Both boys had only recently left school and Nicko had fled with his chum to St Petersburg to fill in his gap year before starting university, leaving Uncle Frank to pick up the pieces of his shattered krater when he returned from his holiday.

In St Petersburg Nicko had shared a flat with Viktor, who had already been set up on his own by his astronomically rich parents. But a ready-made fortune did not turn this spoiled young Russian into an indolent lie-abed. On the contrary the business bug was already coursing in his veins and the itch to trade was irresistible. His experience of an English public school had opened his eyes to the opportunities for a niche market of New Russians in search of the trappings of what might loosely be defined as an English upper-class lifestyle. This covered all sorts of things from traditional countrywear to household antiques.

And this was where Nicko fitted in. In that gap year with his friend he had helped him set up in a shop off the Nevsky Prospekt. It was Viktor's first venture and he had to feel his way. Nicko had no entrepreneurial skills to offer, but while the Russian boy managed to run merchandise to earth from goodness knows where - Nicko never really found out - the English one provided the business with a gentle face, charming Russians by his Englishness and at the same time proving adept at dealing with foreign tourists on the lookout for Russian things. Viktor had a plentiful supply of those - hand-painted lacquer boxes, matrioshka dolls and even icons - all of the very best quality for the upper end of the market.

Meanwhile Nicko's father kept him appraised of the consequences of the outrage committed in Uncle Frank's flat, above all of the fate of the Athenian krater. He was suitably stern with his son and insisted on paying the cost of restoring the piece himself while threatening to deduct the entire sum from the young man's allowance. Nicko duly expressed contrition and on his return to England, having grovelled, was received back into the bosom of the family - his mother having poured a great deal of oil on some very choppy waters. After which he went up to St Andrews University to read History where he managed to keep his nose clean for the duration.

Viktor meanwhile missed out on university altogether - he was far too busy running a business.

It went without saying that Nicko's father had not much time for Viktor, seeing him as the kind of spiv, which, as the descendant of an aristocratic White Russian officer, he heartily despised. He never could forgive what the Bolsheviks and their minions had done to his family's fortunes. At the same time he was concerned about Nicko - who unlike his younger sister - seemed to have no clear sense of direction in his life. He left university with a lower second and no real idea of what to do with it, but his year spent in St Petersburg with Viktor inclined him in a vague sort of way towards something in the Fine Arts field. He had specialised in the Italian Renaissance for his history degree and wondered if he could make something out of that.

His father had an old friend who worked in the antique trade, mostly buying up stuff at country house sales and the like and selling it on, so he approached him about Nicko.

Freddie Ryedale was what was euphemistically described as a confirmed bachelor who readily took to the pleasantly polished young man just down from university.

'I don't suppose I have to warn you about Freddie,' the father cautioned his son.

'You mean I have to keep my bum against the wall Dad?' replied Nicko.

'In a manner of speaking yes, but I wouldn't have expressed it in quite, such vivid terms.'

'Having managed to survive an English public school I daresay I can handle it.'

'As long as you bear it in mind, that's all. Actually I believe Freddie's a perfectly harmless old thing. If he is a homosexual he's almost certainly the repressed kind.'

'A bit like Uncle Frank, you mean? He was gay, wasn't he?'

'And another thing,' Nicko's father went on, ignoring the mention of Uncle Frank, 'he won't be able to pay you very much either. It'll be pocket money and nothing more.'

Freddie Ryedale worked from a large old farm house in Norfolk, not far from Aylesham, but his forays with a van sometimes took him as far afield as the North Riding of Yorkshire. He could have been said to work the east side of the country and was prepared to take anything that caught his eye. And it was a reasonably good eye too, especially for seventeenth century English oak furniture and, by way of contrast, eighteenth and early nineteenth century topographical paintings and landscapes. He had made one bad mistake in his life though, when an early Constable had come his way, which had only been properly identified after it had passed through his hands for a tiny fraction of its real worth, It was the kind of gaffe he vowed never to repeat. His friends in the trade looking at his relatively modest returns tended to hark back to it among themselves and talk about 'Ryedale's luck', but Freddie did not repine as long as he could go on visiting the places and mixing with the kind of people he liked. As a one man band he made just about enough to keep himself afloat, but no more than that.

And now, warmed by Nicko's good looks and manners, he reined back whatever less than Platonic thoughts he might have entertained about the lad. Nicko was urbane and not the least bit of a threat to the tenor of Freddie's existence.

He gave him the spare room in his house and took him out straight

7

away on his expeditions to learn the trade, in the course of which Nicko soon began to pick up a lot about old furniture, china and of course something of provincial painters of landscapes and topographical pictures as well.

Nicko felt at home in the countryside and enjoyed the work except for one thing. He didn't earn a bean.

He had already sacrificed one summer to working with Freddie and, despite the pleasure he found in the work, he felt he deserved a break. He had no money put by from his notional salary to afford a holiday while at the same time he hardly liked to go to his father cap in hand. The Greek vase incident cast a long shadow. So, perhaps inevitably, it came down to Viktor with whom he had kept in fitful contact by e-mail ever since their time together in St Petersburg.

They had eyed each other's progress with curiosity, Nicko probably revealing a great deal more about his circumstances than Viktor about his. The latter had expressed interest in Nicko's attempt to get into the world of antiques, especially as it was a line he appeared to be most actively pursuing himself. Nor could it have been hard to guess why the young Russian entrepreneur should have wanted to keep in with his former school fellow. Nicko saw it too, of course, but his feelings for his old chum - with which his wistful vision of the lost land of his ancestors was inextricably mixed up - still worked their magic. Moreover his friend was rich while he was still relatively poor. He wanted a holiday and Viktor offered him the chance of one- in Russia - when he could meet his wife and the new baby for the first time.

Viktor had shifted his base from St Petersburg to Novgorod which put him closer to Moscow and was a pleasantly green open-looking city. He had left Nicko to make his own way there on the night train from Moscow and to meet him at a fashionable restaurant in the old kremlin walls at midday, pleading an engagement which had taken him out of town overnight and prevented him from meeting his friend at the station, but he assured him that he was expected to stay with him in his flat on the other side of the river.

So Nicko had left his bag at the station and wandered through the park near the river in the morning sunshine, stopping a couple of times for a coffee and a beer, before inspecting Novgorod's great medieval kremlin at leisure, and eventually making his way to the restaurant where he was to meet his friend.

It had occurred to Nicko as he approached Viktor across the dimly-lit cavernous restaurant that the Russian had contrived it this way: standing behind the table with its snow white cloth and napery and its gleaming cutlery and glass, his arms half-raised, ready to embrace his old school chum.

The vodka got things moving, blinys and caviar followed and a white Georgian wine, then a run of Russian dishes, whose rich flavours were not easy to identify, but were subtle and rather mysterious, a bit like Viktor himself. In spite of his cautiousness, something he had managed to maintain surprisingly well during the months in St Petersburg living with his friend in the shocked aftermath of the infamous symposium, Nicko found himself drinking a good deal. Red wine followed the white while brandy arrived with the coffee. The bottle was placed on the table and Viktor plied his friend.

'When do we start playing monkeys on the chandelier?' he joked.

'My great-grandfather and his brother officers used to take pot shots at them with their revolvers,' said Nicko.

'My people smashed a good few in their time too,' supplied Viktor, determined to uphold the Stalinist service nobility's reputation

9

for drunken vandalism against the pretentions of the more effete Tsarist Officer Corps.

They giggled like a pair of small boys as fresh coffee arrived: the waiter was in no hurry to bring the bill despite the fact that it was almost the middle of the afternoon, Viktor had seen to everything.

'Now,' he said, placing an affectionate hand on his friend's shoulder, 'Tell me all about it.'

'All about what?' asked Nicko. The drink had made him expansive, but had not destroyed his ability to think straight. It was enough nevertheless to make him just a shade reckless.

'Your work, buying and selling nice things, the places you visit, those houses in the beautiful English countryside.'

'I'm still learning Vik, but slowly, gradually building up the knowledge. It's the only way to do it, not to try to cram it in all at once. I suppose Petersburg gave me a taste for it. I have you to thank for that.'

Viktor dipped his head in a patronising gesture of acknowledgement, which seemed a little odd coming from one who was almost exactly the same age as his friend.

'But...'

'Ah, but.'

There's still no bloody money, Vik. Freddie's a super chap and all that, but can only pay me a pittance.'

'Tell me about Freddie,'

'About my father's age. Perhaps a few years younger. Unmarried, lives for his work.'

'A bit like Uncle Frank maybe?'

'Possibly, but more down to earth than him, I guess.'

'I see.' Viktor did not develop the thought that was apparently passing through his mind.

'He loves his work, but never has any fucking money or so it seems. Mind you he might once have done - if he hadn't let the thing slip though his fingers.'

'Let what thing slip though his fingers?'

'A Constable. You know Constable? One of our two finest nineteenth century landscape painters.'

'And he lost it?

'Sold it on for next to nothing before anyone knew what it was. He's never had another break like it- or so he claims.'

'Poor old Freddie. Even worse than Uncle Frank's vase being smashed by the sound of it. At least he was left with the pieces.'

'Shut up about that fucking vase, Vik.'

'Is he Uncle Freddie?'

'No, of course he's not.'

'So plain Freddie then, who could do with a bob or two? Have said that right?'

'Spot on Vik. Do I have to keep telling you?'

'And you're fond of Freddie?'

'Sure. He's a decent enough guy.'

Viktor looked thoughtful and reached for the brandy bottle.

'Steady on,' Nicko warned him. 'Remember I've still got to meet your wife and the malchik.'

'Good thinking,' said Viktor. 'Does that sound right?'

'Fuck off, Vik. You know it does!' replied Nicko testily.

'I'd rather tike to meet your friend Freddie,' mused Viktor, 'but then perhaps that mightn't really be necessary.' He eyed Nicko thoughtfully.

'Oho? What cunning plan is this?'

'Do you feel up to it?'

'Up to what?'

'You mentioned who was it? A painter. Constable.'

'Freddie Ryedale's blackest hour.'

'Freddie deals mostly in pictures?'

'Among other things.'

'We must think more about this,' said Viktor. 'But now it's time to meet my dear wife and the Tsarovich, my little Nikoshka.'

He called for the bill which he settled with a credit card, leaving the waiter a generous cash tip at the same time.

'Are you steady on your feet?' he asked Nicko.

'I think so.'

'We'll take a taxi anyway. You have a bag?'

'At the station.'

The girl at the cash desk rang for a taxi and they wandered down the wide stairs that led to the entrance built into the inside of the kremlin wall.

Having collected Nicko's luggage, the taxi took them across the river, skirting the religious heart of medieval Novgorod to a pleasant street of stuccoed nineteenth century houses. Little gardens lay behind them, rather unkempt in the Russian way that Nicko liked. It was late in the afternoon and the street was empty.

Viktor led the way through the big double door of one of the houses that gave onto the broad pavement.

'We live on what you in England call the first floor,' he explained, 'the one above the ground.'

'I like the look of this,' said Nicko, glancing down the street with approval as they entered.

'It's not the whole story. Yes?'

'Yes Viktor. You mean there's something else as well.'

'Kaneshna. Tomorrow I will take you to see our dacha.'

'You have a dacha? Already? But of course you have. I might have guessed. You're not letting the grass grow under your feet, are you? Now work that one out.' Nicko gave his chum a playful nudge.

'Fuck off, Nikoshka,' said Viktor.

Despite the house being spacious and predating the great flat building era of Khruschev's time, the stairwell was dingy with the faintly sour, unventilated smell common to so many Russian stairwells. Viktor was conscious of the anomaly.

'The usual thing,' he told his friend. 'We Russians are all the same. We won't - how do you say? - lift a finger to look after the what-do-you-call-it, the communal space?'

'That's one of the things that makes you so exotic. The squalor on the outside and then lo, it's opposite once you get inside.'

'Russia in a nutshell? Right?'

'Quite so, Viktor.'

'We curl up in the warmth and comfort of our homes and shut the nasty world out. Like - how do I say? Returning to the womb?'

They reached a large door with a finely carved frame on the landing where Viktor rang the bell.

Soft slippered footsteps approached it and Vera opened it.

'Welcome,' she said to Nicko in English.

'Try him in Russian,' said Viktor, giving his wife a peck on the cheek. 'He likes to call himself one.' This was said in English for the benefit of the guest.

Nicko gave Vera a peck on the cheek as well.

'The malchik has been asleep. He's just waking up now,' Vera informed them.

Viktor meanwhile slipped off his shoes and Nicko did likewise.

'Try these for size,' said Viktor, offering him a pair of slippers.

Nicko shuffled into the house through the ample vestibule and into a living room, the double glazed doors of which Viktor threw open before him with a ceremonial flourish. It was a good deal larger than the rooms in most Russian flats. It had a high ceiling and a cornice from which several oil paintings in heavy gilt frames hung by cords. The floor was a polished parquet with several Turkish rugs distributed about it. A large round mahogany table with a lace-ringed cloth stood near the window where the light filtered gently though the lace curtains which were stirring in a slight draught. There were a couple of deep leather upholstered sofas and several chairs covered in throws with pleasantly-faded oriental patterns. On a bulky, almost baroque dresser stood a vast samova. An ikon and lamp were set in one corner of the room.

'What do you think?' said Viktor.

Nicko nodded his appreciation in a way that left no doubt about its genuineness.

'Not bad for a New Russian, wouldn't you say?' Viktor ventured with the sly lowering of an eyelid.

'I wasn't going to say that.'

'But you were thinking it all the same. Anyway, it was Vera who set it up,' Viktor explained. 'She has a very good eye.'

'So I can see. I'm impressed.' Nicko looked round for Vera who had not followed them into the room. 'Where has she gone, by the way?'

As he spoke Vera appeared in the doorway, carrying a sleepy child in her arms.

'I hope you haven't woken him up for my sake,' Nicko said.

'He was starting to wake up anyway.'

Vera spoke clear, almost accentless English.

'Where did you learn your English?' asked Nicko.

'In the Pedagogical Institute in St Peterburg,' Vera replied, 'and then I worked as a tourist guide. I've done a couple of trips as well.'

She handed the baby to her husband. 'Tea?' she asked.

'Kaneshna,' said her husband.

'Kaneshna,' repeated Vera as she left the room for the kitchen.

Viktor bounced little Nickoshka in his lap who stared at his namesake with big round eyes.

'He's enchanting,' said Nicko. 'I'm trying to figure out which one of you he's like'

'His mother,' said Viktor.

'Hm, more like himself than either of you, I'd say.'

'Here. Get some practice.' Viktor handed the child to his friend.

The child wriggled a little at first, resisting the transfer, but soon settled down when Nicko tapped him gently on the end of his tiny snub nose and bounced him on his knees.

Vera returned with the tea and a large bowl of raspberry jam and looked pleased at what she found.

'I see you've made friends quickly,' she said.

'He's gorgeous. You must be terribly proud of him,' gushed Nicko.

'Kaneshna,' said the child's father.

'I'd like to take him back to England with me. May I?'

Both parents laughed. Vera poured the tea and supplied a bowl of lemon slices, then retrieved the child. She dipped a spoon into the jam and fed it to him. All the time she asked Nicko questions about England: his university and what he was doing now. Then, offering Nikoshka to her husband again, she took Nicko to his bedroom, having pointed the way to the bathroom.

'You must be tired,' she said. 'I can never sleep properly on trains.'

'I'm all right,' Nicko replied, 'but I nearly fell out of the bunk.'

'It was a hard carriage?'

'I'm afraid so.'

'When you return to Moscow we must make sure you have a better one,' she said. 'But it's so good to see you. Viktor has told me such a lot about you.'

Nicko laughed and said that he hoped it was the right things.

'Kaneshna - of course.'

'This room looks comfortable,' said Nicko. 'It's so much bigger than you see in most Russian flats.'

'The house is old and was the home of a bourgeois. I love its big rooms.'

Nicko concurred.

'Would you like to rest?' Vera asked.

'It might be nice to stretch out for a bit, though I don't suppose I'll sleep,' said Nicko.

Vera left him and he lay down on the bed.

A few minutes later she put her head round the door.

'Not asleep?' she said.

'I'm afraid not, but your bed is very comfortable.'

'Shall I draw the curtains?'

'One of them,' said Nicko, 'but leave the other. I rather like the light at this time of day.'

He looked at Vera as she crossed the room, really for the first time.

She was the opposite of Viktor who was square and dark, and already running to fat.

Vera was also Slavic, but in a different mode. She was slim for a start, fair haired and blue eyed with a slightly repoussé nose and high cheekbones which seemed so typically Russian. Nicko approved of the way she dressed, nothing showy. He liked the muted lilac of her slacks which came to just below her knees and her chunky pale grey sweater. She wore a small pearl in each ear lobe, but no make-up. She didn't need any.

'Better?' she said, turning back to Nicko.

'Perfect,' he replied.

Nicko caught himself wondering what a girl like Vera was doing married to a spiv like Viktor.

'Have a good rest,' she said, leaving the room once more.

Nicko lay there, woolgathering. Though he still knew practically nothing about Vera or even where his friend had first met her, he found himself thinking about her to the exclusion of anything else. She had a simplicity which appealed to him as well as seeming to be acute. He wanted to try her on Russian literature - something which Viktor had always shied off. In Nicko's eyes he redeemed himself by appearing as a character out of a Russian novel. He could not make up his mind which one, but Dead Souls by Gogol seemed the most likely. With Vera he felt that he might actually be able to discuss artistic questions without attaching monetary value to them - or least that was the impression she had given him on this first encounter.

Nicko took a book from his bag and read a bit as the light eventually began to fade. He thought he would wait until his hosts summoned him. And sure enough, when his watch told him that it was seven o'clock there came a tap at the door.

'Yes?' Nicko called.

It was Viktor this time who stuck his head round the door. 'Not in - how do you say it - a state of nature?'

'It wouldn't matter if I was, would it? You've seen me that way often enough before.'

'All boys together - like in our Russian banya. Do you fancy one, by the way? We can get one going up at the dacha.'

'I'm on,' said Nicko.

'Good. We eat in a few minutes.'

'God, I don't know where I could put another meal.'

'Tomorrow you can walk it off with some sightseeing - before we go out to the dacha,' Viktor told him, as he slipped away.

Nicko put his feet into the slippers - which were a size too big for him, and shuffled out into the vestibule. It was starting to get dark, but there was a light on in the living room. Viktor was in there alone, poring over what looked like a sheaf of accounts.

'Come and sit down, old boy,' he said, at the same time reaching into the dresser cupboard for a couple of glasses.

'Golly,' said Nicko. 'I don't know where I can put any more drink. I'm sure Vera is a brilliant cook, but I hope she isn't preparing a big meal. We can leave that till tomorrow at the dacha, can't we? Twice in one day is more than I can manage.'

'What kind of a Russian are you?' laughed Viktor. 'But Vera understands. She won't overload you. As a matter of fact she thinks I'm getting too fat.'

'She's quite right Vik - if you don't mind my saying so. You might spoil your good looks if you're not careful.'

'Fuck off,' said the Russian in a whisper, deferring, it seemed, to his wife who presumably was within earshot.

He went out and returned with what looked like rollmop herrings on a plate and a decanter of chilled vodka.

'You bloody man, you're quite impossible,' groaned Nicko.

Viktor charged the glasses. 'Nasdarovia,' he said and downed his in one.

Nicko only sipped his glass.

'Now,' said Viktor. 'About Freddie?'

'What about Freddie?'

'He buys up pictures, and sells them on, right?'

'Right.'

'I might be able to help him there. What I mean is I could make a lot more money for him than he does now, if what you tell me is true.'

Nicko frowned and his friend noted the mistrust in his face.

'Look old boy, it isn't very difficult. There are plenty of people I know who would be willing to pay a hell of a lot more for the sort of thing he has to offer than the folks do in his own country. Believe me, Nikoshka, I do know my own kind.'

'I don't doubt that for one second, Vik.'

'I've been thinking - quite seriously. But I think we can talk about it at the dacha. After that banya.' He recharged his glass and threw it back in one. 'Nasdarovia,' he said again. You're not drinking, Nikoshka.' He put a hand on Nicko's arm. 'But don't worry. Take your time.'

Vera appeared and said something to her husband in Russian. 'Would you like to eat?' she said to Nicko in English.

'You really should try him in Russian,' her husband told her rather peremptorily. 'He can speak it perfectly well - if he bothers. But I know my Nicko from the old times. He's a very lazy boy. You have to be strict with him.'

Nicko and Vera smiled at each other.

'I'm sure it'll be lovely, but I don't think I have room for very much,' he said to her.

She nodded and smiled and Viktor lead the way into the dining room.

Vera had got it right. Instead of loading Nicko with a lot more food, she had scrambled some eggs which she served up with dark rye bread. This was followed by a good old-fashioned compot.

'My babushka's recipe,' she told Nicko.

'And how can you improve on that?' he enthused. 'Grandmothers' recipes always turn out to be the best. God save the Tsarovich, Nikoshka!' he declared, raising the remains of his vodka which he had brought through with him from the living room in a toast to the infant sitting in the high chair.

Vera looked wistful and sighed. Then Nicko remembered the fate of the last Russian Tsarovich, the child Alexis, murdered in cold blood by Bolshevik fanatics. It was still an unhealed wound running through Russian life, still the occasion for maternal sighs that such an atrocity should ever have been committed in the name of so-called progress - a crime, moreover, unforgiven by his own family.

They did not sit about for long. Tomorrow at the dacha would be the occasion to open out in the proper Russian fashion.

'An early night?' suggested Viktor and Nicko concurred.

'Have you got everything you need?' Vera asked her guest.

'Kaneshna,' said Nicko. 'Spasibo.'

She followed him into the room and instead of going straight out again Vera sat down on the bed and, locking him in her arms, hugged him tightly and planted a kiss on his lips.

Nicko's head swam and he prolonged the kiss as their tongues met to release a further charge. 'You're a beautiful boy,' Vera whispered.

'And you're a beautiful girl,' he murmured.

'I hope my Nikoshka grows up to be just like you.'

'He's beautiful as he is.., like his mother,'

Vera got up without another word and left the room, shutting the door quietly behind her.

Nicko switched off the light and lay back. That he might have cheated on his old school friend never crossed his mind.

It was a while before he slept. In the matter of girls Nicko was surprisingly, indeed quite unfashionably, innocent. He had kissed them enough times before, but had always fallen short of a final consummation. It had been fleetingly pleasurable, but this time something remained. It was almost as if Vera was still there, her head resting on the pillow beside his own. He turned to caress the place where it would have been and his loins throbbed insistently.

Eventually he went to sleep with Vera hovering on the edge of his dream - never quite at its centre, but always present, colouring it.

When he woke it was Viktor looking down at him with little Nikoshka in his arms. The child reached out and tugged a loose lock of hair hanging over Nicko's brow.

'He remembers you,' Viktor said. 'His Uncle Nicko.'

'What time is it?' said Nicko, sitting up.

'Not late,' his friend told him 'It's just gone eight o'clock. Vera's doing some breakfast.' Nicko could hear someone singing softly in the kitchen.

'She's got a nice voice,' he said. 'She's a woman of parts.'

Having said it he wished he had expressed it slightly differently, but any innuendo seemed to have been lost on Viktor.

Vera busied herself in the living room while the two young men idled through their breakfast in the kitchen.

'I'll show you a bit of Novgorod, Viktor told his friend. 'For lunch we can have a beer and a kebab and then in the afternoon we will go out to the dacha. I will have to get the fire going.'

'I like the look of Novgorod,' said Nicko. 'It was a good idea moving down here.'

'I still keep the shop in Petersburg,' explained Viktor, 'but this is quieter - and more private.'

'I must see more of it after the dacha,' Nicko said.

'And you and I must put our heads together while we're there. Yes?'

'Yes, Viktor.'

Vera had remained in the living room and her husband dumped their dirty plates in the sink. Little Nikoshka who was starting to crawl appeared on the threshold to be scooped up by his father who made baby talk to him.

'That sounds much the same as it does in English,' Nicko pointed out.

Viktor whisked the child through to his mother who remained busy in the other room.

As he went out of the flat with Nicko he called 'Goodbye darling, we'll be back at two,' in English to Vera.

Vera answered and as they shut the door she started to sing.

'She doesn't usually sing so much,' pointed out Viktor. 'That's something you must have done to her.'

Nicko blushed and did not reply.

They walked back towards the river and the Kremlin through the park where Viktor lead his guest off into what was known as Yaroslav's Court. It had been old Novgorod's market, as Viktor explained, but all that remained of that now was a seventeenth century arcade fronting the Volkov River. It stood there, looking oddly pointless in an open space.

Nicko was struck by how green and spacious Novgorod looked, especially under the benign summer sky. There was a soft breeze which gently eased a scattering of cumulus clouds along.

'You did well coming to live here,' he told his friend.

Viktor took him into the Court Cathedral of St Nicholas. 'Your very own saint,' he said. 'And its all that's left of the palace complex of the Princes of Novgorod.'

It had recently been restored and together they looked at the fragments of the twelfth century frescoes, including the one of Job covered with boils while his wife passed him food on the end of a pole.

'I hope my wife will do the same for me when I'm in that condition,' joked Viktor. Then they crossed the footbridge that lead to the main east gate of the Kremlin.

At the end of the bridge opposite the Kremlin gate was a large cafe tent which sold draught beer and kebabs. They went inside and sat at one of the tables.

'Let this be on me,' Nicko said.

But of course Viktor wouldn't hear of it. 'Later,' he said, 'before you go home.'

Nicko didn't argue.

'Tell me,' said his friend, taking a big pull at his beer, 'what do you think of Vera?' Viktor looked at him closely as he said it, but there was nothing in his tone to suggest that he suspected what had actually passed between his wife and their guest.

'Impeccably good taste on your part,' his friend assured him, trying to make light of it. 'I couldn't have got it better myself. And little Nikoshka. He's a delight. You're a lucky sod, Vik.'

Viktor nodded and beamed a trifle complacently. 'Yes, I suppose I am.'

After they had eaten they wandered into the Kremlin itself, but did not go into the Cathedral of Saint Sophia, Viktor suggesting that they stored it up until after they had back from the dacha. Instead they ambled under the trees in the extensive park that lay along the river bank. They drank a coffee at a small open air cafe where they lingered before Viktor took his friend into the streets that lay behind the kremlin.

'It's so peaceful here,' Nicko said. 'It makes me feel quite drowsy.'

Then they wandered back to the footbridge and stopped to gaze along the great wide Volkov River to the south where it flowed through a grassy plain scattered with copses of birch and other trees. The golden cupola of a church caught the sunlight a short distance from its bank in the middle distance.

'This is almost a cliché of Old Russia,' declared Nicko. 'Levitan might have painted this scene.'

'Probably he did,' said his friend. 'And while we're on that subject...' But he didn't continue, he paused and looked at Nicko in his rather watchful way instead.

After that they wandered slowly homeward.

Vera had been busy, packing up for a couple of days at the dacha. She had loaded two big plastic containers with food and drink, which her husband opened again and inspected.

'What's the matter?' she said. 'I haven't forgotten your vodka!' She grinned at Nicko as she spoke. 'We Russians,' she added.

'Careful what you say. He thinks he's one too, don't forget,' put in Viktor. 'A Count Orloff, no less!'

Together they loaded up the car, Nicko carrying down a large bag holding the baby's things. He carried a big teddy bear under his arm and it occurred to him that it might have been a good idea for him to have brought a present for the child from England. It was something he wouldn't forget in future.

The car was in a lock-up at the end of the street and Viktor went to fetch it. Then he drove them in a southerly direction along the river bank.

'We are right out in the country,' he explained to Nicko. 'I don't like being too close to other people.'

'Me neither,' his friend assured him.

The dacha stood on its own, screened on two sides by copses of birch trees. 'Pure Levitan,' declared Nicko, trying to sound as au fait with Russian art as possible for the benefit of Vera.

'You know Levitan?' she asked.

'Of course. I love his work.'

'You have visited the Tretyakov?'

'Once.'

'We must go there together.'

Nicko wondered if the 'we' included her husband.

But now he was climbing out of the car and admiring the dacha. It was spanking new, but not built by his own hands Viktor informed him. 'I know some people do,' he said. 'But I'm not one of them. If I can pay someone to do a thing like that I will.'

It was built in the traditional style of a Russian isba with elaborately carved and brightly painted window frames, a steeply-pitched roof with wooden tiles and finials above each gable. But unlike most isbas it had two storeys and an outside staircase leading up to a balcony, also rendered in a folkish style.

Nicko wasn't quite sure about it at close quarters but managed to say the right thing. 'Most impressive,' he said.

'It needs time Vera,' said. 'Things always look better when they have got a bit older.'

'Exactly so,' enthused Nicko. 'In two or three years time it's going to look great. It'll be real Levitan then.'

'The garden's round the other side,' Viktor said, 'and the banya.'

He lead the way up the stairs onto the balcony.

There was a central fireplace in the middle of an open space. A table with chairs whose backs were carved in a folk style like the windows occupied one side. A sofa with a Turkey rug pinned on the wall behind it and a couple of armchairs were on the other. A couple of small rooms lead off it. The place had an air of pleasantly-contrived simplicity about it.

The kitchen is downstairs and there is a cellar, Viktor explained. 'Oh and the loo - I'm afraid you have to go outside for that. We live very simply in the country, you see,' he said with a cynical shrug.

'And the banya?'

'Across the yard.'

Nicko offered to help his friend to get it started, but Viktor insisted on doing it himself.

'Stay and talk to Vera,' he said. 'She likes to practise her English, but it mightn't do you any harm to try speaking some Russian for a change.' He dug Nicko playfully in the ribs.

'Da, kaneshna,' Nicko replied.

'Come on you can say a bit more than that! Or did the Orloffs only speak French?'

'Fuck off, Vik.'

'Now say that in Russian!'

Viktor went to light up the banya while Nicko strolled down to chat to Vera in the kitchen. Little Nikoshka had been laid on a bench propped on some cushions and was conveniently dropping off to sleep.

'This is lovely,' he said.

'You really think so?'

'Well don't you?'

'Yes, I suppose I do. I love - how do say? - the nature.'

'The countryside.'

'The countryside. But I'm not so sure about Viktor. I think in his heart he is a city person.'

'He seems to like playing with his banya.'

'Oh he's very Russian - in spite of his English education. He loves Russian things. That's the reason you like him, isn't it?'

'It's one of the reasons.'

'And I like some English things - but I mustn't forget, you're a kind of a Russian too.' She stroked his hair tenderly, almost as she would have done with her own child.

Nicko laughed. 'I'm really a bit of a fake. I can't even speak the language properly.'

'You're not a fake,' Vera told him emphatically. 'I think I know what a fake is,' she added softly. 'I ought to by now.'

She did not elaborate because at that moment Viktor, who had set his fire, came in looking for a box of matches.

'Having a good gossip?' he said in English. 'In about an hour the water should be ready.'

'I'd like to see how you do this,' said Nicko.

'Come along then. You might learn something useful - what every true Russian should know: How to fire up a banya.'

Nicko and Vera exchanged nods and he followed his friend out into the yard at the back.

Viktor had filled the small furnace with kindling from the woodpile and newspaper. He had also added a touch of paraffin.

'Ready?' he said to Nicko.

'Fire away.'

Viktor struck a match and the newspaper flared up.

'It draws well,' Nicko said.

'Which reminds me,' said Viktor.

'Of what?'

'Of your friend Freddie and his pictures.'

'Very droll, Vik.'

'No I'm being serious. There's a lot in this for him and for you too. But we'll talk about it later and then, when we're back in town, there's someone I'd like you to meet.'

'You're being very secretive,' said Nicko.

'Remember where I've come from.' Viktor grinned. 'Come on, let's have a beer while the water heats up.'

They retreated indoors, Viktor collecting some bottles of Baltika Number Nine on the way.

'The strong stuff,' said Nicko.

'Kaneshna.'

They sat on the balcony drinking the beer from the bottles.

'So Nikoshka, I'm waiting for you to ask me some questions?'

'What kind of questions?'

'Things like what am I selling, who to and how are my profits.'

'God Vik. I think I can guess.'

'Can you? You know I'm interested in pictures - seriously interested.'

'And that's where Freddie's supposed to come in?'

'Kaneshna. But not just English pictures. They can be French or Dutch or German ones - from anywhere.'

'Can I ask you Vik, do you know anything about pictures?'

His friend shrugged. 'Not a lot, but enough - for what I want, anyway.'

'And what do you want?'

'What the people I sell to want. My New Russians.' He grinned broadly. 'But enough! I'll take you to meet someone back in town. No more till then, I think you'll find him interesting.'

'You're not going to tell me about him now?'

'Nyet, so you can just fuck off, Nikoshka.'

They downed a couple more beers before wandering over to the banya for the ritual of steppe cleansing. Viktor had eveything laid on - the heated stones for generating the steam, the birch twigs and jugs of cold water. When the time came for it, he plied the birch twigs on Nicko as, naked, he lay stretched on the slatted bench. Viktor was adept, the twigs passing crisply from the base of his friends thighs up to his shoulders. It felt good and Nicko wished that he could have performed as well for his chum, but Viktor, after his cautious essay, took the twigs and beat himself down effectively. Afterwards the two friends sat in the steamy heat and reminisced about their schooldays, the talk largely consisting of smutty appraisals of how their former peers had looked in the showers. Nicko felt mildy guilty at this retreat into his adolescence, but enjoyed it all the same.

Finally Viktor dashed cold water over him and he returned the favour. It was supper time.

The two days at the dacha passed placidly: Nicko walked out a couple of times with Vera and the baby, but although Viktor remained at home they did not repeat the brief intimacy of the flat in town. Nevertheless it seemed to be built into their relationship and their talk rattled along very happily. Vera's English was well nigh perfect and not given to the sort of occasional pedantries that Viktor's was. it went without saying that Nicko's Russian made no progress.

Otherwise Nicko played with the child and spent the time chatting to Viktor - about all sorts of things: Russia and its future; Viktor's own plans; their ancestral forebears - Orloffs and Nikishovs, though it was a topic that had already been exhaustively aired, And they drank much too much of course and enjoyed two more banyas.

Meanwhile the business of Freddie Ryedale and the buying in of pictures for the Russian market was not raised. Viktor, it seemed, was holding his fire until they had got back to town and the meeting that he had in mind for his friend.

It was an overcast day when they went back, but pleasantly cool. Nicko rather liked the grey tones that the landscape had assumed. Grey had always been his favourite colour - its subtle gradations and the fact that it set off brighter colours so well.

In the afternoon Viktor walked with him to a street not very far from his own. It was near the church of the Apostle Philip and ran off the Ulitsa Nikolskaya. By now the sun had started to break through the clouds, sending out rays. It was a magical effect.

The little side street seemed to be completely deserted. The houses and the fencing that separated them had that rather unkempt look which

Nicko admired, as if somehow Russians were spiritually superior to the fussy neatness of the Germans. Near the end of the street, Viktor pushed open a wooden gate which scraped noisily on the pavement and lead the way into a courtyard.

At that moment the sun sent out a great burst of light that irradiated the scene before them.

Nicko gasped. 'This is wonderful Vik. This is the real Russia! Not even in Petersburg did I see anything like this! Who's the painter?'

Viktor grinned. 'The painter? You'll meet him in a minute if he's in. He's called Igor, Igor Pavlovich Peshkov.'

'No, no, the one in the Tretyakov gallery. What's his name? Vera would know.'

Viktor looked blank.

'Polenov!' exclaimed Nicko. 'That's the guy, Vik. You must know that marvellous painting of his in the Tretyakov.'

'Kaneshna,' answered Viktor, as he looked at the scene with a rather more critical eye than his friend or at least tried to give the impression of doing so. 'Maybe you've got a point there, old boy. Yes, really think I can see what you mean. It does remind you of Polenov's picture, doesn't it? Russia in a nutshell, wouldn't you say?'

He lead the way past the children, pausing only to ask them if Igor Ilyich was at home.

'Da,' replied a flaxen-haired cherub, pointing in the direction of the open door.

'Are these his kids?' asked Nicko.

'No,' said Viktor. 'They belong to his landlady.'

'His landlady?'

'Oksana Andreevna.'

On the ground floor was a cluttered kitchen, with a vast Soviet era fridge where a young/middle-aged woman was slicing vegetables. She nodded at Viktor and pointed to the worn wooden staircase, leading to the floor above.

'Spasibo, Oksana Andreevna,' Viktor called out, starting up the stairs without bothering to introduce his friend.

On the landing a door was ajar past which a shaft of sunlight filled with motes of dust thrust its way into the dark interior. Viktor put his head round the door. There was a whispered conversation before he turned to his friend. 'Come,' he said.

It was a large room with a window facing north and another to the west where the sun was just starting to sink through a now clear sky. A couple of paintings were perched on a pair of easels while a large table was spread with colour photographs - mostly close-ups of trees, Nicko noticed. There was a large piece of board acting as a palette with different pigments arranged around its perimeter, jars of oil and clumps of brushes of all sizes.

Viktor introduced his friend to Igor, using Russian and the conversation went forward in that language with occasional offerings from Viktor in English to keep Nicko fully informed.

Igor was short with an untidily-cropped grizzled beard. He wore a large apron of what looked like sailcloth covered with daubs of paint. Smiling pleasantly at Nicko, he revealed a gold front tooth and dipped his head graciously as Viktor introduced his chum, not omitting to mention his Russian aristocratic connection which seemed to make a favourable impression on the artist, for that was clearly what he was.

Nicko's eyes drifted to the easels and the pictures on them. One was an exquisite rendering of a stand of birch trees in a forest glade.

They were catching the late afternoon sun which possessed the same intense luminosity as he had just witnessed in the yard below. He nodded his appreciation to the artist, who smiled and returned his nod.

Then he looked at the other easel and saw what was quite clearly an old picture. At a glance it could have been a Dutch or a Flemish landscape - flat with clumps of trees. like parkland almost, retreating into the distance under billowing clouds. There was the telltale windmill and a few cattle were grazing in the middle distance, while two figures appeared to be fishing on a canal bank in the foreground. It was a little jewel and Nicko could not say which of the two works he liked best.

'Do you understand?' Viktor asked him.

'Two beautiful pictures,' replied Nicko. 'But no, I don't think I do quite.'

Viktor grinned and exchanged a knowing look with Igor. 'I'll explain it to you, then. But I think it's fairly - obvious.'

'To me it isn't, but I'm listening.'

'Are you familiar with the works of Shishkin?'

'I think so. Nineteenth century Russian painter who specialised in woodland or forest scenes. I've seen them in the Tretyakov.'

Viktor nodded in the direction of the painting on the easel.

'Is that a Shishkin?' said Nicko. 'It's a gem whovever painted it! How did you - or he - come by it?'

Viktor nodded in the direction of Igor who seemed to be following what was said, despite the conversation being in English. The painter smiled and shrugged his shoulders in a self-deprecatory fashion.

'You mean...?'

'Yes, I do mean. He painted it.'

Nicko looked at the picture closely. 'It's beautiful. But... doesn't that make it a forgery? Technically speaking? I mean if he says its by Shishkin?'

Viktor shrugged. 'Not necessarily. Why should it? It's a matter of opinion, isn't it? It isn't an actual copy of another picture, if that's what you mean. Painted in the manner of Shishkin, that's all - which isn't quite the same thing. And if it's just as good as a Shishkin and people like to think it is one, who really cares but a few experts?'

'But to say Shishkin painted it is a lie, surely? Will you sell it as one?'

'If that's what people want to think it is, I won't deny it. If it makes them happy believing that and they are willing to pay a price which makes me happy. This talk about forgery is just a game for the experts.'

'An interesting way of looking at it.'

'A realistic way.'

'What does Igor himself think?'

Viktor spoke to the painter softly in his own language and the man shrugged, spread his hands and grinned. He used the Russian word for money which Nicko picked up.

'I think you got that,' said Viktor.

'He's a bloody good painter all the same,' declared Nicko. 'Isn't he wasted playing this kind of game?'

Again it was put to the man who shook his head.

'He doesn't think so,' Viktor said. 'He's perfectly happy for people to go on believing that his pictures are by Shishkin and appreciating them for that very reason when all the time he knows they're the work of Peshkov. The idea amuses him.'

'Well I suppose it tells you something about art critics,' said Nicko.

35

'It probably does.'

Nicko took the picture, which was about eighteen inches square, from its easel and examined the back. 'This is already an old picture!' he exclaimed. 'At least the canvas and the stretcher look as if they are.'

An old picture sure - but with a few refinements added to meet the needs of today's market. You can take it from me that Shishkin's in great demand these days - especially with our New Russian friends, They might be new, but they like their pictures to look old.'

'Very droll, Vik. And this one?' Nick pointed to the Dutch or Flemish landscape. 'You're not going to mess about with this one, surely? You really, mustn't, Vik.'

Viktor put on a token display of being affronted. 'Igor would be very upset if you accused him of messing about with any picture,' he protested. He explained what he had just said to the painter in his own language. The man simply grinned and shrugged his shoulders in a matter-of-fact kind of way.

'I grant you that he's done a superb job with the - er - Shishkin, but it would be sheer vandalism to alter this one in any way whatsoever!' declared Nicko with a flourish that almost swept the picture off its easel.

'You should see what Igor can do to cows,' went on Viktor. 'He can turn them into bears or even camels if he wants to. He's a real magician.'

Nicko shook his head.

'What's the matter? Most painters down the ages have been prepared to touch up or even paint over earlier works, haven't they? However good they were reckoned to be- as long as they were paid enough for doing it. Even the very best of them. You see, old boy, it all comes down to money. Artists need it the same as everybody else. Their art is - how do you say it? - merely their bread and butter?'

'Quite so, Vik.'

'And I'm sure your Freddie Whatsisname is no exception either. When he sells a picture he wants the best price he can get for it. And he doesn't have the labour of having to paint it. And what about you? You're in the business yourself, aren't you, Nikoshka?'

'So what are you asking from me, Vik?'

'Nothing very difficult, Nikoshka. You can see for yourself how good our friend here is. I defy you to say that his version of a Shishkin is any less good than one by the hand of the master himself. In fact it might even be better.'

'But all the same its not a Shishkin. It's an Igor.'

'A Peshkov. Sure, but does that make it any less good? You still have some way to travel, my dear Nikoshka. That is if you're serious about selling pictures.'

'I'm not sure that I'm very keen to travel down that particular road,' said Nicko.

'You see Igor he has an unusual talent. To take an English landscape, say, your English countryside, and to turn it into a Russian one.'

'Why not leave it an English one and sell it as such?'

Viktor sighed. 'The market, dear boy. They want Russian ones that are old, and preferably by famous artists. And people like your Freddie .... Whatisname?'

'Ryedale.'

'Ryedale can supply old pictures - in sufficient quantity - for a man of Igor's genius - and I don't use that word lightly - to turn into something that people want badly enough to pay a lot of money for. It takes a special kind of genius, like Igor's, and you can be sure that usually something better comes out of it than was there in the first place.'

'But leave that other picture alone. It's far too good to tamper with.'

Viktor sighed. 'For your sake Nikoshka we might do as you ask. Just this once. But you can't afford to be sentimental, you know. I'm quite sure the great Michelangelo wasn't.'

'Thank you, Vik. You really are a cunt, aren't you?'

Viktor punched his friend affectionately. 'Do you want to see how Igor works? I think you ought to. It can only increase your respect for the man's genius.'

Igor took them behind a small screen where he had a collection of small vats, rather like a canteen serving unit, each one containing a different pigment.

'It goes without saying that Igor mixed his own colours,' Viktor explained. 'Each to a formula appropriate to the supposed age of the painting.'

On a work bench were bottles containing what looked like small lumps of rock of different colours and a glass mortar and pestle. Viktor picked up a piece of dark blue glass.

'The lapis lazuli stone,' he declared. 'The precious ultramarine from beyond the Caspian!'

Igor explained something in Russian which Nicko understood.

'He says he was a chemist before he became a painter?'

'Just so,' said Viktor, 'and a museum conservationist.'

'Conservator. So he really does know his stuff, then?' Nicko dipped his head to the painter in deference to his undoubted skills. 'You leave nothing to chance, do you?' he added to Viktor.

'What have we got here?' said Nicko, pointing to what looked like an oven door set in the wall. 'Does he bake his pictures as well?'

'Exactly so.'

Nicko frowned and raised his eyebrows.

'He does it to provide - you should know - you've studied the thing, haven't you? Craq...'

'Craquelure,' supplied Nicko.

'Your French is better than your Russian,' said his friend.

'It refers to the network of tiny cracks that forms over the surface of an oil painting as it gets older. I take my hat off to you, Viktor.'

'Say that again. Take your hat off to me?'

'Fuck off, Vik'

When they got home Viktor suddenly announced that he had some business to attend to that very evening and would be taking the car. He would not be back before the morning.

'This is a bit sudden, isn't it?' said Nicko.

'I'm afraid that's the way these things go,' his host explained. 'But I'm sure Vera will look after you well enough. She can practise her English, or you might even try your Russian,' he added with a twinkle. 'And you can always talk to the baby. It won't do him any harm to start learning English - the sooner the better and from a native speaker too.'

'Where are you going?' asked Nicko.

'The other side of town. The trouble is that it's the sort of business that has to be washed down with a good deal of vodka and I'd prefer not to drive home until I've slept it off.'

He seemed to be going to a considerable length to justify his sudden departure. Vera looked at him as he spoke without saying anything.

'Goodbye, darling,' he said to his wife as he kissed her on the cheek and left the flat.

'Well, well,' said Nicko, 'he never stops, does he, your Viktor? As we say in England, always on the go.'

Vera sighed. 'Sometimes I wish he'd just settle down, but then I don't suppose he'd make so much money if he did.' She sighed again. 'There are times when I wonder if it's really worth it. You're not a bit like that, are you Nikoshka? Do you mind me calling you that?'

'It's what you call your baby so I'm flattered.'

'You say such sweet English things.' She leaned across the kitchen table and stroked his hair.

'I like it when you do that.'

'Do you really, Nikoshka?' She kneaded his hair in her fingers and gave it a little tug.

'Ouch.'

'Did I hurt you?'

'Only a little bit. I liked it as a matter of fact.'

They had eaten before Viktor's departure and the baby was asleep. Vera went into the living room and turned on the light.

'Tea?' she called.

'Please,' said Nicko, 'and some of your delicious jam.'

Nicko settled himself on the sofa and Vera returned to the kitchen to make the tea. She came back with a pot, cups and saucers, two spoons and a large bowl of raspberry jam on a painted metal tray.

'This is the best way to drink tea that I know,' Nicko declared.

'I'm so glad you like it, Nikoshka,' said Vera. 'It's nice. Isn't it? -

the two of us, by ourselves. What is your English word for it? Cosy?'

'It'll do.' Nicko edged away ever so slightly, which did not go unnoticed by the Russian.

'You mustn't think about Viktor,' Vera admonished him. 'There's an English proverb - I like English proverbs - how does it go? 'When the cat's away, the mice...''

'...come out to play.'

'When the cat's away the mice come out to play. But I'm being serious, don't think about Viktor. He's not a jealous kind of man. He's too busy making money to worry about things like that. And anyway, he's quite a naughty pussy cat!'

'Oh he is, is he?' said Nicko. 'It's something he's never talked to me about.'

Vera ran a finger down his nose. 'You're so English,' she said, 'in spite of having a Russian name.'

'I'm very proud of my Russian name,' replied Nicko defensively.

'Of course you are,' Vera said. 'And so you should be, but you mustn't get cross. You're really so English. That's what I like about you. It's what makes you sexy.'

Nicko took a large sip from his cup. 'And I like my tea hot. Very hot. Does that make me English - or Russian? Certainly my English grandmother liked hers very, very hot.'

Vera laughed and filled a spoon with a generous dollop of jam which she pressed to his lips 'Open your mouth wide, Nikoshka,' she ordered.

Nicko did as he was told and she pressed two more spoonfuls home.

'That's a good boy,' she said.

'Hm,' he murmured. 'I like it when you do that.'

'Do you, my little Nikoshka? You're such a good little boy. Not all of the time, but for some of it.'

He nestled against her shoulder with a contented sigh.

'A good little English boy. Or are you a Russian one? A malchik?'

'Either will do. You must choose.'

'My little Nikoshka!'

Nicko did not really have much idea how to proceed, but he hardly needed one. Vera handled him as if she was handling her own child, firmly, and tenderly, taking the initiative entirely. And that was exactly what the callow young man had been needing someone to do for a very long time.

It was the middle of the morning when Viktor returned, ample time for the two naughty mice to be up and about, with the baby clean and fed and chuntering happily on Nicko's lap.

'Quite the dad,' said Viktor.

'He's sheer delight, Vik,' replied the other. 'I envy you this more than anything else.'

'We still have to make a man of him. He must follow his father to his Old School.'

'Hmm, I'm not so sure about that,' said Nicko. 'But it's none of my business. What does Vera think?'

'She wants him to grow up an English boy. She has rather definite ideas of what English boys are like - as you've probably found out by now.' He grinned at his friend, who glanced away and said nothing.

For the time being nothing more was said about the piece of

business that had been broached in Igor's studio, but even Nicko could sense that his friend, having planted the seed, was giving it time to germinate.

Together the two young men visited more of the churches that dotted the old city and drove out several times with Vera and the child for a picnic in the surrounding countryside. There were a couple more barbecues and banyas at the dacha, of course, and on one occasion they went fishing together on the river in the direction of Lake Limen. Viktor proved an adept fisherman - yet another talent which had hitherto not been revealed to his friend - but Nicko, who had fished for salmon in a Scottish river a number of times - was able to hold his own sufficiently and though the catch - strictly of the coarse variety - was meagre, he felt that he had kept his end up for once with the brash New Russian.

The fortnight passed off happily with Viktor staying away for two more nights, tacitly leaving the mice to play - which they did with increasing abandon.

At the same time Vera laid bare her hopes for her child to Nicko in a manner which he suspected she did not do with her own husband.

'I do so want him to grow up an English boy,' she kept insisting.

'Like his father?' said Nicko. 'After all he went to school in England.'

Vera shook her head and frowned. 'No, not like his father,' she replied firmly. 'He's a Russian - New Russian.'

'And you don't approve of that? He's making plenty of money for you, isn't he?'

'Kaneshna. But I think you know what I mean, Nikoshka.' She stroked his hair and pinched his ear. 'He's not like you. You're so gentle.'

They sank back onto the pillow and let the matter drop.

Before flying home Nicko, together with Viktor, drafted a letter to Freddie Ryedale which the latter signed. In it Viktor said that he would be in London in October and that they ought to get together. Effusive praise was heaped on Nicko, most of which he managed to tone down. Viktor, despite his years spent in England and his business acumen still hadn't got the hang of English reticence.

Nicko realised that he would have to tread carefully. Freddie certainly could do with a bob or two, but shady deals had never been in his line. He could be described as a guileless snob - affable, content not to push his luck too far as long as he could continue moving in the kind of circles that he found congenial. It was small wonder that he had missed the Constable. Nicko reckoned that it would probably be wiser not to inform him of the likely fate of any of the pictures that he might dispatch to Russia. He merely needed to be told that in Russia there was a growing appetite for English landscape painting, that was all.

Viktor of course knew his friend's character and made a shrewd guess at Freddie's as well.

And so it turned out. When Nicko quoted the kind of sums that very modest works fetched on the Russian market, Freddie took the bait. He had a residual reluctance about selling homegrown works of art abroad, the dispersal of what he termed our island heritage, but at the same time he approved of the idea of disseminating his notion of Englishness among unenlightened foreigners. Freddie Ryedale was an old-fashioned romantic imperialist. He could be quite hardheaded and drive a decent enough bargain at a local level if he needed to, but he was distinctly fuzzy when it came to thinking about the wider world. For one thing he never took a holiday abroad.

Nicko explained the Russian market while Freddie tugged at his bowtie and tried to look knowing. He usually tugged his tie when he was trying to impress someone with his expertise. Before him was Viktor's letter.

'Your Russian chum seems to think pretty highly of you,' he observed.

Nicko shrugged his shoulders. 'Russians tend to lay it on a bit thick,' he replied. 'It's all or nothing with them.'

Freddie frowned in a businesslike manner. 'Are they really as interested in English landscape painting as all that?' he asked.

'It would seem so,' said Nicko. 'They are very romantic about things British, you know. Big Ben, Scotsmen in kilts, the Queen, that kind of thing.'

'Would they like some highland cattle? I get lots of them. I'd be only too glad to offload a few. Most of them are just wallpaper.'

'I'm quite sure they would.'

'Good,' said Freddie, putting on a display of decisiveness which combined tapping his hand on the table with giving his bowtie an extra tug. 'I think we might do business with your Russian friend, don't you? Providing we can sort out the paperwork, of course.'

Only that morning he had received a statement from his credit card company and the interest he was due to pay was terrifying.

Freddie met Viktor in London - a meeting that tied up a number of loose ends- and trade began with a batch of highland cattle which Viktor informed them he was able to sell for a moderately good price, because there was apparently a demand for them, but landscapes with rivers and trees was what he was really after, because these could be most readily modified for the Russian market - something which of course, was not explained to Freddie. The names of the Russian painters he talked to Nicko of most were Levitan and Shishkin. Having seen Igor's skill at running up one of the latter, Nicko was fired up to join the hunt - especially after the money he saw made out of the transformation of a very mediocre Midlands landscape into the work of a Russian master. The fields of Warwickshire had become a great sweep of steppe through which a river snaked its way with a forest fringing the horizon. The original nineteenth century English painter was a provincial whom Nicko had never heard of, so his conscience was undisturbed. Certainly the image of the transformation that Viktor e-mailed to him looked impressive. Viktor usually sent him a pair of images - one taken before and the other after Igor had gone to work. Nicko's admiration for the Novgorod Master, as he dubbed him, knew no bounds. But he never showed these images to Freddie who went on believing that what he sent to Russia was satisfying a sentimental craving there for things British. Indeed he felt touched by it. Nor did any of the people from whom Freddie acquired the pictures ask awkward questions either, trusting his reassuringly homegrown manner as they always did, and accepting the kind of valuations that he placed on them in an English market place.

So Freddie was able to settle his credit card debt while his visits to house sales reached out ever further. He grew to relish the hunt and seemed to have shed some of his old languor. His associates noticed the change and most of them put it down to the young thruster he had taken on as his assistant. Rydedale's luck seemed to be turning.

It was almost too easy and eighteen months on from their first dispatch of highland cattle, Nicko was packing up three or four canvasses at a time for transport by the channel which Viktor had discreetly arranged. He left the selection to Freddie, adding only the occasional comment in passing. The truth, of course, was that Nicko was still somewhat green and had a long way to go in the matter of judging the merits of English landscape and topographical painting by himself. He loved Igor's transformations that Viktor sent to him and was amazed at the Russian artist's ability to turn an English thatched cottage into a Russian isba. It was done with such finesse that he felt that no violation had taken place - quite the opposite if anything. It was a wonderful piece of magic, the frog being turned into a prince.

One day when Autumn was drawing to a close and giving way to winter, Freddie approached his assistant with an anxious frown. He had an ancient saleroom catalogue in his hand.

'Nicko? I turned this up by chance. It was in a job lot of books I was going through and I found this.' He pointed to a colour plate of a woody landscape.

Nick glanced at the title page of the catalogue with dated it to the mid fifties.

'Do you recognise it?' said Freddie. 'It looks familiar, doesn't it?'

'It certainly does. It went off with that last batch. It'll be in Russia by now.'

'I don't suppose there's any chance of getting it back?' asked Freddie anxiously.

'What's the problem? It's a bit late in the day, but I could e-mail Viktor and find out whether he's sold it or not.'

'I wish you would,' said Freddie. 'You see who it's painted by, don't you?

'Not another bloody Constable, for Christ's sake?' said Nicko with a groan.

'No, not this time,' said Freddie miserably, 'but just about as bad. I can't think why I didn't spot it.'

'Gainsborough,' said Nicko. 'We can't let that one go. I'll get onto Viktor at once.'

' God,' groaned Freddie. 'It's probably worth a bomb - far more than they'll ever pay me for it. There's not a moment to lose.'

Although Nicko recognized the picture from the catalogue, he recalled that it had not struck him as anything special when he had set eyes on it. It was a small oil sketch and had come out of a tied cottage on a large Lincoinshire estate, where it had probably been a kind of thank you gift to a retired housekeeper or someone of that ilk. But the Fifties catalogue was quite specific in naming Thomas Gainsborough.

Nicko e-mailed his friend in Novgorod asking about the picture and a day later got a reply from Vera saying that her husband was in Novosibirsk, of all places, and it would be a few days before he got back. 'A very good time for the mice to play, my little Nikoshka,' she cooed. 'I'm sad that you're not here.'

Nicko explained the delay to Freddie who wrung his hands miserably. 'I simply can't believe it,' he moaned. 'I fucked with the Constable and now I've done it again with a Gainsborough.'

It was unlike Freddie to utter such profanities.

'It was easy to miss,' commiserated Nicko. 'It didn't look very much.'

'That's not the point, is it? It's one thing to export dross, but this is one of our greatest painters, our national heritage. It makes me feel a traitor.'

'It might find a good home,' suggested Nicko, attempting to sound hopeful, 'with someone who loves it. And, anyway, all is not yet lost. Viktor might return it.'

'God, I hope so,' moaned Freddie. 'Bloody Ryedale's luck! Have you e-mailed him again?'

But Nicko did not need to. When he got home there was a message already waiting for him from his friend who at considerable length described his trip to the Siberian capital where things were really opening up. 'You mentioned a picture,' he said after everything else. 'I'm not sure that I know which one you mean. It was difficult to tell from your photograph. I will need more information. And here are two more works by the Novgorod Master for your approval, by the way. I hope you like them. And Vera sends her little English boy her love. I wonder what I'm supposed to make of that? What can she possibly mean?'

A couple of Igor's transformations were appended to the text. One of them was a woodland scene in the manner of Shishkin and it did not take Nicko long to work out what almost certainly lay hidden beneath its surface. English ash trees had been turned into birches and a shepherd, in the best shamanistic fashion, had become a mother bear, and a pair of sheep her cubs, while the remainder of the flock had simply vanished. It was a miracle and Nicko had no doubt which version of the picture he liked the better. But then, of course, Nicholas Orloff claimed to have a Russian soul.

Aunt Dot's Teeth

When Aunt Dot's body was being prepared for her funeral no one could find her teeth. Her husband, Geoff, who should have known where they were if anyone did, only mumbled something vague about the night nurse probably having chucked them out by mistake. For Aunt Dot had died under her own roof tree, a little sooner than was expected - she was just short of eighty - though her end had been peaceful. Despite that, her husband seemed strangely affected by it. He had always assumed that his wife would outlast him, although there was only two years difference between them, but his reaction seemed extreme for one who had always appeared so rational. From the time of Dot's death though he did not show any obvious signs of grief - something that he would have considered to be out of character - his speech became horribly confused. His syntax fell to pieces, which was quite unlike him.

Dot and Geoff had suited one another. She was a throwback to a type of feminism that had come into its own in the first half of the twentieth century in circles like the Bloomsbury Group and in a sense Virginia Woolf had been Dot's own exemplar - since she painted in a boldly expressionist manner with sweeping brushstrokes and wrote poetry of appropriate obscurity, some of which she had published in a slender volume. Above all, she talked. Talked relentlessly.

She and her husband, Geoffrey Fairclough, lived in a large converted farmhouse in the North Riding of Yorkshire - once the home of a gentleman farmer - and had enough money to live comfortably without having to do very much about it. Geoff's career in the Colonial Service had ended rather abruptly, when he was still comparatively young and he had done nothing full-time since, but he hadn't really needed to. He had remained a bachelor - a confirmed one in some people's eyes - throughout his career and then suddenly surprised them all on his return from the Sudan by marrying a bluestocking friend of his childhood, though the term sweetheart could hardly be applied to one like Dorothy Hetherington, who was in her late thirties, nearly the same age as Geoff himself. However, sufficient funds welled up steadily to keep the pair of them in comfort, Dot's considerable family investments being the principle source. The marriage had turned out childless which was also convenient, to Dot at least. While it might have been a cause for regret in Geoff 's case, it had been the opposite in hers, for she had thrown herself into her artistic pursuits more wholeheartedly than she might otherwise have done, declaring that life was much too short to repine over trivial matters like not bearing children, and, anyway, had she had been given a choice in the matter, she would have wanted it no differently.

Geoff, though he treated his wife's enthusiasms with the open-mindedness of a man with a sound university degree and an awareness of cultures other than his own, gleaned in large measure from his years in the Colonial Service, was able to pursue his own interests in parallel with hers. Parallel because his great passion was gardening and, despite her artistic leanings, Dot never lifted a trowel or a spade or so much as deadheaded a rose, though she did do her husband the honour of rendering in her expressionist manner views of the vistas and beds that he created.

Geoff's love of gardening was largely rooted in History. He had left Oxford with a First in the subject in the early fifties before embarking on his short career in the Colonial Service in the Sudan where the cream of the postwar generation of colonial servants was being sent. The Whig Supremacy of the eighteenth century had been his speciality and from it had emerged his interest in landscape gardening. In fact he considered himself a sort of Whig - which fitted in rather well with Dot's own quaintly old-fashioned progressive opinions.

'If I'd lived then I think I would have known where I stood,' he explained to her, 'but living when I do I'm at a bit of a loss, I have to confess. I can hardly call myself a socialist.'

Dot could not so readily disavow the most progressive political creed of her time, but she probably felt much the same, because, despite her declared beliefs, she was a snob.

'One of the things I like most about Max,' Geoff remarked one day of his favourite great - nephew, 'is that the boy isn't a snob.'

'No, he isn't very observant, is he?' replied Dot. The broad principle of lifting up humanity at some unspecified and safely distant date in the future had always suited her better than the unsettling and messy business of attempting to do it in the present. Of course it went without saying that she wished the lower classes every success in the Millenium when it eventually did arrive, while preferring them to keep on their own side of the fence in the meantime.

Geoff relished Dot's riposte. Sharp in its way, it was also a pretty fair reflection of her own personality. Geoff liked consistency of character. It fitted in with his own intellectual disposition, which his time in the Sudan, where he had allowed nothing to surprise him, had failed to modify. He prided himself on being a fair-minded sort of man who was in control. Above all, he liked to wrap problems up in reasonably watertight, intellectually-consistent, explanations. As a district officer anthropology had become an abiding interest. In fact if he had pushed it hard enough on his return he might have found a university post teaching the subject, but he had settled instead to write a couple of moderately well-received books on the Madi tribes of Equatoria. In his Whiggish way Geoff remained a gentleman amateur - with a private income sufficient to maintain the part. His wife, meanwhile, was perfectly free to fly her own kites. So there was room enough for both of them in their very agreeable corner of the earth.

But the garden was where Geoff felt best able to combine his brand of creative self-expression with the enlightened principles which he had once tried to practise in the Colonial Service. Laying out a garden, along rational Whiggish lines, he felt, had much in common with administering and developing a district in the Sudan. When it came to the former, on the whole he liked the more regulated, less natural look best, with crisp axial walks radiating from a central point, while planted woods with serpentine paths winding through them separated the garden from the countryside beyond, to add a marginal dash of mystery. But clear lines and good order were the principle feature of Geoff's classical view of the world, while Dot was more inclined to the Gothic and going through the motions, at least, of romantic spontaneity.

There were fifteen acres of ground to play with, ground that undulated and had a small stream running through it - most of it grass, rented to the neighbouring farmers who grazed sheep on it. Geoff visited some of the well-known gardens in the North Riding and consulted a number of the eighteenth century manuals on the subject. He drew plans and talked to experts and at a later stage began to involve his great-nephew, Max, the grandson of his older sister Muriel, who had expressed an interest in a career as a landscape gardener - something the childless Geoff was eager to encourage.

And gradually over the years the garden was established. Its critics were a little ready to dismiss it as a pastiche of an early eighteenth century landscape garden with its serpentine paths winding through bordering woods, its broad axial canal and demi-lune ponds. But Geoff also struck a modern note with some abstract sculpture as well as pieces done in a primitive vein, reflecting his own anthropological interests. He felt the need to appear catholic in his tastes as an enlightened man should, but his heart remained at home in the ordered world of the eighteenth century. His excursions into modernism of course were taken up by Dot who was allowed to select several of the pieces and even provided one of her own.

It was physically demanding work, of course, but it kept Geoff fit well into his old age and he never lost his trim waistline. Two men and usually a youngster assisted him, Indeed he was inclined to employ as many as he reasonably could, an old-fashioned sense of noblesse oblige going hand in hand with his notions of improvement.

One of the men he employed was the single remaining thread connecting Geoff to his old Colonial Service days. He was Joe, who had been his Madi houseboy when he first went out to Equatoria back in the Fifties and had remained with him ever since. Roughly the same age as Geoff himself, he had never married, but instead had followed his adopted master everywhere his career had taken him and had eventually returned with him to England where Geoff had made attempts to school him, though Joe had preferred the role he had been used to in Equatoria, as Geoff's personal household servant. A roof over his head, a comfortable billet, plenty of good food and a familiar type of work were sufficient. And Scrabble: Geoff had taught Joe to play Scrabble and he took to it like a duck to water. Moreover, he seemed to have an uncanny knack for the game and even held his own against Geoff. Meanwhile Dot accepted Joe's presence as part of the household in her usual high-minded fashion. As well as coming from what was soon to be known as the Third World he made himself useful in so many ways. Not least in the garden where hard physical work was required.

Max was the one most privy to his great-uncle's schemes and usually spent a good part of his university vacations at Thoresby. If anyone knew what Uncle Geoff had in mind it was most likely to be the boy who was turning into something of a surrogate son.

'We really must find Aunt Dot's teeth if we possibly can,' Max's mother had said to him at the time of her laying out. 'I'm afraid we're not getting much sense out of Uncle Geoff just at present. In fact I'm quite surprised at the way he's taking it. He seems to be letting it get to him a lot more than I ever thought he would have done. Strong feelings hardly seemed to be a feature of that relationship. It always struck me as a pretty low key affair.'

Max was inclined to agree. He had never witnessed his great-uncle in the grip of a powerful emotion before. He wasn't maudlin exactly, more like punch drunk and unable to focus on even the simplest things of life.

'Are Aunt Dot's teeth really so important, Ma?' queried Max. 'I mean she's not likely to need them, where she's gone, is she?'

'She seems undressed somehow,' retorted his mother. 'It sounds stuffy, I know, but I think people ought to be properly turned out at the end - especially if they're going to be buried.'

'That does surprise me a bit, I must say,' said Max. 'I would have thought with all her progressive opinions Aunt Dot would have opted for cremation.'

'Not nearly so progressive as you might think,' his mother pointed out. 'She was a throwback - a dyed-in-the-wool traditionalist when it boiled down to it - in a word, a snob, who adored playing the great lady.'

Feeling that it rang true, Max did not argue, but he was reluctant to press his great-uncle in the matter of his wife's dentures all the same, and Aunt Dot went down into her grave with naked gums - which of course was apparent to no one else except her immediate kin and the undertaker - or so it would seem.

But it was odd how quickly Geoff seemed to crumple without his wife, especially as they had never seemed emotionally close. Overnight almost, he grew querulous and slapdash when before he had been so incisive, and he was pathetically concerned that Max should take up where he must shortly be leaving off. Max's parents were divorced and he lived much of the time with his mother in York - which made it relatively easy for him to visit Uncle Geoff at Thoresby. His time at university was nearing its end and the matter of a career was exercising his mother and himself. She was a little suspicious of him going in with Uncle Geoff, feeling that he needed a serious professional qualification of some sort before he made his mind up. His grandmother, however, urged the connection, saying it was an opportunity not to be missed and hinted broadly that there would be resources to match should the boy decide to do the sensible thing.

So Max followed up his university degree - like his great-uncle he had read History - with a year studying horticulture - which made him feel more comfortable about taking on the running and development of a landscape garden. Uncle Geoff had already opened it to the public which yielded a modest return - he had never been one to hide his light under a bushel, and Max was keen to maintain the tradition, for it was assumed by the rest of the clan that he would be the inheritor of Thoresby. And now in his rambling old-age Geoff seemed to be confirming the fact. The problem of other possible claimants was cleanly dealt with - obviously Geoff had thought about it well in advance of his own strangely sudden dotage and when the time came for him to pass on - which he did almost exactly a year to the day of his wife's death - there were no serious mutterings, though a couple of Hetherington cousins did remark on the fortuitous way in which Max had managed to complete a diploma in horticulture in time to step into his great- uncle's shoes at Thoresby.

He settled into Thoresby two months after Geoff's funeral and was pleasantly surprised at the good state of things: both the house itself and the garden which after a wet summer was almost rampant. But the grass and the hedges were freshly trimmed and the crisp lines of his great-uncle's scheme were still firmly in place. This, as well as upkeep of the house, had been the work largely of Joe, the erstwhile houseboy turned butler, and the gardener, Bob Bottomley, who, assured of his wages, continued to keep things in good order. Joe had even provided a few conducted tours, adding an engaging African touch to the delights of an English country garden. But the best landscape gardens have generally contained surprises and the Madi tribesman explaining things in his rich African accent added an unusual twist. Max was not unimpressed, having taken the tour with him, but it was the hint of hidden depths in Joe that intrigued him: and the occasional respectful yet mildly cryptic references to Uncle Geoff that his now-grizzled houseboy let fall from time to time.

Joe had maintained the house itself in tiptop form, assiduously polishing floors, dusting and even draping the furniture with sheets in the rooms that had been shut up; a consideration he would hardly have learned in Africa. And he had acquired a bearing to match, coming across to Max as a kind of black Jeeves. Indeed he had dispensed the hospitality at Geoff's own funeral with a sombre discretion which almost suggested a power behind the throne. And now with the arrival of Max it was apparent that he had expectations of being retained, advanced in years as he was. Max, who had no experience of running a house bigger than a students flat before, was not one to look a gift horse in the mouth and, besides, the man had aroused his curiosity.

'By the way Mr Max sir,' Joe asked him deferentially, 'do you like to play Scrabble? Mr Geoffrey liked a game.'

'Scrabble?' reflected Max. 'Sure from time to time, I do, Joe, but I don't think I'm terribly good at it.' He recalled Uncle Geoff telling him how he used to play with Joe who always managed to make it a good contest.

It was a novel experience for Max, living in the large old house along with Joe who seemed to carry everything on in an unassertive way: all kinds of housework, including cooking as well as occasionally helping Bob Bottomley in the garden. He never obtruded on Max, but slipped away in the evenings, presumably to his own quarters, always making sure that drinks were left out, in proper decanters, for Max and any of his chums who might be stopping over. And Max had quite a few of those who came to enjoy the big house and the suggestion of a bygone style of life with its Scrabble-playing African butler. Indeed, Thoresby in the months after Max entered it became something of a cult destination among his former university friends.

And usually a couple of times a week, in the first part of the evening, Max would pour Joe a whisky - which the African sipped delicately - and play a game of Scrabble with him. It was uncanny the obscure English vocabulary the man seemed able to summon up - and, not only that, but like the best players, he also had the knack of matching his numbers to his words as well. So often it is one or the other, but Joe could bank words up against other words and always hit the high-scoring squares with the big numbers at the same time. As music had seemed to flow through Mozart from some mysterious outside source, so too did the ability to score at Scrabble through this former African houseboy who had never had a formal English or Mathematics lesson in his life.

And yet he was modest about it and was reluctant to show off his astonishing skill to any of Max's friends. Somehow Joe still knew his place.

And Joe cooked - most of the usual English dishes - stews, roasts and so on, but when he could lay hands on the ingredients African things too - matoke and some of the hot spicy Arab dishes. His couscous was mouthwatering and he was only too happy to lay on a feast for Max and his chums.

Max had a girlfriend, Cordelia, with whom he had been going steady for over a year and in her university vacations she came and lived with him at Thoresby. Cordelia, who had many of the instincts of a chatelaine, found it to her taste and as she was completing a degree in Archaeology and Anthropology at Cambridge, she was intrigued by Joe, where he had come from, the story of his life with Max's great-uncle, the cultural conundrum he represented and so on. He was good enough for a thesis on his own and in her visits to Thoresby she tried to probe him.

But Joe, while remaining as deferential as ever, was giving nothing away and even when Cordelia quizzed him on his culinary skills he answered her only in general terms.

One day Cordelia went into the kitchen where she found Joe preparing a meal. The large old cupboard was open, revealing the ranks of jars and containers that crowded its shelves.

'My goodness,' exclaimed Cordelia, 'You've got enough stuff in there Joe.'

Joe nodded and smiled politely.

'You could concoct a real witch's brew with that lot.'

Joe gave a little chuckle. 'What do you know about witches, Miss Cordelia?'

Cordelia immediately felt the need to be tactful and unpatronising, having touched on a possibly delicate topic for an African. 'Not all that much, I'm afraid, Joe, but I've been studying the practices of some of the African tribes in my course at university,' she explained. 'In a different part of Africa from yours, I hasten to say. In Ghana and Nigeria mostly.'

'They said my grandmother was a witch,' said Joe with a grin and a wink.

'Did they really, Joe?' Cordelia frowned. 'I hope they didn't do anything unpleasant to her.'

Joe laughed outright. 'No, they didn't kill her or anything like that, if that's what you mean, Miss Cordelia. The witch doctor handled it. That was what he was there for. You have to understand everyone was putting spells on everyone else all the time. If you had a toothache it was because someone had put a spell on you.'

Cordelia nodded. It tied in with some of what she had been

reading. 'But tell me about your jars and tins, Joe,' she asked. 'What have you got in them? Herbs and spices?'

'Most of them.' Joe took the lid off a can and handed it to her. 'Smell that,' he said.

Cordelia sniffed the deep reddish powder. It was not quite like anything she had ever smelled before.

'Is it hot?'

'Try it,' suggested Joe. 'But only a little bit on the end of your finger.'

Cordelia licked a finger and dipped it in the can and tasted it cautiously. 'Yes. it is hot,' she said. 'Like curry powder, but it doesn't taste the same. Rather too sweet if anything.' She laughed. 'I might get to like it. I've got a sweet tooth.'

Joe chuckled and put the lid back on the can.

'What else have you got in there Joe?' Cordelia reached up to the shelf and took down a can.

Joe gently, but firmly took it from her and removed the lid. He poured some of the contents onto the chopping board in front of him.

'Good God,' exclaimed Cordelia. 'Scorpions! You surely don't cook those, do you?' She wrinkled her nose.

Joe laughed and picked one up. 'Like to taste one?' he said.

Cordelia took the shrivelled creature from him and sniffed it.

'The sting is the best part,' laughed Joe and crunched one in his teeth. He scooped up the dead creatures and replaced them in the can.

'I was right,' said Cordelia. 'You have got the ingredients for a witch's brew. But tell me, Joe, where do you lay hands on them? Hardly in your local Sainsbury's I'd have thought.'

Joe only grinned and closed the cupboard door. 'I have my own ways,' he said.

Cordelia believed him and felt it was time to leave him to get on with his work.

'What are you going to do tonight?' she asked.

'What about spiced spiders? They're very nice in a chili sauce.'

Cordelia pulled a disgusted face and left the kitchen.

'Joe has got some weird stuff in that cupboard of his,' she told Max later.

'Such as?'

'Well, dried scorpions for a start. Has he ever served them up?'

'Not that I know of,' said Max, 'but maybe he grinds them up first, and makes a sort of paste. And I don't suppose we'd know then, would we? And anyway, they might not taste bad. Possibly a bit like prawns?'

'I told him he had everything for a witch's brew there and he told me that his grandmother had been a witch.'

'Oh really? It doesn't surprise me. Perhaps that explains his amazing skill at Scrabble. He hammered me last time we played.'

'I'd like to base my thesis on Jo,' said Cordelia.

Max laughed. 'You'd better ask him first.'

They decided to go to bed early.

Spring was turning into summer and the garden was coming to life. Max of course had made his number with Bob Bottomley, the gardener, while his great-uncle was still alive and the pair of them got on well.

'It's beginning to look great, Bob,' enthused Max.

'Thank you. We do our best.' Bob was an old-fashioned doer who was not given to more words than he felt were necessary.

'I'm wondering what there is to do,' went on Max. 'Something new. I'm sure there must be something. We owe it to Uncle Geoff, don't we? I mean to keep things moving.'

'There is something he once talked about, started and then dropped. We might have another crack at that.'

'What was that, Bob?'

'The grotto.'

'A grotto? He never told me about that.'

'It was a long time ago. He was still quite a young man then and I'd just come out of the Army. He started it, then gave up. Filled it in and left it - just like that. He never really said why.'

'Rather a funny thing to do, wasn't it? I wouldn't have a clue where it was and I have been over the place with him.'

'I can show you if you like, but I haven't been in that part of the woods myself for a while. Nothing really to take me there. But it's an idea.'

'Yes,' said Max. 'I rather fancy a grotto. But why would Uncle Geoff start building one simply to chuck it in, I wonder?'

Bob only shrugged his shoulders. 'Buggered if I know.'

'Did you know about Uncle Geoff's grotto, Joe?' Max asked him that evening. 'Bob tells me he started to build one and then gave it up.'

'I helped him, Mr Max' said Joe. 'Helped to lay the stones for it.'

'Why did he give it up Joe? Have you any idea?'

The man shrugged. 'I don't really know. He said something - how do you say it? - about it being a bit over the top. I'm not quite sure what he meant by that.'

'I do, Joe. At least I think I do, but I'd like to see it all the same,' said Max. 'Do you remember where it was?'

'It's a long time ago and we filled it in again. There's nothing to see now. Would Miss Cordelia like to join us in a game of Scrabble tonight sir?' Joe kept up his deferential manner - he always addressed Max as 'sir' or 'Mr Max' - but he seemed not particularly willing to talk about Uncle Geoff's grotto.

'I'm intrigued about this grotto of Uncle Geoff's,' Max said to Cordelia. 'He starts digging it out, then chucks it in. Joe helped him and they simply filled it in again.'

'So? He changed his mind, that's all. Nothing very peculiar about that, is there?'

'And Joe changed the subject when I asked him about it.'

Cordelia laughed. 'He's a dark horse is your Joe - if that's not too racist a thing to say - but quite honestly I can't think there's anything odd about your Uncle Geoff changing his mind about a thing like that. Perhaps he felt he was biting off more than he could chew.'

'Maybe,' said Max.

Bob pointed out the site of the intended grotto - in a small hollow in the woods bordering the garden where it met the neighbouring farmland. It was a good distance from the rest of the garden.

'I would have thought Uncle Geoff would have chosen somewhere a bit more conspicuous for a thing like a grotto,' said Max.

'That's where he said he wanted it to be,' Bob said, 'so that's where we dug it out.'

A low mound with a few fragments of weathered limestone poking through its surface was all that could be seen of it now in a tangled mass of brambles.

Max contemplated the inconspicuous feature. 'Hm. I think a grotto is a nice idea but this is hardly the right place for one, is it?'

Bob shrugged his shoulders and did not reply.

'Tell me, Bob,' went on Max, 'is there much of the stone left inside? Underneath there? I can see a few quite good pieces sticking through the surface. We need to dig it out to see what's left of it. It might save us a bit of expense.'

'Most of it was taken away - if I remember rightly,' said Bob. 'Better to forget this one and start afresh, I'd say. Let sleeping dogs lie.'

Max glanced at him. 'Oh? Are there any? Sleeping dogs, I mean?'

Bob merely shrugged his shoulders and said nothing.

'You make it sound very mysterious.'

'Leave well alone I'd say.'

'You say Joe helped Uncle Geoff?'

Bob nodded.

'But if a grotto's what you want I can show you a much better place for it, if you really want one, that is.'

They returned to the path through the trees and made back in the direction of the house.

Bob led Max to a small glade where the trees let in a bit of sunlight.

The young man eyed it thoughtfully. 'Hm, nearer the house certainly and still among the trees. I take your point, Bob. This makes a lot more sense. What on earth possessed Uncle Geoff to stick it right out there, I wonder?'

Neither of them spoke for a moment and Bob started to whistle softly, his way of saying that there was something else he wanted to get on with.

'Did Joe have anything to do with choosing the other site?'

Bob shrugged. 'He may have done, I can't remember if he did or not. He certainly didn't discuss it with me.'

Anyway, said Max. 'Let's give it some thought, Bob. I think your suggestion is worth considering.'

For the time being the matter rested, while the idea of constructing a grotto continued to grow on Max and he started to put together as much information of the subject that he could lay his hands on, from eighteenth century sources mainly, of which there were plenty, starting with an account of Alexander Pope's grotto at Twickenham. He liked the element of connoisseurship that a grotto implied, of scientific curiosity combined with its Classical or Gothic connotations: a grotto, after all, could equally well be the home of nymphs or of a hermit.

Max visited the surviving specimens at Painshill in Surrey and Goldney at Bristol, taking photographs and writing detailed notes, as well as looking at what was left of Pope's Twickenham one - which wasn't a great deal - but he studied the descriptions of it closely. Soon Bob was even fired up in his own taciturn way. Joe, too, talked about it, but had nothing more to say about Uncle Geoff's first essay. Max concluded that with his severely rational outlook on the world a grotto indeed might have seemed just a trifle over the top for one like Uncle Geoff. He started to sketch plans and elevations with Cordelia beside him adding her own deliberately perverse suggestions.

The Goldney grotto from Bristol provided a good place to start and Max even toyed with the idea of a river god or perhaps some more relevent modern equivalent. He did not feel he had to be too slavishly tied to the pastiche of an eighteenth century Whig garden. But one thing that appealed to him was the idea of lining the grotto's walls with curiosities as Alexander Pope had done, bright natural objects like pieces of quartz and even manmade things which would exercise an increasing fascination with the passage of time. It was another small way, perhaps, of providing an outlet for quirkiness in the formality of a reconstructed eighteenth century landscape garden. It could add a touch of early twentieth century relevence as well and bring the thing forward.

But first of all the stone. Deeply pitted limestone was what was needed to provide the proper effect of a grotto, be it classical or Gothic. He talked to Bob about it.

Bob knew a supplier and reckoned he could talk down the cost if he was allowed to do it in his own way. 'Leave it to me,' he said.

Max said no more about digging out what remained of Uncle Geoff's earlier attempt. He realised that with Bob it was better to give him his head in what might be termed the logistics of the operation while he concerned himself with its aesthetics.

The limestone rocks were duly delivered - good waterworn, tortured-looking specimens.

'These look great,' enthused Max.

So they went to work with a couple of extra hands, Joe helping out too, quite willingly, it seemed. Max all the time was tweaking his plans, but liking the way it was turning out. His ambition grew and he felt that to complete the effect there must be running water. What did Bob think of that? Not much at first, but Max became more pressing. There could be no half measures and there was even a small feeder stream that might be diverted. Max felt sure that it would work and could not for the life of him think why it had not occurred to him earlier, but luckily the site they had selected made it possible. Joe thought it was a great idea as well.

But behind his mounting ambition, something else niggled.

'I'm sure there's still some perfectly good stone left at the other site,' said Max.' It seems wrong to waste it somehow.'

'Nothing there to speak of as I told you,' Bob replayed. 'Joe would tell you the same I'm sure.'

Joe affirmed as much.

But what did you do with the stones you were using? Max persisted.

'There weren't many stones there, Mr Max,' said Joe. 'Mr Geoffrey stopped the work before we could put them in.'

Bob shot Max a cautionary glance which had the opposite effect to the one that it was meant to have.

Max could not articulate even to himself why, but he felt he needed to look at that site again.

When he set out the following morning, by himself, he took just a trowel, not even a spade. It was bright day with dappled sunlight falling on the path as it twisted its serpentine way through the trees.

It took him a moment or two to locate the particular spot again. 'Well and truly off the beaten track,' he told himself. 'That's what so odd about it.'

But he found what he was looking for, the pieces of limestone protruding from the bramble patch.

He grasped one and it felt loose under his hand. When he inserted the trowel it lifted easily, exposing a cavity below. Then scraping away the loose earth he came across a plank which was rotten, but which with a little prising he managed to shift.

But Max stopped when he heard footsteps brushing through the uncut grass and old leaves. He turned to see Cordelia standing beside him.

'I wondered where you were going, sneaking off like that,' she said.

'It's Uncle Geoff's attempt at a grotto,' he informed her. 'I just wanted to check it out, that's all. I thought there might be a few decent bits of stone left in here. But it looks a bit more interesting than that.'

The only sound was of a wood pigeon somewhere in the trees above them. And yet, Max had the feeling that they were not alone.

'The stone lifted out easily,' he explained to Cordelia, 'and now there's this.' He tugged at the edge of the rotten plank which started to crumble.

'Let me give you a hand.' Cordelia leaned down and took one end of it.

'There's something down there,' said Max.

'Sssh!' Cordelia stood up suddenly.

Max frowned and looked round at the bushes and trees. They were perfectly still and apart from the sound of the pigeon he could not hear anything.

'What the matter?'

'I heard a sort of rustling, like something or someone brushing against the leaves.'

'Well I didn't hear anything.' Max addressed himself to the plank once more. 'And in any case, we're in wood, aren't we? Natural sounds and all that.'

Cordelia took one end and they both heaved. It came away suddenly in their hands. They stood staring into the cavity beneath where it had been and both heard the movement in the bushes this time. Max strode across to where it had seemed to come from.

'Nothing there, he reported to Cordelia. A squirrel or a rabbit, most likely. There are masses of them about.'

'Look down there,' said Cordelia, pointing into the cavity. He leaned over and could see a pink and white object. Gingerly he lifted it out.

'Good Lord!' he exclaimed. 'It's a set of dentures! These must be Aunt Dot's teeth!'

Cordelia looked baffled. 'Aunt Dot's teeth?'

'Yes. They went missing just before her funeral. We couldn't find them anywhere and Uncle Geoff was in no state to do anything about it. Now they turn up here, buried in the ground! And, moreover, I know exactly where they're going to go - right onto the wall of our new grotto! The first of many strange and fascinating objects!' Max's eyes lit up at the prospect.

'That's not all,' Cordelia said. She was fishing inside the hole and produced a what looked like a small blackened twig.

'What have you got there?' Max took the object from her and scrutinised it carefully. 'It looks like a bone.'

But Cordelia was already kneeling and working at something else. Slowly and with tender care she lifted it out.

It was small and blackened like the bone and round. But instead of passing it to Max she started gently to rub the earth off it.

'Poor mite, I think I know what you are,' she murmured. 'I've handled others like you in the Arch and Anth department.'

Max frowned and eyed the object. 'Man or beast?'

'Man - or at least the early stages of one.' Cordelia brushed the dirt gently from the rounded surface. 'Do you see? That's what's called the fontanelle - the space on the skull where the sutures have not yet closed. It's a membrane covering the brain. This is the skull of a foetus or of a very young baby. And at a guess I'd say it's the former....'

Dead Men's Clothes

As soon as Reg Hancock got home he took the suit out of the plastic dry-cleaning bag and put it on a coat hanger. He reckoned he had done pretty well for just twenty quid. It was a dark grey suit with a thin pinstripe and a double breasted jacket. The material was not the best quality - it lacked body and was a bit too shiny - but it was a genuine well-worn, run of the mill nineteen-fifties suit. He had held it up against himself in front of a mirror in the secondhand shop - 'Dead Men's Clothes' as he liked to call it - and it seemed to fit him more or less. Nothing that Alice couldn't fix anyway. The owner of the shop, Mr Haslehurst, told him that he would need a pair of braces to keep his trousers up.

'Men always wore braces to keep their trousers up in those days,' he explained.

It was exactly what Reg had been looking for: a real nineteen-fifties suit. Now back at home, instead of putting it in the wardrobe, he decided to try it on straight away. He did not have a pair of braces, but he thought he could hold the trousers up with a belt in the meantime so that Alice could at least see what needed to be done. The jacket was roomy and the loose-fitting trousers felt comfortable. It was nice, too, to have proper flies instead of a zip.

'What do you think of that then?' he asked his wife, when he presented himself in the kitchen.

'Good heavens, Reg, what have you dug up this time?' was Alice's immediate response.

'A suit.'

'I can see it's a suit, but what kind of a suit? Not a very new one by the look of it, Where on earth did you find it? In a charity shop?'

'I got it from Haslehurst. You know - at Dead Men's Clothes.'

'And it looks as if a dead man's been wearing it too,' Alice observed dourly. 'It certainly could do with a clean. But anyway what do you want another suit for? You've got two already. Isn't that plenty?'

'But this is the real thing, love. A real nineteen-fifties suit.'

'If you ask me it makes you look like a spiv in one of your old black and white DVDs.' Alice was unimpressed and shook her head. 'No, Reg, I can't say it does anything for you.'

'It'll need some adjustment - then it'll look fine.' Reg eyed his wife hopefully.

'In that case shouldn't you take it to a tailor?'

Reg said nothing, but looked at Alice with his best puppy-dog expression.

'Oh all right then.' She gave in as she always did. 'But you'll have to get it cleaned first. I won't touch it till you have. You've no idea who was last wearing it.'

'Thanks love,' said Reg, giving her a peck on the cheek. He had been born in the nineteen-sixties but he sometimes tried to affect the cheeky-chappy manner, as he conceived it, of an earlier generation when he addressed his missus. Alice managed to put up with these laboured attempts at facetiousness with an astonishing good grace.

Reg already had a plan for his new suit. It was to have its first outing at a forthcoming Fifties event in a local hotel. He had never been to one before, but he belonged to a club that met once a month to look at films of the Fifties and to discuss and exchange memorabilia. Needless to say they dressed in what they hoped passed for the right gear for the occasion. There were a dozen of them, nine men and three women. But Kennie Handslip - who acted as a kind of correspondence secretary for their circle, came up with a fresh idea. He had contacts with other Fifties circles and had recently attended a nationwide convention near London which had thrown up some good ideas. So Kennie arranged a Fifties weekend where everyone was to get up as a well-known character of the time and to act out the part. The idea was to guess who people were supposed to be without anyone letting on. The evening would kick off with a sausage sizzle, out of doors, weather permitting, followed by a game of murder in the dark on two of the hotel floors which had been booked and set aside specially for the purpose. A singsong of favourite Fifties hits would round off proceedings before bedtime. A similar programme was laid on for the next day, a Sunday, including a teatime film show, after which there was to be a hop including a bit of vintage rock and roll as first performed by Bill Haley and his Comets. Wives and any other guests who were prepared to enter into the spirit of the thing were of course more than welcome and Reg knew that Alice, who was a good sport, wouldn't let him down.

But before she would attend to his suit it had to be dry-cleaned. A day after leaving it at the cleaners when Reg went to collect it, the girl who packed it up for him handed him an envelope.

'We found this in the inside pocket,' she told him.

'Really? I've no idea what that can be,' said Reg.

'It's a photograph,' explained the girl. 'Something from down Memory Lane by the look of it. It might be your mum and dad.'

'No. I'm afraid that's hardly likely, but it sounds interesting all the same.' Reg pocketed the envelope without opening it. He would examine its contents at leisure when he got home.

Reg hung up the suit in the kitchen for Alice to find and sitting down at the table opened the envelope. Inside was an old black and white photograph, creased and dog-eared at the corners. It was of a middle-aged couple, taken, by the look of it, in a photographer's studio. The woman had a dumpy homely sort of figure and tightly arranged hair. She looked a little tense, while the man had a slight smile on his rugged face. He had a high balding forehead, and a mildly quizzical glint in his eye as if he wasn't the kind to give very much away- a man who held his cards dose to his chest. His tie, Reg noticed, was spotted and tied in a tight knot. For some reason that he could not explain to himself Reg's attention focused on the tie and the way it was knotted.

But what was more interesting, the man appeared to be wearing the very suit in whose pocket the picture had turned up, or at least one like it. And the face was vaguely familiar too. Rag was sure that he had seen it somewhere, but couldn't place it.

Something told him that despite the couple's rather humdrum appearance the man at least had been a personality to be reckoned with. Was he a Labour politician from the time of Clement Attlee? His rugged working class features looked authoritative. A powerful trade union leader maybe?

Then a thought struck Reg. Could it possibly be? It was hardly likely, a very long shot indeed, but he had an idea where to look, on the bookshelf in his glory hole up in the attic. Reg climbed the ladder staircase to the attic and took a paperback book from his shelves. He liked to keep all his books together and refused to lend them to anyone if it meant them leaving the house.

There was a simple black and white photograph on the dark ground of the book's cover - a head and shoulders portrait of a middle-aged man. Reg set it by his photograph. The two seemed to be about the same age and the likeness was striking though the man on the cover of the book was wearing a trilby - the kind of soft hat that men wore in the Forties and Fifties - but it was difficult to say about his suit - not enough of it could be seen to be sure if it was the same one or not.

'It's certainly very like him,' mused Reg. 'It might almost be his spitting image, but, of course, I can't be absolutely sure. Anyway it's given me a great idea.'

Reg had been looking at a picture of Britain's most famous hangman of the twentieth century who had published his memoirs in the nineteen seventies - and a riveting read they had turned out to be too, especially his account of the hanging of the Belsen war criminals. Needless to say Reg had lapped up all the technical details of the process of a judicial execution as it was carried out until the early sixties when the death penalty was finally abolished. He knew all about varying the length of the trapdoor drop, the metal washer that had taken the place of the traditional hangman's knot - even the rubber one, an extra added by this selfsame executioner, to prevent the prisoner from jerking the noose loose once the metal washer had been set under the left side of his jaw. Oh and soaping the rope to make sure that there was the minimum of friction when it drew tight as the trapdoor was sprung. Reg was very taken with that particular detail.

The prisoner was always hooded of course. And another detail that had tickled Reg's fancy: the executioner carried the hood like a large white handkerchief in his breast pocket and whipped it out to place over the prisoner's head on the trapdoor just before he set the noose. That showed style. Reg knew that this particular executioner liked to look his best for a hanging and, despite the brief time it took to dispatch his victim, to invest the occasion with a proper sobriety. He always wore a suit for the job, rather as an undertaker might have done. So what about Reg's suit? And what had been in that breast pocket, if indeed the suit had belonged to the hangman? Reg was going to take his part at the Fifties event. His choice of character had been handed to him on a plate.

Picking up the jacket, Reg put his fingers inside the breast pocket. It may have been his imagination, but the cloth forming its lip seemed to have been stretched as if it had held something rather larger than it was made for. He imagined the white hood dangling foppishly from it, and, running his fingers around the lining, Reg's spine tingled slightly at the thought. But then of course he did not know for certain if this really had been the hangman's suit.

When he informed Alice of his intention to go to the Fifties event as the public hangman, she eyed him and shook her head. 'You're a morbid bugger, Reg Hancock,' she said. 'And you expect me to tag along as his missus, don't you?'

'Unless you'd rather go as one of his customers. He topped a good few women in his time,' Reg chuckled, a trifle unpleasantly, Alice felt.

'And he wasn't such a gloomy devil as you might think either,' he went on. 'He kept a pub and was a very cheery landlord. There was nothing he liked better than a good singsong and playing Father Christmas at kids' parties.'

'That's creepy.'

'It depends on your point of view,' said Reg.

'It gives me the shivers. But if that's what you want, I'll trot along as Mrs Hangman just as long as I'm allowed to look like a normal human being.'

'You couldn't look like anything else,' said Reg giving her a peck on the cheek in his usual perky manner.

'Enough of your soft soap you daft bugger.'

And so it turned out. Alice studied the photograph and contrived an outfit that was similar to the one in it and on the day of the event in the Beechgrove Park Hotel even attempted to do up her hair in the style of an elderly or middle-aged woman of the Fifties.

'I won't wear lots of war paint,' she told her husband, 'I draw the line at that, but a dab of rouge and a dollop of the old lipstick would be in order, I daresay.'

Reg felt deeply touched by his missus being so supportive.

It was a warm evening in late May and the turnout at the Beechgrove Park was good, at least twice the number of the group's core members. A whole floor had been booked and set aside for the occasion, to maintain the illusion as far as possible.

'The Fifties seem to be catching on,' Reg observed enthusiastically. 'It would be really nice to see them come around again in a big way.'

And immediately the guessing of people's identities began. Denis Cornpton was the first to be rumbled - it wasn't difficult. Eddie Street, who took his part, was known to be a mine of Fifties cricketing lore, a walking Wisden, and was wearing the proper gear, including cream flannels. He was even padded up ready for the crease, but the real giveaway for those who knew anything at all about the iconography of the time was his hair - Brylcreamed exactly as it had been in those magazine and billboard adverts featuring the famous cricketer. The film star Richard Todd, played by Leslie Tyler, was rapidly unmasked as well, mainly because of the bomber pilot's gear he was wearing and his well-known passion for war films of that time, and the bulky Labour MP Bessie Braddock followed, betrayed by her large red rosette. She was played rather pluckily by the ample Judy Hodge. The film star Alan Ladd, in his role as the gunfighter Shane, played by Paul Wood, bit the dust quickly too.

But some of the others proved more tricky. The game was to drop small clues, but not make them too obvious. And Reg in his nondescript suit could not be cracked, despite his having stuffed a napkin in his breast pocket which he allowed to hang ostentatiously down his front. No one seemed able to pick up the clue. But he went no further than that. From his reading he knew that the Hangman had been understandably reluctant to discuss his craft, so when he was pressed, Reg only provided broad hints about keeping a pub in a strong north country accent. Not that Reg was pressed as hard as some of the others who had adopted more glamorous roles, after all drabness was of the essence of the part he was trying to play and provided a good mask.

So by the time main programme got underway, Reg had still not been rumbled. He intended to drop broader hints as the evening wore on and of course all would be revealed anyway in the Hercule Poirot style post mortem concluding the game of murder in the dark. Alice maintained her part too, keeping mum, the loyal back-up to her man.

Reg meanwhile enjoyed himself guessing who the other remaining characters were and was very proud of identifying Fred Truman who wore what turned out to be a Yorkshire County Cricket Club Blazer with grey flannels, instead of full cricket gear. An ostentatiously large briar pipe had been the giveaway in his case. But Diana Dors arriving late was instantly unmasked. She was just too good a lookalike.

There was a cool breeze and the sausage sizzle was got through fairly briskly before the party retreated to the annex bar which had been set aside for them. Reg was intrigued by another blonde who had slipped in late, and placed herself at the table where he was sitting with Alice and a few others. She was apparently on her own and got up in full war paint, as Alice would have expressed it. Reg couldn't place her and she did not say much. But she seemed curious about him, more so than in any of the others, and she even leaned over the table and fingered the napkin drooping from his breast pocket.

'A nice touch. I remember it so well.'

Reg looked backed at her, startled. 'What do you mean you remember it so well?'

The woman shrugged and smiled. 'What I said. After all, I should know, shouldn't I? If anyone does.'

'Then you've guessed who I'm supposed to be?'

The woman smiled and shrugged her shoulders again. 'It's hardly very difficult, is it? I mean for someone in my position.'

'But I'm afraid I can't place you,' said Reg. 'I know I should, because your face rings a loud bell, but I can't.'

'You surprise me, but then I might have expected you to say that, mightn't I? I'll put you out of your misery before the fun's over,' she replied. 'All in good time. There's no hurry.'

'Perhaps we've been reading the same book,' said Reg.

'Perhaps we have. But I would have known you anywhere with that thing stuffed in your breast pocket. Now if you'll excuse me, we'll chat later.'

She got up and crossed the room to talk to Bill Winterton who was endevouring to pass himself off as the racing driver, Stirling Moss.

'Fancy her knowing a thing like that, I mean about my breast pocket. She's the only one to have rumbled it,' remarked Reg to Elsie Swatridge on his right. 'Who is she by the way? I haven't met her before, but I feel as if I ought to know her. I presume she must know somebody here.'

'I've simply no idea,' said Elsie. 'I've never set eyes on her before - though she reminds me of someone too, from the Fifties, I mean. Another film star or someone of that kind. They all seem much of a muchness to me with their heavy make-up. They certainly liked to lay on the lipstick then.'

Kennie called for silence and explained the game of murder in the dark which was about to follow. The lights would go out on the two floors above which had been specially set aside for the occasion. Everyone was to scatter, but of course remain within the area. One of their number had been designated the murderer and was equipped with a loaded starting pistol and a pencil torch. Once the selected victim had been tracked down, a tap on the shoulder and the whispered words 'You're dead' would follow. The victim was then be expected to slump to the floor while the murderer fired the starting pistol. Darkness would reign for another minute to give the killer time to distance him or herself from the immediate scene of the crime. With the discovery of the corpse the entire caste would decamp to the lounge bar for the post mortem and denouement conducted by a detective in the manner of Agatha Christie's Hercule Poirot.

'Have I made myself clear?' said Kennie.

There was no dissent and they all trooped up to the next floor where Kennie turned on a sinister soundtrack to generate the right kind of atmosphere.

'Now scatter,' he told them. 'The lights are going off now.'

And on cue the lights went off, plunging them into darkness. A few gasps and muted squeals followed.

'Be careful on the stairs,' warned Kennie. 'No broken ankles please. Good hunting!'

Whispers and giggles could be heard as people groped about and bumped into each other, with the menacing music pulsing away behind it all.

Alice had been holding Reg's hand when the lights went out, but he quickly lost her.

'Are you there, Reg?' he heard her call anxiously as someone bumped into him and caused him to step back and to stand on another person's toe.

'Ouch,' said a female voice. 'That's my toe!' Reg thought it might have been the girl playing Diana Dors and was trying to think up a saucy riposte, but he put out a hand instead which came to rest on a well-formed bosom and its cleavage at the top of a low-slung dress.

'You dirty thing - whoever you are,' shrilled the female voice again, followed by a giggle and a playful slap on Reg's wrist.

Reg emitted a throaty chuckle.

'You old groper!' came the phony reproof.

'Reg, where are you?' Alice's anxious voice came from further away now.

'I'm over here, love,' Reg called back. 'But watch out. There are some pretty dodgy characters about this evening.'

Reg felt his way along the wainscotted passage, trying to remember if there were any tables or chairs to be negotiated. Giggles and whispers could be heard on all sides and bumps as people blundered into pieces of furniture. And one couple were already taking advantage of the dark to engage in a little love play. Rather dirty jokes occasionally reached Reg's ears as he groped in the direction of the foot of the staircase where he bumped into the couple whose lovemaking he had heard. They were sitting on the bottom stair and he could hear the smack of a kiss and an affectedly husky female voice, but he could not recognise its owner. Was it the girl playing Diana Dors? Or possibly the one whom he spoken to in the bar? She had looked the type, certainly.

Reg decided he would creep up to the landing above which was also blacked out. He guided himself by the bannister rail. There were no sounds coming from above and it crossed his mind that he might be the first to venture up the staircase. Where the murderer was he had no idea. So far he had been in complete blackness and there wasn't the faintest glimmer of a pencil torch. It was all going to take time. Meanwhile the original sountrack had been replaced by The Ride of the Valkyries of all things. Kennie's choice of music was somewhat idiosyncratic. It sounded a little faraway on the upper landing and to Reg vaguely sinister as a consequence. Otherwise he could hear no movement, not a whisper even, nothing. Why had none of the others ventured this far? he couldn't help wondering.

Then along the end of the corridor he saw a tiny pinprick of light, but too small to be able to make out the person carrying it. Reg wondered whether he ought to feel his way back to the stairs and return to the lower landing, but beside him the wall ended suddenly where a second passage met the one he had entered. He decided to slip into the side passage and wait for the presumed murderer to pass. As quiet as a mouse, he felt his way into it, pressing his body close to the wall as he inched his way up it. In spite of it only being a game, he was scared. He was the possible prey with a predator on the prowl. He remembered as a child the terror of playing hide-and-seek when the searcher got nearer and nearer to his hiding place. He had known it wasn't for real, but the feeling of terror at his imminent discovery used to be too much for him all the same, so much so that he usually gave himself away to get the suspense over and done with.

He pressed himself hard against the wall and felt a bead of sweat running down his cheek. The person holding the pencil torch was moving silently, advancing with feline stealth. Reg stifled the urge to call out and end the suspense just as he had done as a child. Then the light drew level with the end of the side passage and stopped. He still couldn't see the bearer, only the tiny pinprick. Then horror of horrors. It turned into the side passage where he was hiding. Reg started to inch his way along the wall towards the end of the passage, passing bedroom doors as he went. The dot of light came on, silently, relentlessly. Reg prayed to himself that he would find another staircase and make his escape that way. But no, only more doors until he reached a window at the end of the passage.

'I'm here,' he called out, a frightened child once more.

As the light came closer he could now make out that its carrier was a woman. Her heavily made-up face with its bright lipstick illuminated in the sliver of light. At once Reg recognised the woman who had identified him during the meal. Somehow he was half-expecting her. It was shrewd of Kennie to appoint her as the killer and for the Hangman to be her victim!

'I surrender,' called Reg, trying to make a jest out of his fear, which for some reason had not left him as it normally had done in his childish games of hide-and-seek as soon as he had been discovered.

The woman did not speak as she came right up to him.

'Mr Pierrepoint?'

'Hancock. Actually it's Reg Hancock.'

'Mr Albert Pierrepoint,' she repeated.

'Oh all right - if you want it that way.'

'That's the way it was.' She smiled showing a row of even white teeth, that gleamed in the torchlight.

'Are you going to murder me?' Reg asked. 'Just give me the word and I'll be a good boy and lie down. It's quite a good joke, isn't it? I mean the hangman being the victim for a change. So who's going to top his killer then?' Reg chuckled, yet it did not feel at all funny.

Suddenly the woman thrust her face forward and planted her deep red lips on Reg's mouth. It was a long, hard, determined kind of a kiss with her tongue forcing a passage though his lips. The smell of her perfume was overpowering. Reg felt dizzy.

Then she equally suddenly thrust him away and, with the pencil torch pointing full in his face, she eyed him critically, almost reproachfully. The deep shadows under her cheekbones and in the wells of her eyes gave her features something of the quality of a death mask.

'Do you still not remember me?' she asked in a soft almost

caressing voice. 'Surely you must by now.'

'No,' Reg faltered, 'I know I should, but your name has escaped me.'

'I don't believe you. You want to kid yourself that you've forgotten me, but you haven't - you can't have done.'

'All right,' gasped Reg, the sweat breaking out on his brow, 'I'll tell you then. You're Ruth Ellis, the last woman I - I mean Albert Pierrepoint - ever hanged.'

'There you are. What took you so long? But now we have to round off this little charade, haven't we?'

She pressed her cheek against his and nibbled his ear, tenderly. 'You're dead,' she whispered in a husky voice. Then, taking a small pistol from her shoulder bag, she placed the muzzle on Reg's chest over the napkin that was drooping from his breast pocket and pulled the trigger. There was a report, too loud for a starting pistol, shouts and cheers from various points in the darkness. But when the lights went up they found Reg, lying where he had fallen - stone dead and a deep crimson stain spreading over the while napkin and the front of his suit.

The Ghost

There were times when Leo felt that he had taken the wrong turning in life. He had left university with a young man's literary aspirations, which was nothing unusual, and to a limited extent he had lived up to them for, now in his mid fifties, he did make a living of sorts with his pen, but alone it would hardly have been sufficient. Some home tutoring and a meager occupational pension, realised a bit too soon to be worth much, were necessary to keep him afloat, but at least he could claim to have a creative output of a kind with his ghostwriting. And that is how he chose to describe himself - as a ghost.

How spooky, came the inevitable tacky reply at which he would try to raise up a ghostly smile.

It was hack work of course and his current assignment was fairly typical. This time its subject was a recently deceased Regular Army colonel, though just occasionally he might have to tell the story of a minor celebrity sinking into obscurity, who would clutch him in a forlorn attempt to check the descent.

Colonel Akhurst's widow had commissioned the work which was

to be offered up in the form of a memoir written by the deceased warrior himself. And it was all so predictable.

Mrs Akhurst had already done a lot of the spadework by the time Leo first called on her at her home in the North Riding of Yorkshire where her late husband's family had long been settled. In her diligent fashion she had written down the salient facts of the Colonel's schooldays, as she saw them, and of his early career in the Royal Artillery before the war. But for the wartime years themselves she was relying on his own letters addressed to herself which provided her with the justification for telling his story in the form of a personal memoir.

Leo was unimpressed. The letters were stodgy and unrevealing, though he was tickled by the nicknames they used at that time - in particular he liked Fruity Pears - and he admired, too, the reluctance of Colonel Akhurst's generation to blow their own trumpets. He appreciated how they played down quite fierce actions by talking about them as shows and came out with schoolboyish euphemisms like 'Jerry got a good licking.' It was the authentic voice of an age that had passed, but at the same time it opened no doors onto an inner life. Colonel Akhurst was hardly a Sassoon or a Blunden.

Having waded through Mrs Akhurst's neatly-tabulated account of the Colonel's schooldays at Rugby - mostly a list of the teams he had played in and his sporting honours - the very bald record of the prewar spell in India and the years at home leading up to the Second World War, Leo finally came upon a possible nugget. The Colonel in one of his letters to his wife from the Western Desert in 1942 mentioned an encounter with the then General Montgomery. He used the sentence, 'he seems a bit of a showman, but he might just do the trick.' And that it seemed was as far as he was prepared to go.

Leo thought it might be worth a trip to the family seat near

Harrogate to see if he could draw the Colonel's widow out a bit further on that one. Maybe he had said more to her at a later time of what had passed between him and the General than was contained in the letter. But when he rang Mrs Akhurst Leo merely said that there were a number of points that he needed to go over with her and made no mention of General Montgomery. He enjoyed these trips out to visit his clients in their own homes; he was always curious to see the insides of other people's houses, telling himself that it provided him with an insight into their personalities, something very necessary for a good ghost after all, while on this particular occasion it gave him an excuse to visit Harrogate and to poke around in some of its antique shops.

He found that Mrs Akhurst had moved into the gatehouse since his last visit and the big house was already in the hands of a developer who was converting it into flats. Privately he wondered about the funding of the Colonel's memoirs, but felt that this was not the time to raise it.

'Like most of his generation your husband wasn't given to talking very much about himself,' he said to her. 'He kept himself under wraps, which is a quality I admire, but it doesn't help me very much.'

'Men of Edward's kind didn't waste time talking,' Mrs Akhurst explained, 'but simply got on with the job that had to be done and didn't complain.'

'The laconic Spartans,' said Leo to himself, but not uttering the thought aloud as he felt it might be lost on the Colonel's widow.

'And in any case,' she went on. 'You're a writer and it's your job to supply the dash of romance, isn't it?'

'The dash of romance?'

'Indeed. It's something that should shine through the man's own

91

modesty, shouldn't it?'

'In other words I've got to spin a good yarn, even if it's meant to be the man telling his own story?'

'Of course you have, but you still have to remember that it's Edward speaking and he was very much a no nonsense kind of a man. When it comes to his later life that should be plain enough.'

'I'm sure it will be.' Leo grimaced inwardly at the prospect of the later life. 'But with respect, Mrs Akhurst, you don't make it sound very easy.'

'You are a professional writer, aren't you?'

'I like to think so.'

'Well there you are then.' Her eyes opened wide in her shrivelled face. They were old and watery ones now, but might once have been quite beguiling.

'There is one detail - possibly a rather important one, I would like to discuss with you, if I may, Mrs Akhurst.'

'Fire away, as Edward would have said.'

'Monty. General, as he then was, General Montgomery.'

'Yes. Indeed. Edward met him.'

'In one of his letters he describes him as a bit of a showman.'

'Well wasn't he? A lot of people said that at the time.'

'Did he ever, how shall I put it, develop the idea with you?'

'I'm not sure that I follow you,' said Mrs Akhurst. 'How do you mean develop the idea?'

'A lot of people, especially some of the ones who'd served under Auckinleck before him thought Monty........ frankly - forgive the word Mrs Akhurst - a bit of a shit.'

92

Mrs Akhurst frowned severely and Leo knew that he never should have uttered such a word. In fact he could not think what had possessed him to do it.

'I'm sorry,' he said. 'I expressed that rather badly.'

'More than rather, I'd say very badly, Mr Summers,' Mrs Akhurst admonished him, 'but I think I know what you're trying to say. No, Edward was completely loyal. He liked a winner. After all, he was one himself. As you know, he was a very keen games player.'

Leo wondered for a second if he should not be writing a footballer's life rather than the memoirs of a retired colonel, the former being a genre that he found particularly irksome, as he had never been much of a games player himself. He wasn't going to get very far with General Montgomery, he could see. But somehow the furrow had to be ploughed.

Meanwhile he turned the talk to Mrs Akhurst's new domestic arrangements and the future of the big house.

'I feel a bit like that woman in - what was that television show called? - you know the one I'm talking about with Penelope Keith.'

'To the Manor Born?'

'That's the one, but there's no Mr Whatsit... the Czech or the Pole, the man who'd bought the Manor.'

'Czech - Mr de Vere.'

'There's no Mr de Vere in my life.'

Leo laughed and assured her that she hardly needed one and after a little more scribble talk of that kind, excused himself and left for Harrogate. He remembered a shop there from his last visit that had some good pieces of Bristol Blue Glass, one of his passions, and he felt in a spending mood.

Once back in the capital he started a tentative account of the Colonel's schooldays at his Yorkshire prep school then at Rugby. Clearly they had meant a great deal to him because as well as her outline of his achievements Mrs Akhurst had provided an album with a good supply of school photographs, including some team ones. In them young Akhurst looked a handsome lad with neatly-cropped fair hair and the smile of someone in the full flush of his own schoolboy success, especially on the rugby and cricket fields. A decent, transparent sort of boy, without a flicker of self-doubt on his face. All was as it should have been in his world. A touch of arrogance that went with the genre, perhaps, but Edward Akhurst was clearly no Flashman. Leo felt that he needed to mug up on Rugby School in the late Twenties and early Thirties.

That promised to open up a fascinating and for Leo a hitherto unexplored territory, the world of the pre-war preparatory and public school. It could be a book in its own right, he thought, probably one with a wider appeal than the Life and Times of Colonel Edward Akhurst O.B.E., Royal Artillery was likely to have, while the Colonel himself might be turned into a useful peg on which to hang it.

But there was Mrs Akhurst to be reckoned with, and she seemed to a have pretty clear idea of the kind of book she wanted written about the man who was such a perfect knight in her eyes. There would be a copy of it proudly displayed on her own shelves, of course, another in the county library and one in the regimental archive, while relatives, friends, members of the golf club and leading lights in the County Show would each have a copy. And not forgetting Rugby School, who would get theirs as well.

The more he thought about it, the more Leo knew the sort of book he himself prefered to write and that the worthy but dull scion of Rugby

94

School, Edward Akhurst, might possibly provide a focal point for part of the story at least... .the story of an English public school from the years before the war up to the Sixties... told to the general reader for whom such a world might only have existed in the books or comics of childhood. It was going to need a lot more research than he had been used to doing. But then he was not unfamiliar with the process because providing background was an essential part of a ghostwriter's work. And it would need to be colourful and rich in anecdote, which would mean landing some more exotic fish than Edward Akhurst - a thing that surely would not be too difficult given the subject of the book.

So Leo started by visiting Rugby School. He had been a day boy at a London independent school himself, and had been spared the Spartan rigours of boarding, especially in such a robust age as Edward Akhurst's, and the thing had an almost voyeuristic fascination for him. In many ways, too, he thought of the Thirties and Forties, and also of the Fifties, when he had been born, as rather a good time for children to grow up in, all the better for being relatively unsophisticated, and he wanted to do them justice, even if it meant using a stuffed shirt like Edward Akhurst to do it.

The people at Rugby were helpful, even laying on a boy to show him over the place while he was given access to the school's main library and archive. He came away fired up, with a mountain of notes, but also with a feeling that he might be biting off more than he could chew. Meanwhile his visits to Mrs Akhurst became less frequent and, perhaps, more ominously, she contacted him less, until a point came when his telephone calls and letters to her went unanswered.

Leo was in a quandry. He had met none of her family: there were a son and a daughter as well as three grandchildren that she liked talking about, especially her son Robert's boy who also bore the name of Edward and was said to be the image of his grandfather. The likeness was 'really quite uncanny' she had insisted, dropping her voice to a kind of awed whisper as if young Edward was a reincarnation of the Colonel himself.

How the kin could be contacted Leo did not know. But it did not take him long to find out about what had happened to Mrs Akhurst since he regularly cast an eye down the deaths columns of The Times and there her name was. She had died peacefully a week earlier and presumably there had been a time before that when she had been in hospital or a nursing home and in no condition to answer his queries about her husband's memoirs. Anyway Leo decided to drop what he was doing and go to her funeral which was to be held in her village church.

It was a bright, blustery April day with daffodils in full bloom on the green and there was a respectable turn-out of forty or so people, from the village and what might be described as the County Set, exactly what Leo would have expected to find there. Everything about the Akhursts seemed worthily predictable, but hardly the grist for his own particular mill.

'No,' Leo said to himself. 'This has got to be made into something bigger; a kind of history for which the Colonel is merely a peg, or one of a number of pegs.'

But what was going to happen to the book now that Mrs Akhurst was dead was a more pressing question. It was very possible that it would die with her, unless she had set money aside for it and he sensed that by the end she had none too much of that.

The funeral was not a grief-stricken event, the old lady having passed away ripe in years, so Leo felt free to probe some of the mourners at the drinks party which was held in the local hostelry afterwards, since the gatehouse where she had lately resided was deemed to be too small.

There were Mrs Akhurst's immediate family and some farming folk, several of them the kind of County grandees among whom the Colonel had been numbered. As well as being active in organizing the County Show, he had of course been a foxhunting man, but hardly one in the mould of Siegfried Sassoon, needless to say; if he had ever felt any of the hunt's poetry, he would have been incapable of expressing it.

Leo had to introduce himself to the others there since he knew none of them, but Mrs Akhurst's son had picked him up after the burial and invited him along for the drinks. He was there with his wife and their teenage son, the one who, bore such a striking resemblance to the Edward of the school photographs and whom Mrs Akhurst had talked about so warmly. Leo felt that that a remark on those lines might be a suitable opener.

'Robert Akhurst,' said the father, introducing himself, 'and my wife Pru.'

'Leo. Leo Summers. I'm supposed to be writing your father's memoirs.'

'Yes, I've heard about you.' Robert gave him a searching look and his right eyelid dropped almost in a conspiratorial wink. 'Oh young Edward, by the way,' he said remembering the boy.

'You don't have to tell me - the same name as his grandfather,' Leo said. 'And his spitting image as well - if the old photographs are anything to go by.'

'As his grandmother never ceased reminding everyone. In fact she got to be a bloody bore on that subject. But then we mustn't speak ill of the dead, must we? Especially the most recent ones,' he said with a second conspiratorial lowering of an eyelid. 'But tell me about the book.'

'I suppose it's all in the air now that your mother has passed on.'

'Oh I don't think so - not necessarily.'

Leo looked at the man and at his wife, who had so far said nothing. Robert Akhurst if anything appeared to be the 'city type', probably in his later forties, his waistline starting to bulge, but with a crop of thick blond hair which was streaked with grey in places. He wore a well-cut pinstripe suit, a Jermyn Street shirt and a knitted black silk tie for the occasion.

Leo raised his eyebrows at what Robert had just said. 'Oh?'

'Seriously,' said the latter. 'I'm sure that between us we could manage to market the old buffer, with a bit of repackaging.'

' The way you talk about your own father!' expostulated his wife, speaking for the first time.

'Well wasn't he an old buffer? At least I didn't call him a buffoon.'

'Your mother thought the world of him,' Leo reminded him.

'But she would, wouldn't she? And anyway she's safe on the far side of Jordan by now, in a manner of speaking.'

Leo glanced at the boy who, with a sulky frown on his face, had said nothing, but now took the opportunity to sidle off to the table where the drinks were laid out and to help himself to a fresh glass of wine.

'Go easy on it, Teddy, for God's sake,' his mother pleaded with him. 'You remember what happened the last time.'

The boy scowled at her and by way of answering took a big pull at his glass.

His mother looked at Leo and released an exasperated parental sigh.

'It's that age,' he tried to reassure her, 'but he really does look astonishingly like his grandfather - in the photographs I've seen of him - but without his triumphant expression.'

She glanced anxiously at her husband who flashed a warning to her which Leo also picked up.

'That's as far as it goes, I can assure you,' he said to Leo. 'But let's talk about the book instead, it's a less morbid topic than teenage children. How far have you got with it?'

Leo covered the ground he felt pretty thoroughly and then provided a fairly fulsome account of his recent visit to Rugby School.

'I must say they were pretty decent to me. They couldn't have been more helpful in fact.'

But as he spoke he noticed the faces of Robert Akhurst and his wife cloud over. He fell silent and they did not supply any kind of a filler.

'You must excuse me,' Robert came out with at length. 'It's time I did some mingling. Son of the deceased and all that.'

His wife, Pru, turned at once to her son, who had just helped himself to his second glass of wine, and remonstrated with him in an urgent whisper, while her husband, as he left him, squeezed Leo's arm and pressed a card into his hand. 'We have to talk more about this book,' he said in a low voice. 'I think you and I should meet up in town, don't you? Give me a buzz.'

Then he crossed the room to talk to Sir Paul Lumley, the MOH. Leo meanwhile nodded his goodbyes and set off to enjoy the rest of the day in Harrogate.

He was curious about Robert Akhurst and even more so about the boy, young Edward, who looked so like his grandfather. The boy's sulleness was not really surprising. After all he had been dragged along to a family funeral where he had had to put up with a bunch of stuffy adults who kept reminding him of how like his grandfather he looked. Leo felt a little guilty that he had done that very thing himself and he almost heard the inward groan from the boy while his father had tried to downplay the matter by criticizing his own newly deceased mother for the same offence. And then there was that blip in the conversation when Rugby School was mentioned. Had the boy somehow failed to live up to expectations by not following his grandfather's shining example? Had he possibly blotted his copybook there? Something like that had been hinted to Leo on his visit to the school And what about Robert who had so obviously wanted to duck out of any further conversation while making it plain that he was keen to discuss the projected book at a better time?

Leo liked it. He felt that here were the beginnings a story: one with a plot, possibly more interesting even, than his idea of life in a pre-war English public school.

Back in London he was on the phone straight away to Robert who responded by inviting Leo to his club. It was not one of the more famous ones, but was small and comfortable in the old- fashioned masculine way which Leo felt that gentlemen's clubs ought to be. They settled into the corner of the bar in a couple of deep leather armchairs.

'If you want to smoke I'm afraid we'll have to go upstairs for that,' Robert explained. 'There's a kind of priest-hole in the attic for the sinners like myself. This bloody silly politically correct government.'

'Hear, hear,' vociferated Leo, thumping the arm of his chair. 'I couldn't agree with you more. It makes me feel sick just listening to that ghastly Health Secretary woman banging on in her infant teacher's voice.'

'Anyway, stuff her and cheers,' Robert said, raising his gin and tonic. 'You knew my mother quite well then?'

'Up to a point I did, but how do I put it? She was rather formidable.' Leo pronounced the last word in the French manner.

'You can say that again. A proper old battle axe. She used to terrify the wits out of us as children.' He smiled at his companion as he said it.

Leo was beginning to warm to Robert and felt that they might work together.

'But be honest with me. That book, quite frankly, is a crashing bore, isn't it?'

'I'm afraid crashing bores tend to be my stock in trade.'

'They don't have to be, do they? I mean not all of the time? You can cut loose once in a while, can't you?'

'Much less than you might think.' Leo paused and looked closely at Robert who was scrutinizing the contents of his own glass and giving them a thoughtful whirl.

'Now's your chance.'

'Oh? To do what?'

'To cut loose. I'm being perfectly serious,' Robert went on. 'You see, we could still market the old fart if we wanted to, though it would hardly be the kind of thing Mother had in mind.'

'As a matter of fact I had some thoughts of my own on that very subject,' said Leo.

'You did, did you? Not such a ghost after all, eh? Fire away, old man.'

'Well it seemed to me that something about the English public school in the era when your father was growing up would be rather more interesting. It could be made quite racy as a matter of fact.'

'You mean lots of buggery and beating? That sort of thing?'

'Not necessarily.'

'Oh I don't know - I'm sure buggery and beating would go down a treat. There's a pretty healthy market for it,' said Robert. 'How's your glass, by the way? You look in need of a top up.'

Leo liked the man's frank way of speaking. It was probably the quality his father had possessed also.

Robert saw to the topping up of the glasses.

'Have I shocked you?' he asked unapologetically.

'Hardly. I don't shock easily.'

'I didn't think you did. But can I ask you another thing? Have you ever written anything in that line before? I mean it doesn't have to have been buggery and beating, but for that end of the market?'

'No I haven't, but it has crossed my mind from time to time There must be some money in it.'

Robert laughed before resuming. 'You probably realise, don't you? that Mother left precious little of that, I mean compared with what they once had, Death duties are an absolute killer - forgive the pun if it is one - and they were big spenders. Caribbean cruises, that sort of thing.'

'I got that impression.'

'Well then, surely the old fart can give us something back. I could certainly use it.' Robert winked as Leo had seen him do at the funeral drinks party. 'And no doubt you could too.'

'So what have you got in mind?'

'I don't know exactly. Thats where you might come in. Maybe the schoolboy scrapes of young Edward Akhurst. The ups and downs of school life. Its bumps and bruises. Boys Own stuff, but with a bit of buggery and beating thrown in, because that's what the punters are looking for.'

'Tell me one thing,' said Leo. 'Your own son?'

'Teddy. What about him?'

'Also called Edward and so like your father to look at. What might he make of this?'

'Should he make anything of it?'

'I don't suppose we'd need to use the same name.'

'Oh I'm not so sure about that. There's something, how do I put it, quintessentially English about the name 'Edward Akhurst', wouldn't you agree? So I'd be inclined to stick to it. Also it provides an authentic biographical touch and anyway the surviving holder doesn't necessarily have to be told about it. Unless, of course.....' He paused.

'Unless?'

'He fancies the idea himself. You know, he might find it a bit of a chuckle.'

'This is beginning to run on a bit fast,' thought Leo.

The two men looked at each other with slightly wary approval, without saying anything for a minute.

'You're going to have to fill me in,' said Leo at length.

'What with?'

'Yourselves - the family. How you all fit together, or don't, more likely. Because it's clear to me that it's all a lot more complicated than your mother would have had me believe. I mean your father may have been more or less what she cracked him up to be, but you are not a bit like that, are you? And, I may be guessing, but young Edward certainly isn't. You all sound splendidly dysfunctional.'

'You mean there are skeletons rattling around in our cupboard? Black sheep?'

'Well aren't there?'

103

The other smiled but did not reply.

'I'm sorry, but it's my trade,' said Leo. 'I need to be nosy about things like that - especially if we're to turn this blasted book round.'

'Of course you do and I'm with you all the way. And anyway, we're an old family so there are bound to be a few old bones rattling around in our cupboards or black sheep or whatever way you like to put it,' Robert leaned forward and patted him on the knee. 'Do you fancy a visit to the priest-hole? Sorry, that sounds a bit risque.'

'Not today, thanks,' Leo replied, 'but next time I will - if only as a matter of principle.'

'We mustn't let this thing go off the boil. I'll give you a ring and we'll talk again next week.'

They left it there and each went his separate way: Leo to his flat in St John's Wood and Robert to whatever it was that he did in the City- Leo hadn't worked it out yet, but had felt disinclined to ask him directly.

He wanted to know more about Robert. Was he an Old Rugbeian the same as his father? It was easy enough to check, having been put in touch with the retired master who ran the Old Boys' Society. No, Robert had not been to Rugby himself, nor could he say where he had been. What about his son - Edward the Younger? The grandson. Ah. There was a pause. He was at the school, but he had left early, less than a year ago as a matter of fact. Why was that? He didn't want to say, but putting two and two together it wouldn't be hard to guess, would it? What? The age-old vice associated with monasteries and all-male educational establishments? No not that one - something else - how do I put it?- more contemporary, but I really don't think I ought to be discussing this with you - if you don't mind.

It was enough to be getting on with. Robert hadn't even followed in his father's footsteps at Rugby and young Edward had indeed blotted his copybook there, probably drugs by the sound of it but if Robert had missed out on Rugby who had seen to it that his son had not? Grandparents who had helped out with the fees no doubt - a common enough practice. Leo thought immediately of Mrs Akhurst, determined that the grandchild who looked so like her dear departed husband should prove to be a chip off that old block. Maybe. And why had Robert missed out? Did his eagerness to press on with the book in its new form have anything to do with it? A score to settle perhaps?

He still felt that he needed to know more about the Akhursts - because whatever form the book did eventually take he had to have some real flesh and blood to work with. And all-too-real flesh and blood was what Robert seemed to have in mind.

'Tell me,' ventured Leo when he next met Robert, 'what exactly do you do for a living?'

Robert laughed. 'I wondered when you'd get round to asking me that.'

'Well it's not an unreasonable thing to want to know, is it?'

'Not at all. Perfectly reasonable, but not all that easy to answer.'

Leo left him to continue.

'I - how do I put this? - I do a number of different things and it's a bit tricky to put them in a nutshell - to summarise them like saying I'm a barrister or a stockbroker or whatever. I suppose I've got fingers in several different pies.'

Leo again said nothing but let him carry on.

Robert laughed. 'How do I put this? Basically it's work with the media - of a kind.'

'Of a kind?'

'Sorry if that sounds dodgy - which I suppose it is. If I had boil it down to anything, I could say I run an agency.'

'What kind of an agency?'

'We cover a lot of video material, presentational stuff, most of it .... and books on the same sort of lines.., that kind of thing.'

'Ah. Does it make much money?'

Robert smiled and shrugged his shoulders. 'It can do. Not as much as I'd like it to, of course. It's steady enough in its way, but depends on the talent.'

'I think I can guess, but you tell me. What kind of talent?'

'The writers., the film-makers... the performers... the whatsit?.,. the creative input.., sorry, that sounds pure businesspeak, doesn't it? But that's where you might come in, Leo. There could be an opening for you - as the Actress once said to the Bishop.'

'Tell me more.'

'This book. It doesn't necessarily have to take that form does it? I mean as a book. Have you ever written a script? I mean for a film.'

'No, but I daresay I could have a go.'

'Well then...' And Robert launched himself. He seemed to have a pretty clear idea of what he wanted, not unlike his mother, Leo thought, and it involved the use of some of the same material, but taking it in an entirely new direction which left Leo's head reeling at the man's nerve.

What he suggested was a video, though a book well-supplied with still pictures from it could also be produced - the book of the film. It sounded like a good idea, but begged all sorts of questions. Where, Leo wondered, was he going to find the actors? And if it was going to be a set in the Thirties what about the costumes and other period considerations, none of which would come cheap? And what about the location? It would be difficult to persuade Rugby School that it was a such a good idea.

Robert laughed at that one, 'Maybe we could offer them a cut. And they could flog it to their Old Boys at a discount. Flog is the word too. I'm sure there'd be enough takers.'

'To be quite frank with you, Robert, this is pornography, isn't it? I mean what you said about buggery and beating?'

'That's interesting,' said Robert. 'Where does art end and pornography begin? A hoary old question - sorry about the hopeless pun - quite unintentional of course - probably it's one for the Greeks.'

'I suppose it's the place where the real money starts to be made,' replied Leo. 'But there's something else. I'll be honest with you, Robert, this isn't my field. I mean I'm not averse to a bit of what you might term pornography, but this schoolboy stuff isn't my scene at all, I'm not sure I could deliver. What did Matisse say? 'I paint with my penis.' Well, in this case I don't think I could write with mine.'

Robert laughed outright. 'It would be interesting to see you try.' He paused and continued, 'Two points: there could be a lot of money in it, despite an initial outlay for the things you've been talking about. And secondly - you're a professional writer, aren't you?'

'That's what your mother told me when she wanted me to make your father into a knight in shining armour. You're a professional writer and it's your job to do it.'

'Well she'd got a point, hadn't she?' He laughed again. 'I never thought I'd catch myself saying anything so nice about the witch.'

Leo frowned and did not speak.

'It's a matter of - what's the word for it - empathy. You have to worm your way into the characters whether you like the things they do or not.'

'That's true, as long as the money's good enough. But there's the other thing. Who's going to play your hero? Might we not be straying into the realm of child abuse?'

That's hardly a problem.' Robert fixed his eyes on Leo's. Its already in the bag.'

'You mean?.'

'Just so. He's tickled pink at the idea - even if it means getting a few stripes.'

'But he's your own son, for Heavens sake!'

'Is that worse than using someone else's?'

Leo shook his head. 'I suppose not, but all the same, you're the boy's father. I could never do that to a son of mine.'

'Have you got one?'

'No I haven't, but..'

'Well then. You'll have to meet young Teddy. He's got a mind of his own and knows what he's doing perfectly well. And besides, he likes the sound of his cut, I mean his money, of course. The other thing's all in a day's work as far as he's concerned. And, anyway, think of what they once got up to in these schools, especially in my father's day. Then it was done for all the most righteous reasons. But you can bet your bottom dollar most of them got a kick out of it at the same time.'

'Why was Teddy chucked out of Rugby?'

'Who told you he was chucked out?'

'The School. The guy who runs their Old Boys.'

'What did he tell you exactly?'

'Nothing really, he left me to make a guess. He was perfectly discreet about it. Coy I could say.'

'And have you made your guess?'

'I suspect it was drugs - he made it fairly clear that it wasn't the other thing.'

Robert laughed. 'Well then! We can leave it there, can't we? And anyway Teddy's got his whole life ahead of him. He's not looking backwards, over his shoulder. He says he wants to be an actor, as so many of them do.'

'One more thing,' said Leo. 'What does Pru make of all this?'

'It's the drugs she worries about. As long as he keeps off them.' A shadow crossed Robert's face. 'And I agree with her - about that at least, if not much else.'

Leo said nothing, sitting hunched in the chair with a frown on his face.

'Are you free one day next week? To discuss the money side of things and your possible role in all this.'

'My role?' Leo shook his head as if waking up. 'Yes of course. My role.'

'How about a visit to the priest-hole?'

'A good idea.'

'Like being back at school, isn't it? You realise we could get beaten for doing this?'

Sitting in the carriage of the Underground taking him home Leo mulled it over. 'Christ, what would Mrs Akhurst, the senior one I mean, have made of it all? Did she even have the faintest clue that any of it was going on? The kind of things Robert was up to? But what did she make of young Teddy being chucked out of Rugby? For drugs? Possibly drugs. Or did they cover it up and hide it from her? And how much of it was she capable of taking in by then? She clearly believed the things she wanted to believe. A woman with a great capacity for faith.'

Robert had got the bit between his teeth and seemed to be all fired up. Leo had no doubt that getting his own back on his parents had a lot to do with it. But despite his complaint about them squandering the money that he felt ought to have come his way, he seemed to have enough to play around with and to spend on things like a period video and the hire of actors. Leo wondered about Robert's siblings, two sisters, he believed, and where they fitted into the scheme of things. One was married with two girls, probably not Mrs Akhurst's thing, and the other was unmarried. Did either of them have any ideas about the book and what should be made of it? They probably would be mortified at the use that their late father was being put to. And what would they think of young Teddy's part in it?

Before he settled to provide Robert with his script, Leo insisted on meeting the boy and speaking to him properly, while being careful to avoid any tiresome reference to his resemblance to his grandfather this time round, though of course that was clearly the spice in the stew, for Robert, at least.

It was no problem and Robert asked him along to his club to meet Teddy. And the thing that immediately struck Leo was how much more at ease the boy was in these surroundings than he had been at his grandmother's funeral. Here, lolling nonchalantly in his armchair he was quite the young adult, while in tow behind his mother he had seemed to be hardly out of his short trousers, And Leo noticed too the relaxed relationship that appeared to exist between father and son. They looked like chums.

'It must be his mother who brings out the lad's callowness,' Leo concluded.

Teddy was wearing jeans and a sports jacket with a light check. In spite of club rules he wasn't wearing a tie, but his conservative mildly countrified look enabled him to pass muster, especially in the company of his own father who was obviously popular with the staff and the other club members.

He seemed to have been briefed about his father's plans and was eager to go. Leo had the impression that he himself was the one who would have to be brought round.

'Teddy's happy to be the naughty boy,' said his father, 'as long as he gets a fair deal for his pains.'

Teddy nodded and grinned, reminding Leo very much of his grandfather in the photographs.

'How old are you, Ted?' Leo asked him.

'Sixteen.' He shrugged and took a lazy pull at his half pint of beer. 'But what the shit?'

It was not the way Leo expected to be addressed by an adolescent. He wasn't much taken by the way the boy idled in his chair with his leg over one of the arms either. Leo found himself thinking that he needed to be taken down a peg or two.

He frowned but said nothing.

'You watch it young man,' said Robert with mock severity. 'Mr

Summers'll soon settle your hash for you if you speak to him like that.'

Teddy looked at his parent and they smiled at each other in a way that suggested they were sharing some kind of a private joke.

'Anyway Leo,' resumed the boy's father, 'we want you to come up with a script. Something on the lines of an old-fashioned school story with lots of the idiom of the place and time. Full of all the stereotypes, it goes without saying, A bit of Greyfriars about it. And Teddy here is the hero of the fourth form who's always in trouble, but when the time comes, he takes his punishment like a man. That's important - he's full of pluck.'

'That might take care of the beating,' Leo pointed out, 'but what about the other thing? We can give that a miss, don't you think?'

'What do you think Ted?' the boy's father asked him.

Leo was incredulous that a father could ask his own son such a question, but nevertheless held his tongue.

Teddy shrugged and eyed Leo stealthily, but said nothing.

'Look,' said Leo, 'we could handle it obliquely, surely, if you feel it's necessary at all. A few fleeting shots taken in the showers, that sort of thing, the implication would be clear, but it doesn't need to go any further than that, does it?' He felt rather scared at how far he was being sucked into this thing and something told him to pull out before it was too late. But something else which he couldn't quite put a finger on was drawing him further in - he actually found himself warming to the idea and when he had told Robert that it wasn't his thing he realised that he hadn't been quite truthful. Had Robert read him better than he had read himself? It was a disquieting thought, especially for one as far on in life as Leo was. Had the presence of young Edward anything to do with it? Acted on him as a catalyst of sorts? And then of course there was the money - not to be sniffed at.

112

That would have to be discussed, but meanwhile father and son appeared to be joining forces in putting pressure on him, if in fact much of it was needed. It seemed that they, or at least Robert, were tickling something dormant which he had been unwilling or unable up till now to admit about himself.

One thing he had never discussed with Robert was his own marital status. Leo hadn't got a wife. He had had occasional girlfriends and some of his relationships had even lasted a few years before petering out, but nothing had gelled into anything permanent. He was reluctant to think of himself as a confirmed bachelor and what that term had come to imply in the eyes of the world, but now in his fifties and single he had grown emotionally lazy. Was there any more to it than that? No doubt that was the question that Robert was turning over in his mind during their conversations. Probably he had reached the conclusion that Leo wasn't the marrying sort. Not that Leo had attempted to discuss such questions with Robert, but considering how he appeared to make his money, the man was very likely making some shrewd guesses. He traded in human frailty after all. So was Robert seeing possibilities in him which he was reluctant to admit to himself? Noting his declared interest in writing a book about a boys' boarding school for instance?

'The script,' Leo said. 'Yes we must get down to that when you've spelled out what you want in more detail.'

'And what you want too?' suggested Robert, exchanging a glance with his son. 'After all, you're the one who's writing it.'

These two are as thick as thieves, Leo decided.

Yet when he was back in his study he was surprised and slightly alarmed how readily the ideas managed to flow. He dug out some traditional school stories, Billy Bunter and others of that kind and even Kipling's Stalky and Co as well as a standard history of Rugby School which he skimmed through, but his own imagination raced along so well that he had little difficulty in devising the situations in which his hero found himself. And surprisingly easy, too, even liberating, was the business of writing dialogue and the accompanying stage directions instead of having to hack away at solid lumps of prose. Leo's powers of concentration rose to the task in a way that he hadn't known for a long time and he was enjoying his writing which was a new sensation. He felt liberated. 'Why didn't I hit upon writing traditional school stories before this? And as playscripts to be performed?' he asked himself. 'Because no one has ever asked me to do it before, that's why.'

He wrote it as a conventional school story. Young Edward was a naughty lad, the leader of his peers, whose adventures often involved a licking at some stage, a badge of honour which he wore with pride, needless to say. He was a fag who annoyed his fagmaster by his incorrigible slackness and insouciant attitude. As a sort of finale to the story he was caned by the headmaster, which was a serious business because it was something that did not happen to many boys and singled him out as a cut above the rest. This was the only occasion that corporal punishment appeared in his script and by confining it to this one scene Leo felt he had underlined the solemnity of the climactic event. Otherwise it was a rollicking yarn which he hoped Robert would buy nevertheless.

All this Leo contrived to weave into a plot which left the boy at the end with his already legendary reputation among his peers enhanced. The next thing was to show this first draft to Robert. It had taken him just ten days.

Robert's response was not even to take the manuscript from the brown envelope in which it had been delivered.

'I'll give it to Teddy to look at,' he said. 'I'd like his opinion first.'

Leo's immediate reaction was to feel affronted, but a moment's reflection told him that Robert was right - the boy's impression was the one that mattered.

And the verdict came back three days later. Teddy was over the moon about it and Leo felt a rush of pleasure such as he had never experienced with any of his previous work.

Robert had a few reservations of a purely practical nature. Leo's imagination had run away with him and the thing would have to be cut down to a more manageable size. Costs, after all, had to be born in mind. While he was a stickler for period detail - accurate haircuts, the right fabrics and so on, Robert worked to a strict budget, which in any case did not greatly inhibit the intention of the work as it did not require anything large-scale, but involved comparatively few performers in intimate situations.

How intimate was what concerned Leo who had started to view the thing in a curiously elevated light, as a work of art rather than pornography, while Edward Akhurst grew into a real flesh and blood hero. Had young Edward's rise to stardom begun?

Leo heard nothing from Robert for a week and wondered if he ought to give him a ring, but Robert was onto him first. He wanted to discuss some modifications to the script while he was already setting in motion the practical aspects of the production. Authentic locations were the immediate challenge, such as a Thirties school shower room. He had discovered that boys at Rugby at the time used toshes, a kind of truncated bath in which they bathed in a sitting position. There were showers too, of course, but it was a matter of finding something that looked right for the time. Leo wanted to play down the showers idea, he still felt nervous about nudity, and Robert respected his reservations without going the whole way with them.

Costumes were no problem: a regular theatrical costumier could supply what was required: grey flannel trousers and a sober sports jacket cut in the style of that time, a shirt with a thin blue stripe and detachable collar and a black tie. Brightly-striped school caps, preferably in the authentic colours - each house had its own - Robert insisted on that, Clearly he had a flair for such matters.

And there were the boy actors, about whom Robert sounded somewhat evasive at first, but when Leo pressed him he assured him that there was no lack of takers: Teddy's own school chums.

Teddy was now a dayboy at an independent school in south London and he and his schoolfellows had little difficulty in making the transition to pre-Second World War public schoolboys. Being Londoners they were inclined to consider themselves a sophisticated bunch, more independent than their provincial counterparts, which probably was true of Teddy's set. And some of them. like him, had hopes of becoming professional actors.

All this became clear when Leo met them at Robert's Fulham home. But there was another thing he noticed on this occasion. Pru, Robert's wife, did not put in an appearance.

This troubled Leo who did not want to be in any way responsible for hastening on the breakup of a marriage, which he felt might be at stake. He had rather old-fashioned views about the sanctity of family life and it worried him that he might be a party to it in this case. But both father and son had an air of such bland unconcern that he decided that it was really nothing to do with him how this particular family carried on among themselves. He had never spoken to the boy's mother since their brief encounter at the late Mrs Akhurst's funeral, so how could he say what her true feelings were? But all the same he found it hard to imagine any mother who genuinely cared about her child being entirely happy to see him in the kind of role that he was being asked to play.

Boy parts were apportioned and Robert explained the filming schedule. He had access to a small studio which was already largely set up with the kind of school furnishings that were required for a period piece like this one. Some establishing outdoor shots of Rugby School were needed, such things as views of the School Close, the Chapel and the Speech Room, but these would present little difficulty.

But what about the adult parts? The men who were to play the masters, without whom the story of young Edward Akhurst could not be told? Would Robert use professional actors? There were always plenty of them hungry for any sort of work. Or would he look elsewhere? It was a sensitive matter and Leo decided to take Robert head-on.

As usual Robert was his imperturbable self who had the matter in hand and had no qualms about it. Leo could only admire his insouciance. Father and son were very much alike in that respect and apart from the physical likeness Leo wondered where the old Colonel, who was the starting point of the whole enterprise, got a look-in.

When Leo asked him about the adult parts Robert shrugged it off. 'They're queuing up for it,' he said blithely.

'What kind of people are they? Paedophiles?'

'One or two of them do teach - so they're the genuine article. And a couple of young actors. It's the usual story - hungry for anything. But they're good - I've used them before.'

'What kind of parts did they play?'

But Robert only smiled. 'They're good,' he repeated. There's only one part still to be filled.'

'Oh? Which one's that?'

'The Great Man himself - the Headmaster.' His eyes remained fixed on Leos.

'That shouldn't be too difficult, should it?' said Leo, looking away.

'No, shouldn't think so.' His gaze did not shift from Leo's face.

Leo stared back. 'You're not suggesting...?'

'A passing fancy, but rather a good one. An inspiration even.'

'But I can't do that!'

Robert did not speak.

'Go on then. Tell me more,' said Leo with a resigned shrug.

'Good man. I had a feeling you might,' Robert replied.

So Leo was taken on board to visit the climactic punishment on Young Edward. He insisted on one thing, however, under no circumstances was he going to beat the boy's naked flesh, and Robert assured him that it would be out of character to do so anyway. A suitable gravitas was to be the order of the day.

Teddy approved of the idea. 'Dad said you'd be the right man for the job from the beginning.' he told him.

'Did he indeed?'

'He says he knew it from the time he first met you at my grandmother's funeral.'

'But none of it had even been written then. How did he...?'

'He always keeps ahead of the game and he can read people,' said the boy.

'A clever cove, your dad,' Leo said. 'But tell me something else, Ted. What does your mum think of all this? And in particular of what her little boy's getting up to?'

'Quite honestly, I don't think she really wants to know.'

'A bit odd, isn't it? I would have thought most mums would want to know about a thing like that.'

'As long as it's not drugs. She's got a bee in her bonnet about that. You see her own sister, my aunt, died from an overdose. Heroin. And Mum's never really got over it. And when I was given the boot by Rugby...' The boy grinned - remarkably like his grandfather thought Leo - 'well... that was the last straw and she kind of flipped.'

'So anything else goes as long as it's not harmful substances?'

The boy shrugged his shoulders and did not reply.

'And your Dad. Why does he make use of you like this?'

'I could ask you the very same question, but I won't.'

'I'm a grown man. I'm not his teenage son. And I could do with the money.'

'So could I. You might say it's a way of getting his own back. God, you should hear the way he goes on about my grandmother. He hated her guts, so to filch her precious memorial to her beloved husband and to rewrite it was a chance too good to be missed. Not that she'll know a thing about it, of course. not where she's gone - or hasn't, as the case may be. But I don't think he would have thought of it if I hadn't looked quite so like Grandpa and Granny wouldn't shut up about it. That's what makes it so sweet. And then I went and fucked up at Rugby.'

'Did your grandmother know about that?'

'She was never told.' The boy grinned.

'Who was paying your tees?'

'She was.'

'But how..?'

'She put the money into a special account in Dad's bank. And anyway it was only for a year until she snuffed it.'

'You're just as bad, aren't you? The same as your dad.'

Teddy laughed. 'Perhaps that's why I deserve a beating from the headmaster - for my attitude.'

'You sound as if you do.'

'There you are then. Dad was right. You're quite ready to do it. Any way it's all part of the deal. But I tell you some pretty cool people are likely to be seeing this thing- which could be useful for me. And maybe for you as well.'

'I'm not quite sure how I'm meant to take that.'

'As a bit of a giggle - if you can't think of any other way. That's what I'm doing- for the time being at least.'

'One other thing that interests me,' said Leo. 'Your dad. He missed out on Rugby. Surely he should have gone there too as they were so set on the place. Your grandfather did and then you did, until you fucked it up, of course.'

'He failed his Common Entrance and didn't get in. It was as simple as that. He went to some place in the West Country instead. I don't think they ever forgave him for it - especially his mother.'

'He has admitted to me that he was never very academic and quite hopeless at Maths. He told me that up in the priest-hole. So they paid your fees for Rugby where you were to restore the family honour, so to speak, until.:.'

'I fucked it. Actually Dad thought it was quite funny, but Mum, silly cow, didn't. Hell, it was only coke. Nothing really for her to get her knickers in such a twist about.'

'Between the lot of you, you're a bit of mess, aren't you?' said Leo.

The boy laughed. 'Probably we are,' he said.

Now that he had the picture, Leo felt that he had to take his part seriously. He felt that to write the scene well, and then to follow that by acting it well would raise it to something like the level of art, which was the way he justified to himself what he was about to do. But more than anything he felt he was now involved in his own plot - the saga of three generations of Akhursts.

He did not watch much of the filming of any of the other scenes having once settled the script, but concentrated on his own part. Having committed his lines to memory he waited for the call from Robert.

The costumier fitted him out in a tweed suit and waistcoat with a handsome watch chain and a shirt with a wing collar, like the one worn by the then prime minister, Neville Chamberlain, himself an Old Boy of Rugby School. It set Leo thinking back to the school's greatest headmaster, Doctor Arnold and Teddy's fictional predecessors - in a manner of speaking - Tom Brown and Flashman. Was he dishing out punishment to Brown or Flashman? Neither, of course, but to young Akhurst. And should he carry himself like Arnold, with all the gravitas of an Eminent Victorian? Probably, but remember that Young Edward Akhurst was meant to be a loveable rogue, after all, so it must be done with a bit of a twinkle.

He wore a gown for the occasion and was placed behind a large mahogany desk in what passed for the headmaster's study. As well as Teddy, his father and a small film crew were in attendance. He was shown his main prop, a cane which rested in a corner behind the desk.

'Do you need to practise?' Robert enquired.

'What? On a cushion? I hardly think so,' said Leo.

'Make the boy bend over the arm of this chair,' Robert explained. 'He doesn't have to take his trousers down. But it's got to look like the real thing.'

'Are you protected?' Leo asked the boy.

'No, of course not.' Teddy, who was wearing his school grey flannel trousers, sounded scornful of such a notion.

'You're really entering into the part, aren't you? Shouldn't I be doing the same?' remarked Leo.

'Do what you have to do,' replied the boy stoically. He seemed to be bracing himself for what lay in store for him as if he was getting something he deserved.

They then ran through the scene: Akhurst's arrival; the stern address from the headmaster which Leo had committed to memory, the pronouncement of sentence and the placing of the miscreant over the arm of the chair for his punishment which was suspended for this rehearsal and then his dismissal from the godlike presence, having received half a crown from the head for taking it like a man. Despite it being a mere rehearsal Teddy acted his part beautifully, looking appropriately contrite at the solemn words of the headmaster and remembering to wince ruefully and to clutch his bottom at the close of the ceremony.

'That sounded pretty cool,' he told Leo. 'Now for the real thing.'

'Good,' said Robert. 'Sadly you've missed your true vocation in life, Leo. Just remember to lift back the tail of his jacket before you start to beat him, that's all. Otherwise its fine.'

'How many do I give him?' said Leo.

'Six. Six of the best.'

Both actors played the scene with conviction, keeping straight faces and not messing up their words. The climax came when Leo took up the cane.

'Bend over the arm of the chair,' he said solemnly, but not sepulchurally.

Young Edward put on a brave face and did as he was told, bending as low as he possibly could so that his trousers drew tight across his backside.

Leo folded back the tail of the boy's jacket.

'Go,' whispered Robert.

'Lead on Macduff,' whispered his son.

For Leo it was surprisingly easy. Six stinging strokes which could easily have been heard in the next room. They drew gasps from the boy who had never been beaten in his life before.

After the sixth stroke Leo restored the tail of Young Edward's jacket. 'Well done. You can stand up now.'

As the boy stood up, he looked genuinely shaken by the experience. Leo put out his hand and shook his. 'You took that well, Akhurst,' he said. He put his hand in his pocket for a coin which he pressed into the boy's hand. 'Now go and treat yourself to an ice-cream.'

'Thank you sir,' mumbled Young Edward.

'No hard feelings, I hope?'

'None at all sir.'

'That's what I like to hear. A boy who knows how to face the music when he has to.'

'Thank you sir.' He slipped out through the door.

'Splendid,' said Robert. 'All in the bag. We could hardly have asked Ted to go through that again, could we? You old sadist!' he laughed, giving Leo a friendly punch. 'Anyway it's one in the eye for the old witch. She never dreamed that this was going to happen, did she?'

'But all the same she may not have entirely disapproved of it,' said Leo. He felt drained and a little unclean. It had all been a bit too real and he was disturbed by Robert's elated mood.

He found Teddy in the next room, inspecting the damage.

'Christ, you laid that on a bit, didn't you?' said the boy.

'More than you bargained for, was it? But you deserved to have it for real, didn't you? After all, you'd been a bad lad, hadn't you? I mean snorting that coke.'

'Sure, but I wasn't expecting it to be quite that real. God, it must have been tough in Grandpa's day.' The boy laughed. 'But never mind. All in a day's work. No hard feelings!'

'I'm glad of that,' said Leo. 'I promise I won't make a habit of it. But you know something, Ted?'

'What?'

'Your grandmother.'

'What about her?'

'Your Dad says it's one in the eye for her, but actually I think she would have been quite proud of you. The way you behaved, your pluck. You took it like a man. Quite a chip off the old block after all, eh?'

'So perhaps she got what she wanted in the end, even if the people who'll watch it aren't quite the ones she had in mind,' mused Teddy. 'But then perhaps they are, but aren't too keen to own up to it. Who can tell?'

'That might be the twist in the tale,' said Leo. How old did you say you were, Ted? Sixteen?'

The boy nodded.

'You're a knowing little sod for your age.'

They left it there. Teddy eventually made it as an actor, not quite as quickly as he would have liked to have done, but there were willing hands to help him up while there was no denying he had genuine talent, and Leo in the late afternoon of his life started to make a lot more money than he ever thought he was going to - thanks in large part to the ghost of Edward Akhurst.

It Pays To Keep It Simple

The Pilsudski is a small Polish restaurant near the South Kensington Underground station where it is possible to enjoy a chilled vodka with a fishy snack, and to follow it with a traditional Polish main dish. The customers tend to be middle-aged and a number are probably like myself, passing through and wanting a comparatively simple inexpensive meal before making the journey home. For me it is directly linked on the Piccadilly Line with King's Cross, the mainline station I leave from, which means I can drink perhaps a little more than I should, and linger without worrying too much about missing my train.

I visit the Pilsudski probably half a dozen times a year at the most, not enough to be remembered as one of their regulars and I seldom engage anyone there in conversation, but I like to eavesdrop on the neighbouring tables instead. It is a natural nosiness which I excuse to myself as a good way picking up copy for a literary endeavour I have vague plans for in the not-too-distant future. So on the whole I prefer to be left alone, alert to what is being said around me, but as often as not merely basking in the warm glow of my own vodka-induced thoughts. To me, daydreaming combined with a bit of eavesdropping in a restaurant is one of life's pleasures, every bit as important as the food. And as a rule I prefer not to share my table with strangers. Indeed I have walked out of restaurants where unwanted company has been thrust upon me. But this is not something I have ever had to do in the Pilsudski where my privacy has always been respected. Exchanging a passing banality is usually the limit of my contact with its other customers. So one evening last autumn when a man who looked to be in his late forties or early fifties instead of waiting for a table to fall vacant approached me and said 'May I?' in a rather urgent tone of voice, before sitting himself down opposite me, I didn't feel best pleased.

I had just reached the closing stage of my meal and had ordered a cognac and a coffee, so I felt now that I would be obliged to cut things short by ordering my bill and making my escape sooner than I wanted to. I looked at my watch. It said only five past seven, too much time to kill before my train left, which increased my irritation.

But the man apparently sensed none of my discomfort as he faced me, but nodded, and extended a hand towards me in an effort to be friendly.

'How do you do? My name is Igor,' he said in a stilted manner.

'Igor? You're a Russian then? You sound like one.'

'I'm Russian,' he replied, his musical accent resting agreeably on my ear.

'What's a Russian doing in a Polish restaurant?' I quipped. 'I didn't think you liked each other very much.'

Igor shrugged. 'The vodka is just as good, or nearly, which is what matters the most, isn't it? But you're an Englishman in a Polish restaurant, so why not a Russian?'

'You noticed the name of this restaurant, didn't you?'

Igor shrugged again. 'Not especially.'

'The Pilsudsky. Pilsudsky was the man who gave your Bolsheviks a beating in 1920 when they tried to invade his country. Not exactly a friend of the Russians I should have thought.'

Igor's broad Slavic features lit up in a smile. 'Ah, you know about that, do you?' He glanced over his shoulder at the street door as he spoke.

'I've read my share of Russian history and literature. In translation, I have to say. But your English is very good. Where did you learn it?'

The waitress brought a menu and Igor ordered a vodka without answering my question. 'And another cognac for my friend here.'

'It's very kind of you, but I've got a train to catch.'

The girl looked at me questioningly and I gave in. 'Oh all right then. Just the one. It's very kind of you,' I said once again.

The cognac and the vodka arrived together.

'Nasdorovia,' announced Igor, raising his glass. 'What is your name?'

'I'm sorry. I forgot to tell you. It's Goderic.'

'An interesting name. English I think.'

'Anglo-Saxon. There was a saint with that name.'

'Nasdorovia, Goderic,' said Igor and tossed his vodka back in one.

'Nasdorovia,' I repeated, taking a cautious sip at my cognac.

'You know what it means?'

'Kaneshna, ' I said. 'Of course. Good health, doesn't it? '

'So you speak Russian?'

'Hardly any at all - just a very few words - useful ones like nasdorovia. But you didn't answer my question. Where did you learn to speak such good English?'

'In Russia of course. We have very good teachers.'

'And do you come here often?'

'Kaneshna. I like London.' He glanced once more in the direction of the door.

'Most Russians do. More than the English, I suspect. There are times when we feel like foreigners in our own capital. But you are welcome here of course.'

'Thank you. Spasibo.'

'What do you do? Your job?'

Igor looked round in a furtive, mildly histrionic, manner. 'I'm a businessman.'

'Aha,' I laughed. 'That covers a multitude of sins! Especially Russian ones!'

For a moment Igor looked puzzled.

'Multitude?'

'Many things,' I explained. 'But perhaps I shouldn't have asked. Cloak and dagger stuff, eh?' I gave him what I intended to be a knowing wink, which was out of character for me and quite implausible.

'Cloak and dagger stuff?'

'Like being a spy or trafficking in drugs or the sex trade. You know, something underground.'

Igor's laugh was a trifle forced.

'You mustn't mind me saying things like that. I'm only joking, of course. But you Russians have got a bit of a reputation, so you have to expect it.'

'Not at all,' Igor smiled and called to the waitress to bring him second vodka. He seemed to be in no particular hurry to order his meal. He cast another quick glance over his shoulder.

'Are you expecting someone?'

Igor shrugged. 'No,' he said, 'I don't think so.'

'Then in that case may I recommend the hunter's stew? It's pretty good. A bit like your Russian food.'

'Drink up.' Igor called to the waitress. 'Bring my friend another cognac.'

'Go easy,' I said. 'That'll be my third.'

The girl looked at me to confirm the order.

'Oh all right,' I said. 'Just the one. But you must eat.'

Despite my normal sense of aloofness I found myself being drawn along by this man. It was the old Slavic way of breaking down barriers, I suppose, to drown any tensions that might exist in alcohol, and then to follow up with plenty of soulful, meaning-of-life talk.

'I have a train to catch,' I said. 'I must keep an eye on the time.'

'I'm a business man,' said Igor, ignoring my remark, 'so what are you?'

'An archaeologist. I work in a university - in the north of England.'

'Hmm!' Igor sounded impressed. 'A professor?'

'Alas no, just a humble lecturer. My speciality is the Palaeolithic period. Does that mean anything to you?'

'Sure, it does. It's the time before Noah's Flood.'

God, I thought, what did he have to go and say a thing like that for? It'll be aliens from outer space any second now.

'You don't seriously believe that, do you? I mean about Noah's

Flood?'

'Of course I believe it. Moses described it in the Bible, didn't he? And he spoke the Word of God.'

I said nothing. It clearly was time to be heading for the station. Well have the Givers of Life carrying Egyptian civilization to the New World next. Or even worse - the da Vinci Code.

I looked at my watch. 'I have to be on my way,' I said, 'or I'll miss my train.'

The world is full of mysteries,' Igor observed portentously. The vodka was reaching his tripes by now.

'Indeed so,' I replied, 'but you can generally find a perfectly rational explanation for them if you look hard enough.'

'That is the problem,' Igor rejoined. 'Finding an explanation. But sometimes we have to wait until we are told the meaning of things. Until we are, how do you say, inspired?'

I signalled to the waitress to bring my bill.

'So you're an archaeologist,' Igor went on, lowering his voice. 'Let me tell you a little secret. I used to be a kind of detective, which is like being an archaeologist in its way, I suppose.'

This was a more sensible observation than what had preceded it.

'Yes, I suppose it is,' I replied. 'But what kind of a detective were you? Were you a criminal investigator? The kind of thing I normally think of when I hear the word detective?'

Igor chuckled mysteriously without offering a reply.

'Or maybe you were a spook? Cloak and dagger stuff?'

He gave me a sharp glance, but said nothing.

'Is that where you learned to speak your excellent English? In a school for spooks?'

'In Russia we have many good teachers,' he replied stiffly. 'But tell me about something else.'

I glanced in the direction of the waitress, frowning impatiently.

She arrived with my bill.

'Tell me,' resumed Igor, 'about Princess Diana.'

'What about her? There's so much nonsense talked about Diana. All this conspiracy rubbish about her death when it was a perfectly straightforward case of drunken driving.'

'I don't agree with you.'

I knew now that I had to make my escape as quickly as possible.

Then it got even worse.

'Are you a freemason?'

'Good heavens no - but my father was.' God, was it sinking to this? Any minute now well have the Secret of the Holy Grail.

'I have studied the freemasons,' went on Igor. 'I understand they are an important organization in this country. A lot of very powerful people are freemasons.'

'As far as I know they're quite harmless, but I'm no expert. You'll have to ask someone else about that.'

'But you say your father was a freemason. And don't sons usually - how do you say? - follow in their fathers' footsteps in things like that?'

'Not necessarily. It's a free country - or supposed to be. A few of us have got minds of our own.'

The bill arrived. I paid it with my debit card. My need to escape from Igor was palpable.

'Can you give me my bill too? Igor asked the waitress. 'And

quickly please, I also am in a hurry.'

I put out a hand. 'Goodbye Igor,' I said. 'It's been great talking to you.'

'Wait a minute. I'd like to come with you, if I may - to talk about the freemasons.'

'I'm sorry, but I know awfully little about them. But now, if you'll excuse me, I've got to catch my train'.

Igor went to the cash desk to settle his bill there instead of waiting for the return of the waitress. I patted him on the shoulder in a friendly way as I went past him into the street. For a second he stiffened and shot me a nervous glance.

It was dark now and I turned left towards the Underground station, setting off at a brisk pace without looking back. I really did not want to have any further discussion with Igor about Freemasonry. But it was curious, I reflected, how taken up by it some Russians, especially former members of the KGB, were. No doubt they linked all sorts of conspiracy theories with the Masons, who, no doubt, had succeeded the Knights Templar as the Keepers of the Holy Grail. But once they began to insist on the absolute veracity of such things and all the sinister plots connected with them, it was impossible to hold any sort of rational discourse on the subject. No doubt many of them had stuck to their Marxist faith with the same kind of obtuseness. It was sad how people still had to cling to irrational explanations for things that were really quite straightforward.

Such thoughts were running through my mind as I went down into the Underground station. I had no loose change so I could not use a ticket machine, but had to join the queue at the ticket office instead. It was not a long one, but there was an American tourist before me, trying to buy a rover ticket, who seemed determined to take his time, in complete disregard of anybody else.

Why do other people always have such complicated needs, I thought, when mine are generally so simple?

And then the thing I had hoped to avoid, but was half-expecting, happened. Igor rolled up in the queue a few places behind me. We exchanged glances and I nodded to him without giving him any encouragement to engage me in further conversation.

I reached the counter. 'King's Cross,' I mumbled in a low voice, hoping not to be heard further back in the queue.

But the ticket clerk, who was Asian, asked me to repeat what I had said.

'King's Cross,' I said again in a louder voice.

I paid with my twenty pound note and fled. Igor was a couple of places away from the counter as I passed through the barrier and onto the escalator. I walked swiftly down it and turned left to the platform. As luck would have it, the rush hour being over, it was virtually empty. The next train was not due for another two minutes, so I walked to the end of the platform and stood well back from the edge. The need to escape from this man whose company had seemed to be so intriguing at first, but had turned out to be so tedious, had become pressing. Why, I couldn't exactly say. If he really had been a spook, as appeared to have been the case, it might have been fascinating to have found out more about him, despite his fixation with Freemasonry, and the conspiracy to murder Princess Diana. But I was fed to the teeth with drivel about lost civilisations and similar intellectual ordure, why, some of my students even took it seriously and I did not feel up to facing speculation now on the whereabouts of the Holy Grail and, no doubt, on the matter of alien abductions as well. For that was a popular idea in Russia, dear old credulous peasant Russia! Once it was the Virgin

Mary, now it was aliens from outer space, observed, all too likely, through the bottom of a vodka bottle. Perhaps the Holy Grail had been carried off in a spaceship. Now there was a thought! What would Igor make of that? But I didn't want to find out.

I watched him come onto the platform. Like me he was taking a northbound train. I stepped further back against the wall, hoping not to be noticed among the half dozen or so people waiting there. As Igor walked up the platform, another man appeared a few seconds later, who looked left and right before setting off in the same direction. My imagination may have been charged somewhat by the drink I had consumed, and our conversation, but the fact that he was following in the same path as Igor struck me as significant. It I had been completely sober no doubt I would have thought nothing of it, but on this occasion I had drunk sufficient to heighten my perception but not to blunt it. Or that was the way it occurred to me anyway.

Then Igor spotted me and crossed rapidly to where I was standing. He seemed relieved to have my company once more. 'There you are. I thought I had lost you.'

'No such luck,' I replied.

'We must complete our conversation. You were going to tell me something interesting about the Freemasons.'

'I don't think I was, Igor,' I said tersely. 'I've already told you that I know very little about them. And to tell you the truth, I don't care much about them either.' Immediately I felt that I had been a little too abrupt and that it was necessary to sound more emollient. 'To me, Igor, you are much more interesting than any Freemasons,' I went on. 'You described yourself as a detective: but what kind of a detective? Were you one like Sherlock Holmes, for instance?'

I felt that would strike the right note with a Russian and I was right.

'Ah Sherlock Holmes!' said Igor with a sigh. 'I read all those stories when I was a boy and it was my dream to visit London!' He sighed once more, a prolonged, nostalgic sound. 'I was always thinking about Baker Street, and those - how do you call them? - hansom cabs and the fog... Da... yes... I longed - yes? - I longed to see the gaslights for myself... the gaslights shining through the fog...'

'And no doubt Big Ben and the Houses of Parliament as well?'

'Kaneshna. It was my dream.'

Over Igor's shoulder I could see the man whom I vaguely suspected might be tracking him, but my companion, who seemed to be unaware of him, was standing well back from the platform's edge, wrapped up apparently in childhood memories of the works of Sir Arthur Conan Doyle; of Holmes and Watson and London fog. By the look of him, the fellow appeared to be nothing out of the ordinary; in a short beige overcoat, bareheaded and carrying a small briefcase. If he suggested anything at all, it was a commuter going home late from his office. The kind of man you would hardly look at twice. And that's probably why I did.

My conversation with Igor was interrupted by the approach of a train.

'This is my train,' I said.

'Mine too,' said Igor.

We stepped forward to the edge of the platform.

And then it happened - the way it was bound to happen - looking back on it. As the train entered the station, Igor was already waiting impatiently at the platform's edge. And you had to take your hat off to the guy the one in the beige coat with the briefcase I mean, who bumped him so neatly off the platform into the path of the oncoming train - and then rushed back to the exit before anyone had grasped what he had just done.. it was timed perfectly.

I missed my train home from King's Cross, needless to say, but at least I could fill the Police in a little on Igor.

'Better than Polonium 210. They're learning,' said the Special Branch officer whom I talked to. 'I mean, it pays to keep it simple, doesn't it?'

The Heretic

'We took them to a meadow and there we burned them alive...'

The sentence kept repeating itself in Bernard's head. And the sight of the carousel rotating in front of him, its tinny tune and the words seemed to fuse into a single sensation in the afternoon heat. He was sitting at the Narbonne Gate, the principal entrance to the medieval Cité of Carcassonne. Here was where most of the tourist buses dropped and picked up their passengers and visitors paused for a rest below Violet Le Duc's restored medieval walls. The carousel was suitably situated to placate children for whom the wonders of the old city had only a limited appeal. It was a traditional fairground carousel, with gaudily-painted panels, in this case depicting jousting knights in deference to its setting.

In Bernard it induced daydreaming and an unwillingness to move. It was funny how that macabre sentence with its juxtaposed images, of flower-strewn meadow and hideous death, kept running through his head, keeping time with the roundabout: 'we took them to a meadow and there we burned them alive...' He'd read it in a history of the Cathar heresy and the thirteenth century crusade mounted in the Languedoc to suppress it. In fact he recalled it as a chapter heading. Clearly its contrasting images had affected the author of the book as well.

And now Bernard witnessed a medieval duel of sorts taking place near the carousel. Two small French boys, armed with toy swords and wearing plastic helmets, were going hammer and tongs at one another, with the occasional cautionary word thrown in by their father, who was sitting on the sidelines, urging them not to push it too far, but at the same time quite proud of his sons who were engaging in this manly passage of arms. Only when the larger boy rapped the younger one a bit too hard across his knuckles, causing a yelp with pain, did he decide that tempers were about to fray, so, getting up from the bench where he was comfortably settled in the shade, he impounded the weapons and dispatched the lads to the carousel to test their horsemanship instead.

Bernard pondered this scene and thought of the shop windows he had seen inside the Cité, filled with model soldiers, plastic weapons and pieces of armour, the tacky junk of a tourist jampot trading on a medieval past. What had the violence, the fanaticism and cruelty of those distant times boiled down to after the intervening centuries? Could anyone living then remotely have envisaged the way it was now? Would they have recognised anything in it at all? Probably not much, at least in the form it had taken anyway. But then he recalled something else he had noticed in some of the shops; alongside the childish kitsch there were knives - real knives, as nasty as anything ever wielded by medieval footpad or knight. Why were such things being sold alongside the other harmless tourist bric-a-brac? It was not such a superficial question.

A paradox of human nature, Bernard concluded. In a way not unlike enjoying spring flowers and watching heretics being burned alive at the same time. Meanwhile he observed the children in their bright holiday gear on the carousel. As the horses rose and dipped in apparent time with the music, the small boys in particular fell under its spell, showing off their equestrian prowess as their imaginations went to work. It was interesting how little it took to set them going, boys especially, Bernard reflected. Were they knights riding out to battle? Most likely. Or could they even be cowboys? Less likely in this situation, but at the same time he recalled an incident from his own university days. He had emerged from a cinema, having just watched the classic western Shane, when he and another student had collided with each other on the pavement. They had instantly squared up to like a pair of gunfighters, each ready to punish an imagined insult. It had happened so spontaneously, Bernard recalled, that it had to be something fundamental to the male psyche. Now the two erstwhile duellists were riding out to war with their helmets on and flourishing the weapons that their father had restored to them as soon as they were safely launched on their crusade. As fearless a pair of God's warriors as ever rode forth.

But that macabre sentence about the meadow and the burning heretics kept running through Bernard's mind, timed with the music of the carousel and mingling now with his recollection of those evil-looking knives. There was no doubt about it, they could kill, they were designed to kill.... And the tortuous alleyways in the Cité crammed with summer tourists.., what must they have been like once? At the time the Crusaders stormed the place and set about butchering the Cathars for instance? But at other times also, to stalk a prey and dispatch him in the inky gloom couldn't have been too difficult. And in today's crowds it would be simple enough to press up against another body and slip a blade between the ribs... How would Bernard have fared in the Middle Ages? It was a question he sometimes asked himself. Probably pretty badly, he guessed - unless he had managed to find a bolt hole inside a monastery. He might have survived there, being the particular kind of heretic that he was. Which set his thoughts off on a fresh tack - one that these days he tried to avoid.

He wasn't a heretic in the sense that the term is generally understood, of course. But the word bugger having been derived from Bulgar, Bulgaria being the home of the Cathar heresy before it spread into Europe proper, carried with it the stigma of heresy and Bernard knew that in that sense he might be described as a heretic. But no, he would try not to think about any of that now and certainly not about Roger. Above all he must get Roger out of his mind. After all, he was here for a holiday, wasn't he? To leave behind the ghastly humiliations that had been heaped upon him and the things that plagued his conscience still, because in spite of what people had said about him at the time he did have one.

No, he would try to focus his thoughts on Violet-le-Duc instead. An altogether happier subject and one about which he could not make up his mind. Architectural eclecticism was very much Bernard's thing.

Violet-le-Duc: nineteenth century architect and restorer of the medieval citadel of Carcassonne. For the most part he had only to restore the upper tiers of the walls, of course, and to clear away the accumulated clutter of later building. But there was something which Bernard had heard a teenage English boy say on the guided tour he had taken earlier in the day, that put a finger on the problem.

'It's just like a Disney castle!' the boy had exclaimed in a scornful tone, as he looked at the round turrets with their conical slated roofs.

'Well said,' Bernard had blurted out in spite of never having set eyes on any of these people in his life before. The schoolmaster in him had taken over all of a sudden. 'Did you spot that for yourself? Is it your own idea? Because that's precisely what's wrong with it.'

The family looked a little taken aback at this sudden display of vehemence coming from a complete stranger, but at the same time not displeased. Mum nodded appreciatively, at this public and apparently spontaneous recognition of her son's precocious powers of perception.

'Is that really your own idea?' pursued Bernard.

'I think so,' said the boy, more hesitantly this time. 'It just came into my mind, that's all. It reminded me of Disneyland.'

'Those towers! Well you've hit the nail right on its head,' effused Bernard. 'That's the great criticism of the architect Violet-le-Duc's work- the liberty he took and the cliché he helped to establish. Those grey-slated turrets aren't really at home here in Languedoc at all.'

The boy's family nodded and smiled, somewhat bemused, but did not go on with the conversation, no doubt finding Bernard's plummy volubility just a little unnerving.

And at the same time Bernard had winced inwardly as he felt the curtain falling and his thoughts straying back to Roger.

They always seem to know, to guess as soon as I open my mouth, he thought miserably. There's something about me that gives me away. It could have been his camp-sounding voice, of course, and, indeed, it was odd that Bernard, who was wired into so many of the minor nuances of human behaviour, seemed to have missed this one. No one, apparently, had had the heart to point it out to him, but in his brief spell as a prep school master several of the more brazen boys had imitated his accent in his hearing. But then they'd done the same thing to a master who had spoken with a strong north country brogue as well.

But Roger hadn't minded Bernard's plummy voice. He was a lah-di-dah sounding boy himself and to hear them braying together might have raised a few hackles and caused people to jump to certain conclusions about them. In many ways Roger was such an innocent

143

boy and under the thumb of his mother. Bernard recalled the lay-by incident. It had happened not long after he had first got to know the boy and it was a wonder that it hadn't severed their relationship once and for all. As things turned out it would have been better if it had.

By that time Bernard had reached his middle thirties and was teaching in a public school in the Midlands. His real passion was for some of the more arcane byways of art and architectural history, but he had been taken on to teach politics and economics and as a residential house tutor. Roger Gamble was a boy in his house, nominally in his care. It had started from there.

Bernard lived in a bachelor flat above the boys where he held court. Immediately he set about making himself popular by dispensing generous quantities of wine and complaints of noisy late night revels quickly reached the ears of the housemaster whose assistant he was supposed to be. The boys had soon got the measure of Bernard, as the housemaster, Ted Spicer, had probably done as well. But over the years Ted had grown tired of minding teenage boys and tended to turn a blind eye to a number of the things that were going on in his house as long as he felt that someone else was covering for him - as Bernard was willing to do.

However when word of the late night revels eventually got to the headmaster, who respected Bernard's intellect and enthusiasm for his work, but nevertheless could see perfectly well what kind of a man he was, he felt obliged to ask him in.

'I don't mind what you are, Bernard,' he told him candidly. 'It's what you do that I have to be concerned about.' He left it at that, having fired a single shot across his bows.

Bernard took the hint, and cut out the parties. Instead he would try to see the boys on a one to one basis. This, he told himself, was more in line with the job of a house tutor anyway, but it invariably came down to certain boys between whom and himself there developed a close affinity. Roger Gamble soon stood out as the runaway favourite, a fact that was quickly picked up by the other boys in the house, Gamble being a blond youth, whose beauty excited awe in even his most heterosexual peers. They joked about it among themselves, yet at the same time were not resentful of Roger. Indeed, they took care not to trample on his feelings because they all liked him so much. Everyone liked Roger. His looks, especially his gently flirtatious, Princess Diana eyes, made sure of that.

The lay-by incident occurred during the first half term. Bernard had plotted with Roger to collect him in a lay-by that could be reached by a footpath from the boy's home. The ostensible idea was to visit a stately home in the same county and to spend the day there together. Bernard, who knew the place quite well, thought of its shady tree-lined walks and the little arbours which had once been the settings for trysts. It was the middle of October, the leaves were turning and the visitor numbers would be falling off, though it was the school half-term.

'Play it by ear,' Bernard told himself. 'And anyway think of it as a kind of therapy. That you're doing it for the boy's own good. Therapy or counselling - call it what you will - isn't that the kind of thing a house tutor's for?'

Bernard was not normally given to terms like therapy or counselling, but resorted to them whenever he felt the need to justify his conduct to himself.

Nothing had been spelled out to the boy, but he seemed to take the point immediately when Bernard had suggested the discreet rendezvous in the lay-by. He nodded and even grinned conspiratorially, running a hand coyly through his thick fair hair as he did so. Bernard

145

liked the way the boy's hair refused to lie down and his futile but utterly engaging manner of brushing a hand through it.

The meeting was set for ten-thirty on Monday morning. The half-term had begun on the previous Saturday. And on the dot Bernard drove into the lay-by. At first he could see nobody, but was content to sit and listen to Mozart's Flute Concerto on Classic FM. But as he turned up the volume slightly a figure stepped out from under the trees at the side. It was not Roger, but a woman.

'Mr Swinburne?

'Yes?'

'I'm Roger Gamble's mother.'

'How do you do, Mrs Gamble?' Bernard quickly climbed out of the car and put out his hand, which the woman ignored.

She looked at him with a hard blue-eyed gaze. Her fair colouring and the shape of her nose were not unlike her son's, Bernard could not help noticing. But at the same time he felt just as he had done when he was a boy at his prep school and having been caught red handed in a felony of some sort, was about to be chastised for it. His cheeks flushed crimson.

She was dressed in an ancient Barbour with holes in it and green wellies coated with mud - a country woman - which fitted the impression that Bernard had already formed of Roger's family.

'Surely this is a bit unusual, isn't it? I mean a boy's tutor arranging to meet him on the sly like this in a lay-by?'

'It wasn't supposed to be on the sly, Mrs Gamble,' fibbed Bernard. 'At least not in my mind.'

'In that case, then, why did Roger go to such lengths not to tell me? I knew he was hiding something. Getting it out of him was like

146

extracting a tooth.'

'The arrangement was perfectly above board, Mrs Gamble,' replied Bernard. 'Certainly not what you might be thinking. We were to going to visit Houghton Hall, that's all. Didn't Roger tell you that? As you must be aware, your son is very keen on architecture. Rather unusually so,' he added, warming up. 'And it happens to be an interest of mine too.'

'So why was it necessary to cover it up if it was such an innocent trip? Does the school know about it?'

'I'm your son's tutor, Mrs Gamble. I don't have to have to ask anyone's permission for this kind of thing.'

Bernard was short and already running to fat and the woman was a head taller than him, a fact that only seemed to increase her distaste for him.

'All the same I don't like my son engaging in these sorts of liaisons, Mr Swinburne.'

'It was hardly a liaison, Mrs Gamble. I'm sorry you see it that way.'

'In that case why arrange to meet him here instead of picking him up at his home? If you ask me, it looks jolly fishy.' The woman eyed Bernard with palpable distaste and stalked off without waiting for his reply.

'My son will not be going out with you today, Mr Swinburne,' she called from the back of the lay-by where she was about to take the footpath home.

Stung not only by the implication of what she had said and her all-too-obvious dislike of him, Bernard got back into his car and turned up the music. He was sweating. Where next? What had the boy told his mother and what was she likely to do about it? It was only a fortnight since he had been up before the head and he was wanting to let things bed down in the meantime. But then, Bernard reflected, it was only to be expected if you had a son who looked as ravishing as Roger Gamble did. Lucky Mrs Gamble. Bernard drove back to town and browsed in a bookshop until lunchtime.

After half term Roger was very apologetic about the incident. Bernard told him not to worry, but all the same he wanted to know what had sparked his mother's suspicions.

'She's always been like that,' the boy explained. 'Always imagining the worst about me.'

'I suppose meeting in the lay-by was not such a good idea,' said Bernard. 'It probably set her mind running on the wrong track straight away.'

They said no more about it. Bernard poured Roger a generous goblet of Bordeaux and resolved to play things more carefully in future.

Unfortunately Mrs Gamble had not left the matter there. She complained to the boy's housemaster, and even threatened to withdraw her son from the school.

Ted Spicer passed this on to Bernard and cautioned him in his own rather laidback fashion.

'Not such a good idea,' he said. 'I mean meeting in a lay-by. You know, Bernard, you really can't be too careful - especially these days. I think I managed to pacify the old girl, so with any luck it won't reach the head. And anyway, nothing happened to the boy. Mind you with his looks I suppose it's not unreasonable to be a just a little concerned about him.'

He looked hard at Bernard and appeared to be sharing something with him by means of a slyly- lowered right eyelid. And the latter thought of Ted's wife, Penny, whom he had married comparatively late in his life.

Roger had become a regular visitor to the bachelor flat, though now he usually did not come by himself, but brought a fellow aesthete, Caspian Bruce, with him, possibly as a precaution. His companion was not nearly so engaging as he was, quite his opposite, in fact, being dark, bucktoothed and with an earnest expression which was magnified by the thick lenses of his glasses. He talked fast and furiously about art and architecture and Roger clearly looked up to him. It also suited Bernard in a way, to use Caspian as a screen from behind which to admire Roger, but nevertheless there was always a slight sinking feeling whenever he turned up with his unattractive friend.

Another trip to Houghton was fixed for a Sunday afternoon which Roger's mother did not need to know about this time, but Caspian came along too. Bernard ached to take Roger's hand and to plant a kiss on his lips - an action which would somehow have to be dressed up as a form of therapy and consistent with his role as house tutor. But nothing of the sort was remotely possible with the other boy acting the part of chaperone. And while Roger showed a genuine and urbane appreciation of the things they were looking at together - he had an almost proprietary interest in them as if somehow they ought to have belonged to him - Caspian's comments were more acute. He was clearly the brighter of the two.

But it was early days yet and Bernard looked forward to the prospect of the summer term while in the meantime he tried to keep a lid on things so as to limit the gossip to a minimum. Ted wasn't going to make waves unless he was driven to it. The occasional outing to a pub - at a safe distance from the school - was one way that Bernard decided would be sufficiently discreet. A Saturday would be good time when older boys were allowed out on license and Roger would not be conspicuous by his absence.

It was the beginning of the summer term when disaster struck. Bernard had never been good at holding his drink and had the unfortunate tendency of so many of his kind of having to struggle to keep his end up in a masculine setting. Roger was in a lighthearted mood, free from the duennalike presence of Caspian for a change and letting his blond locks down. The pair of them got roaring - or rather braying - drunk and of course the time duly arrived for them to drive back to school.

It immediately became apparent that Bernard was in no condition to drive while the boy, who had drunk only beer and no spirits, was not quite so far gone as his mentor. He had not taken his driving test, but was shortly to do so. All the same Bernard surrendered the wheel to him, mumbling at him to go bloody carefully. As Roger set off down the country lane, his tutor nodded off in the passenger seat and never noticed the car speeding up.

He came to when his head crashed into the windscreen as the car careered off the narrow road and went smack into the wall of a farmyard. The whole front of the car was stove in and Roger was groaning piteously over the steering wheel. Neither of them had bothered about their seat belts.

'Oh God,' gasped Bernard. 'Oh my God!'

Roger said nothing, but continued to groan. He was obviously in great pain.

Bernard put his hand out to touch his shoulder and to ease him from the steering wheel, and despite his own dazed condition felt the blood on his fingers - lots of it.

There was blood too trickling down his own forehead where it had struck the windscreen, but now he started to feel strangely clearheaded. He could see the full ghastliness of the situation, but at the same time the need to act. They were several miles from a main road and getting help might take time.

He had not brought his mobile phone with him, so he decided to go back to the pub and ring for an ambulance from there. It meant abandoning Roger, so he eased the boy out of the driving seat and laid him as best he could on the back seat. That his face was a piteous and bloody mess he could see by the car's inside light. Murmuring endearments, he tried to make him as comfortable as possible. The boy's eyes were shut and on an impulse as he laid him down, Bernard pressed his lips to his forehead. At the same moment the boy opened his eyes and stopped groaning. He stared into Bernard's eyes with a startled, reproachful, gaze.

'I'm coming straight back, Roger... darling,' murmured Bernard. 'I'll be as quick as I can.' He kissed him for a second time - this time on his lips - and the boy flinched and turned his head away. He started to groan once more.

Bernard took the bandana handkerchief from his breast pocket and tied it round the boy's head in an attempt to staunch the bleeding. For a moment he stood there, almost panicking and uncertain whether to leave the boy or not. Then he leaned over and kissed him on the lips again and the boy despite his pain jerked his face away from him.

'Therapy,' Bernard told himself desperately. 'I must try to settle him before I leave him.' He kissed him for a fourth time and knew that even in that extremity he was telling himself a lie.

And the whole thing rolled out as a hideous scandal. Roger was not dangerously injured, but his once-flawless features were spoiled for life; his nose had been smashed and flattened against his face by its impact with the windscreen while his cheeks were scarred by the

151

splintered glass. Bernard had been responsible for slighting the one thing that he cherished most in the world - Roger Gamble's beauty.

But of course that was only the beginning of it. Needless to say Bernard was dismissed from his position in disgrace and the matter came to court. The boy's mother was quite determined to nail him in any way she could. The whole book was thrown at Bernard's head; humiliatingly his inability to hold his drink was raised and his allowing a boy who was also in an inebriated state and who had not yet passed his driving test to take control of the car. But worst of all, Roger had recalled what had happened in the back seat where Bernard had placed him in his injured condition. It was all dragged out in court: how the boy's tutor, supposedly acting in loco parentis, had taken advantage of his injuries to abuse him. Roger was in court to testify and seemed to have little compunction in doing so. Indeed his tone was one of violated innocence. All his time in the witness box he did not look Bernard's way once, but spoke in a soft accusatory voice.

Bernard could hardly believe his ears. He could only assume that the boy's head injury had affected his brain and that his mother was taking full advantage of it. Throughout the proceedings she sat with a steely look on her face. Bernard could feel her eyes boring into the back of his head. Inevitably she gave evidence about the rendezvous in the lay-by.

Bernard defended his action of repeatedly kissing the boy on the grounds of trying to alleviate his distress, but it didn't wash with the court and he was lucky to escape with a suspended prison sentence. At the same time he was placed on a sex offenders register while his career lay in ruins. He lay low in his parent's Norfolk home for a month, living off their good will and the dregs of his salary. His people went through the business of concurring in the fiction that he had been unfairly treated, but it was more a matter of closing family ranks than anything else. Bernard realised that soon he would have to start earning some money - probably abroad.

All the time the thought of Roger's betrayal - as he saw it - rendered him wretched. It was true that the boy's beauty had been marred, but Bernard still loved him to distraction.

Bernard took a short course in teaching English as a foreign language and managed to find a position in France with the help of a reference from Ted Spicer. He had always liked France and while the pay was lousy, he was not too far from some of the places he still wanted to see. The institute where he worked was in Lyons, not ideal, but he could get across to the Languedoc easily enough. He had never really explored it properly, though he had read quite a lot about it, especially the savage medieval passages in its history. And again with his fascination for some of the more outre revivalist architecture of the nineteenth century, Carcassonne beckoned.

But somehow he had to lay the ghost of Roger Gamble and despite all that had happened since the accident it remained a spectre that haunted his sleep and his waking hours as well if he allowed it to.

In Carcassonne he decided to splash out and booked a room at Le Donjon hotel in the Cité itself. It was in the rue Comte-Roger right in the medieval heart of the place. Bernard was no ascetic and never denied himself creature comforts if at all possible and on this occasion, especially, he felt that he had earned them. The Cité was full of little restaurants and cafes spilling onto its squares and narrow streets and he spent the first two days simply wandering in an unfocussed way, peering into shop windows without making any systematic attempt to examine the architectural wonders at all, apart from visiting the Basilique Saint-Nazaire where he admired its combination of

Romanesque nave, with its carved capitals, and Gothic transepts and choir. As he looked at its richly glowing medieval glass, some of the finest in Languedoc, he thought back to his own Roman Catholic roots. He still loved the aesthetics of his mother church, but had long since lapsed into an agnosticism that amounted virtually to atheism. 'We are only an accident,' he liked to tell people if he was pushed on the subject. He would have liked to have had faith, partly for aesthetic reasons, but also, given his own proclivities, he felt that it might have provided him with an emotional anchor in life. 'Yes,' he told himself, 'in the Middle Ages I would have had to have been a monk - but not of the sterner sort. I'm not one for mortifying the flesh.'

After a lethargic couple of days Bernard took the guided tour of the inner enclosure. The guide was a young school teacher who felt it was her duty to fire questions at the members of her group to elicit their response. Bernard did not hold back and, since he knew much more about the history of medieval Languedoc than anyone else in the party, he impressed them, even if they probably found his voice rather tiresome. It was while they were looking at the Tour de la Justice that he had heard the boy compare the towers of Carcassonne with the ones at Disneyland to which he had reacted so effusively.

Afterwards Bernard had settled himself at the Narbonne Gate by the carousel. The Lists and the outer walls could wait until later in the day when it had cooled off a bit - or even the next day. It felt muggy, as if a storm was brewing. The previous day he had found an agreeable restaurant in the Place Marcose which overflowed onto the square and served fresh mussels at a very reasonable price. Bernard liked moules with a carafe of chilled white wine in the middle of the day. They had also served him with a piece of goats' cheese dressed in honey as a desert. Simple fare to be followed by a cup of espresso coffee and a brandy. And of course the chance to watch the world go past. Some of the French boys certainly justified his lingering there. Now he decided to return to the place since he had plenty of time to try others in the days remaining to him.

Once more he had the moules and a chilled Languedoc white wine, nothing special, but dry and tangy, though this time he followed up with a crème-brullee - one of his favourite puds. He had a generous glass of Cognac and was indulging himself with a second espresso when a couple of passing youths caught his eye. He had watched a number of them go by during the course of his meal, and had admired their slender Gallic figures which compared so favourably with his own chubby thirty-five year old one.

Could it be? No, surely not... not here of all places... such coincidences did not occur in real life and in fiction it would have been dismissed as a most dubious contrivance. The pair had passed and were lost in the crowd further down the square, but for a moment he was able to see one of the boys' heads, a mop of fair hair bobbing through the press of people, before they vanished. But the unnaturally flattened nose... that could be no coincidence surely. He had glimpsed it as the boy had passed his table and glanced in his direction before swiftly averting his gaze. Then they had gone, all in a matter of seconds. If it was Roger, had he recognised him? And did he indeed know that his former tutor would be staying here in Carcassonne of all places?

And if somehow he had got wind of it, why follow him out here? Especially after his performance in the witness box, what more could he want from his former house tutor? Had his need to avenge his lost looks not been sufficiently satisfied by what had already been heaped upon him? It could well be the case... if he held Bernard to be responsible for blighting his beauty... or might he possibly have the opposite intention? To make it up? For reconciliation? To make amends for what had passed in the courtroom - which in Bernard's eyes had amounted to a gross betrayal. That was also possible... or was it a mere coincidence that they happened to be in the Cité of Carcassonne at the same time? It was the height of the holiday season, after all. Roger was unlikely to have known. Unless... unless Ted Spicer... who was the only one to have shown Bernard a shred of sympathy in his tribulations... While Bernard had faced the music, Ted had received a muted reprimand for letting the thing happen under his nose... he had exchanged letters with Ted a few times since and in one of them he had mentioned his desire to see the famous Cité walls of Carcassonne... He tended to talk almost exclusively about neutral things like that and to steer clear of more sensitive subjects... Could Ted have let anything slip to a boy in his house? He was unlikely to have said anything to Roger himself, who had not returned for the remainder of the time at the school since the accident and his subsequent surgery. Perhaps Ted had mentioned where Bernard was likely to be found that August. And word of it had been passed on to Roger Gamble - of all people? It seemed far-fetched. And the other boy who was with him? Who was he? Bernard hadn't seen his face. Roger he had recognised. And if it wasn't him, it was someone very like him. It was difficult to mistake him, even with that ruined nose... indeed it was the thing that drew attention to him in a crowd. Surely in this day and age more could be done to mend it with plastic surgery? Bernard found himself thinking. If he got a chance to speak to the boy he might tell him so. There was no point in beating about the bush. He wished that he could do more himself to give the boy's beauty back to him...

All this raced through Bernard's mind, fuelled as it partly was by the cognac that had followed the carafe of wine. He must pay the bill and set off in the same direction as the two boys...

But it was going to be like looking for a needle in a haystack. Bernard wondered where the boys might be staying. And if, perhaps, they would try to contact him, if that was their intention - through his hotel. It wouldn't be all that difficult to run him to earth if they really wanted to.

He walked the entire circuit of the Cité visiting each of the main gates in turn, despite the enervating heat, but saw no one he recognised. He even thought of going down to the area known as the Lists between the Inner Enclosure and the outer walls. But lassitude, aided by his generous intake of alcohol, got the better of him and he decided to lie up for an hour or two in his hotel. There was always the evening and the following day. And the boys might even have set their own enquiry on foot. He must speak to Roger... and let bygones be bygones about what had passed in court. He would help him in any way he could. After all Roger had more to forgive than Bernard had...

It was evening when Bernard emerged from his room and took to the streets once more. In the west the sun was going down in a blaze which filled the spare, rolling Languedoc landscape with deep pools of shadow between its glowing hillsides. The walls of the Cité were lit up too and from his vantage point above the Tour de la Charpentiere, Bernard was able to pick out in detail the rustication of the walls' masonry which marked off Violet-le-Duc's restoration from the earlier courses. It acted as a kind of architect's signature which struck him as honest - the drawing of a clear line between old and new.

But in the press of the evening crowds there was no sign of the two boys. How could there be? So Bernard went to eat in the hotel restaurant. However at the reception he was giving a message which set his heart pounding. Two young men had called, asking if he was staying in the hotel. They had left no other word except to say that they would be back sometime on the following day. No time was mentioned. Bernard confirmed with the receptionist that one of the boys was indeed fair haired and had a squashed-looking nose. 'Oui, comme un pugilist,' the girl suggested.

The weather broke that night when there was a violent thunder storm with the rain coming down in sheets and Bernard did not sleep a wink, but lay awake, wondering what kind of a gloss to put on Roger's presence in Carcassonne. Exactly what was the boy up to?

He rose early and was the first into the breakfast room, where he gobbled a couple of croissants and drank a large cup of milky coffee before going to the reception to say that he would be in his room if anyone asked for him. If the chambermaids wanted to do the room he would come down and wait in the small sitting room area. But he would be in the hotel all morning.

He went to his room, which had not yet been attended to and sat down by the window where he could watch the street. He had been sitting there for three quarters of an hour when he saw the two boys. It was Roger, all right, there was no mistaking him, but the other he did not recognize - he didn't look English, but a Mediterranean type with black hair and a deep olive skin. Bernard rushed from the room and down to the reception, but even so he managed to miss them.

They left this for you and didn't wait,' said the girl. She handed him a note.

Bernard snatched the note from her hand and dashed outside. There was no sign of the boys. But at least he had convinced himself that Roger was indeed in Carcassonne, so he settled down to read the note.

Bernard recognised Roger's scrawl, but the note said little very little, beginning 'Dear Mr Swinburne' and ending with 'yours R.

Gamble.' Hardly a call for restored intimacy. It said that he and his friend would be waiting at the far end of the Pont Vieux which connected the Cité and its immediate surroundings with the Ville Basse on the other side of the river Aude. It said that they would be there in the left hand bay, as you approached from the Cité and would be there at six o'clock.

Despite its rather chilly formality, Bernard felt elated. At least the boy seemed willing to talk to him, though he still couldn't be sure if he intended to tighten the screw further on him or not. Could he have some extra humiliation in mind? Or was the apparent coldness of tone, a sort of embarrassment at the part he had been forced to play in convicting Bernard? Whatever it was he had to take the gamble - the creaky pun occurred to him for the first time - and find out. It could be joy or still greater anguish. And what of Roger's companion? He was a completely unknown quantity and an unsettling one.

So Bernard killed time impatiently by visiting the Lists and walking on the parapet of the Cité's outer walls until it was time to descend from the Narbonne Gate to the Pont Vieux. After the storm of the previous night, the air felt fresher and clouds passed over the distant hills with long, dappling shadows. It was altogether less oppressive than yesterday and Bernard felt strangely euphoric. At the same time he hoped he wasn't deceiving himself. But he trembled with excitement at the thought of being close to Roger once more, ruined face and all.

So far he had not ventured across the Aude to the Ville Basse. The old bridge with its lanterns arranged in a series of slender iron arcs across the walkway was a fitting link. Bernard crossed quickly to the appointed bay and sat down on the stone bench. He was early, of course, by a good twenty minutes, but better safe than sorry and the view, despite his mingled excitement and trepidation, was well worth contemplating for a few minutes by himself. Like a painted castle in the pages of Les Tres Riches Heures du Duc de Berry, the walls of the Cité standing on the hill across the river were redolent of chivalry and romance. The towers thrust their conical roofs towards a sky filled now with great cumulus clouds, while behind the walls rooftops could be glimpsed, adding further to the effect of a city in an illuminated manuscript. Meanwhile the Aude, which was low at this time of year, dawdled between bushy banks over its pebbly bed, stretches of which lay exposed above its surface. On the Cité side, a path ran along the bank where Bernard noticed that a tent had been pitched. He saw a head appear round its flap. Another figure was standing on the path, with his back to the river, waiting, it seemed, for the person emerging from the tent. Then the two set off along the bank in the direction of the bridge.

When the two figures shortly appeared at the far end of the bridge, Bernard could see for certain that they were the two boys. He felt an impulse to rush forward to greet them before they reached him, but he managed to restrain himself. They were the only people crossing the bridge at that moment, and as the boys approached, Bernard could hear a conversation going on between them in a mixture of English and French. So Roger's friend was not English, French by the sound of it. Bernard wondered whether he should stay where he was inside the bay or at least step out to meet them. He stayed where he was.

And then they were in the bay.

'Mr Swinburne?' Roger's voice had not changed, though there was a hint of shyness in it.

But he did not sound hostile.

'Roger!' said Bernard. 'How on earth did you know I was going to be here?'

The boy smiled. 'I have my ways.'

Though the scarring on his cheeks seemed diminished since Bernard had last seen him, his nose was still painfully in need of further attention, having been twisted almost sideways on his face.

'It's great to see you,' declared Bernard. 'How are you? You're looking fine.'

Roger smiled ruefully and ran a finger down his nose. He shrugged his shoulders and did not say anything.

'You're looking pretty good - well, all things considering,' Bernard tried to assure him. 'But it's really great to see you again - a big surprise.'

'Oh and this is Guy,' said Roger who for a moment seemed to have forgotten his friend.

'Nice to meet you, Guy, Enchanté,' Bernard added in French. 'Vous demeurez ici?'

'Non,' replied the French boy. 'In Bordeaux.'

'His English is a lot better than my French,' explained Roger.

For a moment they all fell silent, looking at each other and waiting for one of them to speak.

'It's fantastic - you running me to earth like this,' Bernard gushed. 'Really it is. I can hardly believe it's happening.'

The two boys glanced at each other, but didn't say anything.

'Well,' said Bernard at length. 'This calls for a drink, wouldn't you say? And no-one's driving this time.' As soon as he had said it, he wished he hadn't.

But Roger did not take up the remark and he decided that it was better not to attempt a retraction which could only have made it worse.

They went into the Ville Basse, which Bernard had barely seen, and to a cafe in the Place Carnot that the boys seemed to know. As they went they spoke hardly a word. Bernard did not know how to mention past events, or if he should even try, and Roger was making no attempt to either. Was the French boy acting as a kind of constraint on him? Bernard was reminded of Caspian, but this one was much better looking. He must surely have some idea of Roger's recent past, but as far as Bernard was concerned he was still an unknown quantity and he did not know where to begin.

It was beers all round which Bernard stood. 'Cheers,' he said in a rather stilted manner.

They raised their glasses, but neither of the boys said anything. They simply exchanged glances with one another almost seemed to suggest that they were approaching the encounter with some kind of a pre-arranged strategy.

'Well,' said Bernard. 'Tell me all.'

The boys looked at each other again.

'There's not much to tell really,' Roger eventually came out with. 'I've taken my A levels and have got a place at York.'

'That's great, really great,' said Bernard. 'And this is your gap year?'

'Sort of,' replied the boy, 'but that idea was rather fucked up by what happened, as you might imagine. You know, surgery and that kind of thing.'

'I know,' said Bernard sympathetically, 'but at least you're up and running now.'

'Sort of.'

It was proving rather heavy going and Bernard felt that it might have been easier without Guy. He looked at the French boy - a dark Mediterranean type - nice looking, with regular, almost classical, features which pointed up Roger's disfigurement in an unfortunate way, he couldn't help thinking. A handsome lad - which spoke well for Roger's eye, but with a hardness in his expression suggesting to Bernard that he was not inclined to befriend the former house tutor. In fact his look was almost accusatory. Or did Bernard just imagine that? The boy had hardly said a word.

'So where does Guy fit in?' he asked Roger at length.

'We met back home,' Roger explained, 'through a friend. You remember Caspian Bruce?'

'Of course I do.'

'Well I have been staying with Guy before coming on here.'

The French boy nodded to confirm what he had said, but still did not smile.

After they had drunk a couple more beers, they strolled through the streets of the Ville Basse, taking in the Cathedrale St Michele on the way, but not saying much. Bernard desperately wanted to open up with Roger, to find out what was really going on in his mind, but the presence of the other boy held him back. He eyed the French boy surreptitiously. Roger had made a good choice, if indeed he had made one. The boy looked good even if he was sullen.

In the end they decided it was time to eat, despite it being early. They found a little restaurant on the Rue Chartran which served them more drinks before bringing a menu. Drinks, Bernard decided, were needed. Indeed it reminded him of some of his sessions in the bachelor flat back at the school before The Fall. He needed to do something to break the ice that he felt was due largely to the unsmiling Guy. It was only a short walk for the boys back to their tent beside the Aude, so he had no compunction about ordering three Pernods - a taste not enjoyed by Guy who winced at the aniseed. Roger however ordered gins to follow which the French boy liked better. By the time the menu arrived Bernard felt that Guy was beginning to melt and things were warming up.

Before the meal's end Bernard and Roger were decidedly tipsy and even getting giggly.

Quite like old times, was Bernard's mawkish thought, though he still did not want to refer directly to the terrible events that had come between them. Guy still did not say much, but he seemed to be holding his liquor rather well for a boy who was probably not out of his teens. He smiled and interjected an occasional remark, though he looked politely bored when the others started reminiscing about the short time they had known each other in Ted Spicer's house. Bernard saw this and switched topics in a timely way and asked Guy about himself. It turned out he came from Bordeaux and was the son of a medical doctor, like Caspian's father, and the families had done the usual exchange for language learning purposes. He was due to go to university in the Autumn to read Mathematics.

After a second large cognac, insisted on by Bernard, the party set off. It was dark by now and so far nothing had been said about the one thing that was uppermost in their minds - probably Guy's as well.

Bernard was at a loss for words and, as he was inclined to do on such occasions, felt the way he had done as a boy at his prep school when he had been caught up to no good and knew he could not escape punishment for it.

The lanterns had been lit on the Pont Vieux, which illuminated it prettily, and the walls of the Cité were floodlit. Together they made a fine sight. There was the murmur of voices and several courting couples passed them, holding hands. Bernard wanted to hold Roger's hand and then felt rather put out when he saw Guy doing it instead. The two boys were whispering together in a way that suggested that it was something that he was not meant to hear. This stung Bernard even more and it was on the tip of his tongue to ask them what they were talking about. He could just make out the mixture of French and English words. The French boy sounded the more insistent and Roger hesitant. The boys had fallen behind and had actually stopped under one of the lanterns in the middle of the bridge. Bernard turned back.

'What's all this about? Something I'm not meant to hear?' It was meant sound jokey, but somehow it did not come out that way.

Roger came forward to meet him.

'Guy and I were wondering...' He faltered.

Bernard did not speak.

'We were wondering if you would like to see the place where we're sleeping.'

'I think I know. I saw you leaving your tent.'

'But I told him it was a bit too dark and could wait until the morning.'

'Well couldn't it?' said Bernard 'I can't see any problem.'

Roger's voice was a bit slurred as if the drink was getting to him.

'But Guy wants you to see it now.'

Why does he think I should see it now?' Bernard was genuinely baffled.

Roger pointed up at the sky. It was a blaze of stars.

'It's a fancy of his,' Roger explained. 'Just to lie on his back and gaze up at the night sky.'

'And he wants me to do that?'

Roger did not answer, but shuffled his feet. It seemed such a strange thing to be asking. Bernard despite the excitement of meeting Roger again so unexpectedly felt drained and ready for his bed. He was confident that he was not going to lose sight of him again in a hurry, and he needed to talk to him without Guy.

'I think we can put the stargazing off until tomorrow night, don't you? We can assume they'll still be there.' Despite his agreeable looks Bernard felt uneasy about the French boy, especially having seen the way he had held Roger's hand.

Guy was still hanging back under the lantern in the middle of the bridge, while Roger talked to Bernard.

Roger was explaining his friend to him. Despite the effect of the drink, Bernard sensed that something had been worked out in advance between the two boys. The French boy remained standing almost ostentatiously in the centre of the bridge while the words tumbled out his friend's mouth, like an ill-prepared speech. What was he telling him? That Guy was a stargazer. Astronomy was, apparently, a passion of his and he could name practically every constellation in the night sky.

'He sounds a bit of a nerd, if you ask me,' said Bernard, trying to keep on the wavelength of a boy of Roger's generation, while at the same time feeling middle-aged and ready for bed.

'Maybe he is,' Roger replied, 'but he's still pretty cool.'

'He's a good-looking boy, I'll give you that,' said Bernard, at the same time wondering if it was quite the sort of thing that he ought to have been saying to Roger of all people. 'But he's a bit of a dark horse, isnt he?'

'Sure. He's a loner, if that's what you mean.'

'That figures.'

Guy eventually sidled back to them, his hands thrust deep in his pockets.

'What are we going to do?' he enquired.

'Roger tells me that you're an astronomer,' said Bernard. 'A stargazer.'

The French boy shrugged. 'It's a hobby of mine.'

'I was telling Bernard that you can tell him the names of all the constellations in the night sky,' Roger put in.

'Not quite all of them,' Guy said. He looked up, 'but it is a clear night. The clouds have all gone away. You could see better from the side of the river where there are no lights.'

'I think it's past my bedtime,' yawned Bernard. 'But I'd be happy to do some stargazing tomorrow night.'

'It might be - how do you say in English? Cloudy again tomorrow?'

Guy seemed to be the one who was pressing now while Roger said nothing. In spite of the drink something told Bernard to be on his guard, but he could not figure out why exactly. Perhaps it was because the night sky, spectacular as it appeared to be, seemed a thin sort of a excuse, for keeping him out of his bed. Then Roger looked at him and under the lantern he could see his eyelids flutter in that old flirtatious way that despite his wrecked nose made him so utterly bewitching. It was no good, the boy held him as fast as ever.

'Oh all right then,' Bernard conceded. 'We'll do some stargazing and then it's bedtime. Tomorrow's another day and I take it you're not rushing off anywhere else. But I warn you Guy, I may not be able to take it all in. My powers of concentration are somewhat impaired. And I expect yours are too.'

The French boy glanced up at the great drift of the Milky Way. 'It's a great night for the stars,' he mused.

Bernard looked at the sky, then at the slow-moving river whose surface glinted with reflected starlight and finally at Roger, softly illuminated in the lantern's glow. The sound of the water on the pebbles seemed louder at nighttime than during the day, yet it was immensely peaceful.

No, he told himself, he couldn't walk away from this. Let the French boy explain the night sky to him as much as he liked, as long as he had Roger beside him while he did so - Roger with his poor damaged nose, but who was as dear to him now as he had been before the accident. And forgiving too, because whatever seemed to have been going on between the two boys, he began to feel that forgiveness and reconciliation were in the air on this night by the starlit waters of the Aude. The hatred of the boy's mother, the verdict and judgement of the court, the ruined career, the ignominy of being a listed sex offender and above the responsibility he bore for blighting Roger's beauty, all were behind him now, the watershed crossed. Indeed leading up to this moment standing under the stars on the Pont Vieux at Carcassonne they seemed a necessary Via Dolorosa towards a final redemption. If he had been in a state of mind to consider the matter more soberly, Bernard may have reached the conclusion, perhaps, that there was still a good Catholic inside him after all.

They crossed the bridge and went down to the towpath that ran along the river bank. None of them had a torch, but there was enough light to see their way.

'It's the first time I've been down here,' Bernard said. 'It's very quiet.'

'That's why we like it,' Roger said.

The way he said it implied a bond stronger than mere friendship.

168

What would Mrs Gamble make of Guy? Bernard wondered. Probably he wouldn't bother her in the least because he was the same age as her son. And again Bernard felt the years creeping up on him.

'You're certainly right about the night sky, Guy,' he said with a sigh that simulated satisfaction.

Guy fell behind with Roger, making no attempt so far to explain the constellations.

'I can see why you like it down here,' went on Bernard. 'Nice and cool by the water. Better than the stuffy old Cité.'

They reached the bivouac tent that Bernard had already seen from the bridge.

'You both manage to squeeze into this?' he remarked. 'It looks rather cosy.'

He unzipped the flap and stuck his head inside.

'Let me find a torch,' Roger said. He pushed past Bernard, pressing his body close to his as he did so. As he rummaged among the sleeping bags, although it was dark, Bernard could see his bottom profiled against the roof of the tent as the seat of his shorts was drawn tight. Bernard longed to put out a hand and touch it. But instead he backed out to where Guy was staring up at the sky. Roger emerged and switched on the torch. He had brought something else with him.

'Fancy a drop?' He was holding a bottle of cognac.

'Christ, I'll never make it home,' protested Bernard, though none too ardently.

'What about you, Guy?'

The French boy bobbed his head. 'Oui. Une bonne idée.'

Roger found a couple of enamel mugs. 'I'm afraid there aren't any more. Two of us will have to share.'

169

He half-filled one mug with a generous dose and handed it to Bernard.

'My God, I'll never find my way back if I drink that lot. Like old times, eh? To old times then,' announced Bernard raising the mug and gulping down half its contents.

Roger took a sip and handed his mug to Guy. And in the light of the torch it seemed to Bernard as if a loving cup was passing between the two boys, a ritual from which he was excluded. What am I meant to do? he thought mournfully, get myself completely pissed and pass out while they make love?

The two boys whispered together so that he could not hear what they were saying. Then Roger stuck his head into the tent - my God, that bottom again! - and fished out a sleeping bag which he spread on the sandy bank. 'Sit on that and make yourself comfortable,' he ordered Bernard rather abruptly.

'Thanks.' Bernard sat down, while the two boys remained standing. 'Well,' he said at length. 'I'm waiting, Guy, for you to tell me all about the night sky. What am I supposed to be looking for?'

Guy squatted down on his haunches beside Bernard and clinked mugs with him. 'Bon chance,' he said.

'Bon chance,' replied Bernard and took a large swig. 'Really, this is bloody stupid, he told himself. God knows where it's going to lead. Then without being able to stop himself he called out 'Roger, dear, why don't you come and sit down beside me?'

And Roger did just that. He had hooked the torch to the ridge of the tent and in its beam Bernard saw the bashful flitting of his eyelids. His lashes were the one truly feminine feature in his beautiful boyish face.

Guy meanwhile stepped back into the darkness of the bushes behind the tent. Bernard could hear the sound of water being passed.

He wanted to do the same thing himself, but was unwilling to leave Roger now that he was so close to him and so perfectly and alluringly illuminated by the light of the torch.

'Better?' he said chirpily to the French boy as he came back into the light.

'Oui, un peu. Merci.'

Roger gave Guy the mug, which he clinked against Bernard's and took a sip.

Bernard felt that he really ought to get up for a pee, but lying on the sleeping bag with Roger sitting beside him he felt reluctant to move. 'Cheers,' he said and took a big mouthful of brandy.

It was one too far and he felt suddenly as if he was being firmly but quite gently propelled backwards down a long tunnel. Roger's torchlit face filled the end of it and as he started to fall into a doze he heard himself addressing the boy as his darling...

At first he tried to fight off the desire to sleep, but it was an unequal struggle. He opened his eyes wide enough to see the two boys staring intently into his face and then glance at each other as if to ask the question well what now?

He closed his eyes and was dimly aware of Roger explaining to his friend that his former tutor had always been lousy at holding his drink, adding the words 'like I told you'. That should have set an alarm bell ringing, but the urge to sleep was just too much for Bernard.

'We took them to a meadow and there we burned them alive...' the words ran for one last time through his mind as he slipped out of consciousness.

But he was spared the full horror of that fate. Roger left the real work to his soi-disant astronomer friend. Guy had that morning purchased a knife in a tourist shop in the Cité with a blade that ended in a vicious-looking fang and, with all the dexterity of a practised assassin, he sliced deftly through Bernard's plump neck and the job was quickly done. Neat work for one so young. The body was bundled into the sleeping bag and dragged into the tent where the hilt of the weapon was pressed into Bernard's right hand to take the print of his fingers and placed next to it on the outside of the bag to suggest the possibility of suicide. Neither boy spoke a word throughout and then, having zipped up the tent, they went further down the river bank and sat under the trees. They made no attempt to sleep, but instead talked in low voices about a number of different things, anything except what they had just done to Bernard. Before it got light they set off with their packs to the railway station on the other side of Midi Canal and took the early train to Lyons and then on to Paris. Roger wanted to visit the Louvre which he had not yet seen. They had bought their tickets the day before, so their presence in the station at that early hour attracted no attention. Meanwhile the sun came up in a cloudless sky over the river Aude as it gurgled peacefully over its shallow bed.

Et in Arcadia Ego

It was said of Sir Arthur Evans, the archaeologist who discovered the lost Minoan civilisation, that his shortsightedness was one of the keys to his success. For when it came to detecting the smallest clues that escaped the general run of observers, his eyes would pick them up. It was the very acuteness of his myopia that seemed to provide him with his first insights into a hidden world.

And as I got older, I discovered a similar thing happening to myself, but in my case it only worked in a single instance: when I examined a particular picture in my possession under a magnifying glass, the image, instead of blurring with the enlargement, as it should have done, did the exact opposite. The details were enhanced and I started to notice things that were much too small for the artist to have rendered: And if I increased the magnification still further even more things emerged. I had the queer sensation of looking into a world quite distinct from the one I was living in.

It was not a particularly good picture, being rather primitive and what might be described as topographical; that is a simple record of a place without making any claim to artistic merit. It was a watercolour by Thomas Robins, an eighteenth century painter of gardens. Like the garden it depicted, it was in the rococo style, the scene being contained within a border of plants, coiled about each other, sweet peas, pinks, honeysuckle, nasturtiums, gold-laced polyanthus, which echoed the serpentine paths that edged the lawn in the illustration itself. It was the kind of thing that was probably meant to grace an eighteenth century lady's album. I had come across it in a small shop of a dealer in secondhand books and prints in my home town and, as it happened, I knew something of the artist about whom the dealer confessed his ignorance. The eighteenth century landscape garden was a burgeoning interest of mine.

In a Voltarian kind of way as I have got older my interests have shifted from the stir of everyday events towards more settled things, like architecture and landscape gardening - probably our country's greatest contribution to the arts of Europe. I began putting together a collection of eighteenth century prints of Britain's finest gardens, though it went without saying that my interest also reached out to the fount of inspiration of so many of them, the great gardens of Italy as well.

I had traced their history from the Renaissance through the formal gardens of the seventeenth century to the so-called rococo ones of the early and mid eighteenth, and on to the great neoclassical and Gothic contrived landscapes of the latter part of that century. Indeed, I have toured the country from end to end, nosing around grottoes, Chinese summerhouses, Greek temples and Gothic follies of one kind or another, trying to worm my way into the minds of the people who expended so much money and effort on such things, because I felt that in some way I too was part of their story.

And I pored not only over pictures of the gardens themselves, but also over the works of art that inspired them, Claude Lorraine being a

174

principal source. In fact that was where I have come to feel most at home, in his world of high classicism, his Arcadia, rather than under the stormier skies of the Sublime. It was his vision touched, it seemed to me, by some of the wistfulness of Watteau, those dreamy, sunlit mid-afternoons, that told me the kind of place where I really wanted to be.

I became immersed in the work of men like Richard Bateman and Thomas Wright - designers who made the break with the French-style gardens that had gone before and who created the more playful rococo ones with their serpentine walks and streams. I delighted in grottoes and summerhouses - Chinese and otherwise - and garden sculpture, starting with the lead-caste works of John Van de Nost, Andrew Carpenter and John Cheere.

And then it was the painters who recorded the gardens with naive whimsicality who drew my attention, especially the work of Thomas Robins whose drawings and watercolours first received serious attention in an exhibition at the Royal Institute of British Architects in 1975, over two-hundred years after his death. They were rendered in a rococo style true to the spirit of the gardens they depicted.

My lucky find in the print dealer's shop shows a Chinese bell-pavilion with an open fretwork screen on each side of it, a fine example of the blending of chinoiserie and rococo. The placing of the trees on either side of the lawn, where six gardeners are labouring, still has some of the formality of an earlier garden style, but the serpentine paths flanking them and the asymmetrically arranged seats and flower-beds are genuinely rococo. And framing the whole scene is that essential Robins feature, the garland of flowers.

But as I said, my eyes were picking out things much too small for the artist to have included, and I became convinced of this when I noticed an extra figure in the picture which I had not seen before....

*****

....She is carrying a lavender parasol and to protect her face from the sunlight wears a broad - brimmed straw hat which she has tied under her chin with a large bow. Her lilac silk frock brushes the freshly-cropped grass lightly as she walks in front of the summerhouse with a slight swing of her hips, knowing perfectly well that she is being watched and admired. I'd recognise Sophie Butterworth's walk anywhere. One of the gardeners who is leaning on his rake doffs his hat to her and dips his head in a deferential bow, which she acknowledges with a brief nod as she passes by. And then, when she reaches the end of the ornamental fence where a twisting path bordering the lawn disappears into the backdrop of trees behind the summerhouse, she turns and glances back the way she has come. She sees me and gives me a wave which I return by blowing her a kiss. She knows perfectly well that I have been watching her all the time from the other side of the lawn, and her laugh tinkles brightly in the afternoon air...

Though I am observing her from behind the shrubs at the far side of the lawn I can see everything about her quite clearly, for instance the way she has tied the ribbon in a bow to set off the dimple in the middle of her chin, and her deliciously impertinent blue eyes. All this I can see as if I was right beside her. At once I set off across the grass while she remains standing where she is, idly twirling the parasol over her head.

'Sophie,' I call out, disregarding the gardeners who notice me for the first time, and exchange winks and grins with each other while they continue to rake the lawn.

But Sophie doesn't bother to reply. Instead, as I draw close to her, she jumps with a light skip down behind the latticed fence onto a path that winds off into the wood. She walks rapidly, twirling her parasol as she goes, and occasionally peeping round it in my direction. Once she even sticks out her tongue at me in a most unladylike fashion.

'So you're still playing the will o' the wisp with me, are you Sophie? The way you always do?' I say to myself as I set off in pursuit. I don't run, the rules won't allow it, not at this stage of the game at any rate, but walk briskly instead, keeping her in sight until she turns a corner in the path and vanishes among the trees. When I reach the place I find myself in a little glade with a moss-grown statue of a satyr in its midst. And there sits Sophie, on the other side, where the path twists off once more into the trees, on a small bench in the shade and, despite the comparative gloom after the sunlit lawn, everything about her still seems sharply clear. I notice, for instance, the gold brooch pinned at her bosom, whose cleavage shows generously above her dress, and the wisps of the curls that have escaped from under the ribbon framing her cheeks, and that ever-flickering, mischievous smile...

Of course I know her game well by now - I ought to, since I've played it often enough - and go along with it just as I always do. I don't call to her again, but strike out into the glade, and by the time I reach the satyr, she is up and away once more. It is a game that I'm only too glad to play with her, chasing her along the winding paths as they go deeper into the wood. Indeed, it seems as if we have all of Time to play our game - Sophie for ever scampering ahead of me, but never letting me lose her whichever turn the path takes.

One glade leads on to another... with a succession of statues of fawns, satyrs, wood nymphs...Ovid's Arcadia. And always Sophie darting ahead, screwing her little parasol in my direction and uttering excited giggles...

And then quite suddenly the wood comes to an end and across a small lake reached by an arched bridge stands a temple in the Palladian style. The Chinese summerhouse by the lawn seems a mere caprice by comparison with the simple majesty of this world of Poussin or Claude. At the same moment a breeze rustles in the trees behind me and wrinkles the surface of the lake while a cloud passes overhead - dark-toned, but edged in burning light. Sophie meanwhile is skipping across the bridge towards one of her favourite haunts, the temple. I know that well enough, because I'm familiar with all of her foibles by now...

For a moment she stands framed in the temple porch beneath its pediment. The resident goddess about to enter her own home? But goddess is much too high-sounding a term for Sophie Butterworth - nymph would be more like it, frolicking in the train of a goddess. She commands none of the deference due to a goddess, being much too childlike. For that is exactly what Sophie is, a capricious child, leading giddy young men like me capering round the garden after her.

She stands in the Doric porch, radiantly lit by the sunshine against the temple's dark interior, and then vanishes inside. What further tricks has she got up her sleeve? I can make a guess. for usually when I get to the step at the foot of the porch she rushes out, weaving between the columns, teasing me, as I try to catch her. Sometimes she almost lets me do it before dashing off with squeals of simulated fright in the direction of the bridge once more... it is always timed to perfection... I never manage to catch her... and then, shortly after that, our game peters out and we trail back the way we have come until at last I meet with a more decorous Sophie on the lawn in front of the Chinese pavilion..., and flushed and a little out of breath we drift back to the house where her mama, Lady Butterworth, presides over a tea urn under a spreading beech tree with her two younger sisters.

But this time she does not emerge from inside the temple, allowing me to advance right up to the threshold instead. Apart from the oblong of light in vicinity of the doorway, the place is in darkness. There is a musty smell of dead leaves, earthy, but not overpowering.

'Sophie?' I call out.

A giggle comes from the gloom.

'It's dark in here. I can't see you,' I say.

The sound is repeated.

I take a step forward, and suddenly feel breath hot on my face and moist lips planted on the bridge of my nose of all places. I spread my arms to take hold of her and to draw her close while the lips wander down the length of my nose until they brush against my own where her tongue forces an entry and a shiver runs right through my body.

'Oh Tom.' she sighs. 'Oh Tom! You've managed to catch me at last, haven't you?' and then she sinks onto the carpet of old leaves, drawing me down with her, unresisting, needless to say.

The smell of dried leaves mingling with the warm sweet smell of Sophie... the tips of our tongues pressed together in an ecstatic oral dance...the little gasps - inarticulate, yet so completely expressive of our joy...the shock waves pulsing from one into the other... and the urgent, utterly overpowering, movement in the loins...

*****

A few seconds, yet an eternity. It should have ended for me then and there, once and for all... in Arcadia... But that didn't happen and now the way back is barred and I'm left only with the memory of a dream about a girl called Sophie in a garden. When I look at Robins' painting of the Chinese summerhouse and the six gardeners raking and rolling the lawn under a magnifying glass the image blurs just like any other. And yet... yet... unless my mind is completely deceiving me - et in Arcadia Ego...

The Vintage

'Well you of all people should be the last to complain, Diccon,' said Yvette. 'I was half - expecting Pa to have written you right out of his will altogether. That was a surprise - about the wine, I mean.' There was a hard edge to her voice though she was not looking for a fight.

'Wasn't it just,' admitted her brother with an awkward giggle. 'You were always the apple of his eye while I was the black sheep. Sorry to mix the metaphors, but that's how it was.'

There were four children, now advancing into their middle age. Diccon was the third, sandwiched between Jane and Yvette. Quentin, the firstborn was two years older than Jane and had in most respects been living up to Giles Malet's expectations for him until he had blotted his copybook by his part in a share dealing scandal in the City which had resulted in the untimely closure of his planned career. Meanwhile Diccon, who was already firmly set in his role as the family's bohemian ne'er-do-well, had brought further paternal opprobrium down upon himself by crowing a bit too openly about it.

The death of his wife, Elizabeth, at the relatively early age of seventy had cast a shadow over old Malet's latter years, expecting as he had done for her to have outlived him. It had fuelled his misanthropy and a sense of the pointlessness of his own existence. He continued to go through the old motions of indulging his pleasures like supping fine wines, but his taste buds had dulled and in other respects too his sense of enjoyment had grown stale. Unfortunately old Giles Malet was not one to settle into an Epicurean serenity for the last leg of his earthly passage. Instead he passed his days in a state of peevishness, going out of his way to be as waspish as he could be to the people around him - especially the hapless Diccon who, being chronically short of money and not infrequently in need of the family milk cow, remained a kind of grown-up whipping boy into his middle age. So by the time he shed his mortal coil Giles was not greatly lamented by his family, except possibly by Yvette, who had, after all, been his favourite.

While high hopes had been placed on firstborn Quentin, in a curiously conventional Victorian fashion, Giles had preferred the company of his daughters who, in a way which appeared to the world as perfectly harmless, were expected to flirt with him. Jane, who emerged from adolescence a gallumping tomboy never took to it, but her more girly younger sister was happy enough to indulge her parent, while at the same time a steady stream of boyfriends started coming her way. If anything, this attention pleased her father, and her mother as well for that matter, though she and her younger daughter were never particularly close to each other. Giles Malet was not the slightest bit put out by these young gallants, in fact quite the reverse. He took a paternal pride in the attention his little girl was receiving, as it seemed to reflect well upon himself as her progenitor.

Diccon, on the other hand, could do nothing right, and the boy for his part dismissed his parent as an egregious bore whose highfalutin talk of fine wines, for example, was a symptom of a deep-seated sense of insecurity. During his teens and before he had fluttered from the family nest to reach his present state of quasi-independence, Diccon and his parent had had furious set-tos on this and other contentious topics, while his mother had made rather pathetic attempts to come between them.

Rather in the way that Yvette was the darling of her father, Elizabeth Malet was inclined to be protective of her difficult second son at the expense of her other children. Thus the Malets parents had distributed their affections among their offspring. If any of them was left out, it was Jane, who, given her proclivities, was relieved to be allowed to go her own way.

The crowning surprise of old Giles Malet's will, therefore, was that he had left a sizeable portion of his celebrated cellar to Diccon, the adolescent tormentor who had told him to his face that he was a phoney. His clarets had gone in bulk to the erstwhile golden boy Quentin and each of the girls received a scattering of German whites and miscellaneous French and other reds. But it was Paul, Yvette's husband, who, like Giles, rated himself a serious connoisseur, and was the most suitable recipient of the best of the old man's cellar. Yet the best - the crême de la crême, old Malet's pride and joy, his great Burgundys, which could only be broached on particularly rare and exalted occasions, all passed to Diccon. Could it have been Giles's way of getting back at his disagreeable son from beyond the grave?

The house which was substantial, standing in two acres of garden in North London, and designed by Voysey at the end of the nineteenth century, was shared equally among all four children as well as its contents and all other assets. In that respect at least, peevish old Giles Malet could not have been fairer.

The family was not a closely knit one, but when its members did come together, they managed to be perfectly civil to one another. Jane remained aloof, working for a publishing house and living with a younger female companion, something which was hardly discussed by the rest of the family, but tacitly understood. The great Quentin, despite the abrupt conclusion to his City career, at least had had the nous to pick himself up again and was making good money in the leisure industry, which enabled him to keep up a decent-sized establishment in Henley-on- Thames and to pay boarding school fees for two boys and a girl at the same time, Yvette's husband, Paul, was a solicitor and they lived in Dulwich with two children approaching adolescence, a boy and a girl, who, unlike their Henley cousins, did not go to boarding schools, but attended good independent day ones instead.

Only Diccon seemed to be adrift, as his father had always predicted he would be. He was still unmarried and had never held down a proper job for more than five minutes. Yvette's husband had even tried pushing him in the direction of an acquaintance who ran a company that made TV documentaries but it was the usual story, he started out full of bright ideas, but nothing came to fruition. Yvette told Paul that her father had been right about Diccon all along, that he was, alas, a waster. While he was very contentious, challenging everyone else's assumptions, often trenchantly, he lacked the capacity to enact anything positive of his own. There were times, indeed, when he seemed to be a raging Thersites, a literary comparison Yvette was rather proud of making, especially when Paul assured her that it was probably a very apt one.

'I really don't know what Dad thought he was up to giving all that wine to Diccon,' she grumbled, having brooded on the matter ever since the contents of the will had been disclosed. 'It was meant to be the best in his cellar. I suppose it was some kind of a sick joke. Or he might have had a brainstorm and got it hopelessly wrong, standing the thing on its head and thinking that Diccon was the great oinologist of the family. Call it a caprice of his dotage.' She was quite proud of that phrase and hoped that her husband had noticed it.

'Possibly,' answered Paul with a shrug and in a tone that was meant to sound as if he did not really care. He preferred not to be dragged too far into his in-laws' family politics if he could help it.

'You at least know something about wine. As it is, giving it to Diccon is casting pearls before swine. Sorry, I didn't intend that to rhyme - I mean the wine and the swine.'

'I'll pretend I didn't hear it,' Paul said patronisingly. 'But I think we can get along well enough without your Pa's pet Burgundys, don't you? We've got plenty of our own stuff which is probably just as good.'

'You know better than me.' Yvette's own views on the subject were probably closer to her brother's than she cared to admit, so she was ready enough to yield the crown to Paul in such matters.

As has been implied, there had not been a scrap of resentment on old Malet's part when he had come seeking his daughter's hand, thus breaking the bond between the father and his favourite child. He had approached it in entirely the right way, requesting an appointment in the privacy of the paternal study, armed with a brief setting out his current financial circumstances as well as his prospects. He had addressed his future father-in-law throughout the meeting as sir, which had gone down well, and finally, the pact had been sealed with the broaching of one of the great Malet Burgundys - a Nuit St George. After all, this was one of those rare and momentous occasions that called for it. Paul had discussed the nectar with an impressively furrowed brow and a sufficiency of expertise tinged with an awareness

185

of the older man's greater knowledge of such matters, thus raising himself even further in the estimation of his future father-in-law.

So it was hardly surprising that Yvette should have felt that the fabulous Burgundys should have come her husband's way, more especially since Paul had not five years before become a member of Giles's own Masonic lodge. But still, a timely word in Diccon's ear might yet set the matter to rights, without undue haste, of course, for it would be poor form to start unpicking their father's will so soon after his death, however perverse it might seem to be. The younger Malets possessed a sense of dynastic decorum not altogether unlike the old man's own.

All the same I hope Diccon hasn't managed to drink it before I've had time to have a word in his ear, thought Yvette. You never quite know with him - he's such a strange creature. Paul of course will pay him the going rate - whatever that is. And in any case, I'm sure Diccon would sooner have the money. He's usually broke.

Diccon had a job of sorts for the time being at least. A chum ran a small gallery in Islington where he helped out for a fee. Diccon had no shortage of chums of this kind and indeed they were the principle means, apart from grudging family subventions, that enabled him to bumble along in life, against the day when he made his breakthrough, though what form that long-awaited event was to take remained anybody's guess.

After three weeks Yvette rang her brother in his rented flat. It was the first time they had spoken to each other since the opening of their father's will. She didn't beat about the bush. Malets seldom did.

'Hullo Lesser Brother,' she said - Quentin was greater and Diccon lesser brother in Maletspeak.

'Hullo Lesser Sister,' returned Diccon.

'About that wine,' she went on. 'The stuff Pa left you.'

186

'What about it?'

'You haven't drunk it yet, have you?'

'Only one bottle,' said her brother. 'But give me a chance. There are three dozen cases of the stuff.'

'What did you make of it?'

'Oh dear, you are putting me on the spot, aren't you? I would probably say the wrong thing. I usually do.'

'Just say what you thought of it, that's all I'm asking - even if it is the wrong thing.'

'Quite honestly, it seemed nothing special, to me at any rate. Would you and Paul like to have it?'

'Actually that's what I was ringing you about, Diccon. We'll pay you for it, of course. The going rate. Paul knows what that should be.'

Diccon was tolerably in pocket for the time being following the family settlement, but was never one to look a gift horse in the mouth.

'That sounds pretty reasonable to me.'

'Done, Lesser Brother?'

'Done, Lesser Sister.'

Paul picked up the three dozen cases the following weekend, making several trips in his four by four, and straight away laid them up in the cellar at Dulwich, while Diccon was glad to have the extra cash in his pocket.

It was superb stuff, there was no doubt about it: Nuits St George, Gevrey-Chambertin, Romanee-Con, Corton-Charlemagne, and some noble whites too: Le Montrachet, Puligny, Chassagne Montrache, all grand cru, of course. Paul knew that he was onto something very special.

He opened a couple of bottles - a Gevrey-Chambertin and a PulignyMontrachet - with a carefully selected company of fellow masons from his lodge and it was roundly declared that old Malet had indeed got it right. It was lucky Diccon wasn't present, because the observations that were made would, in his eyes, have reached new heights of wine-bibbing cant.

It was solemnly decreed then and there that the Malet Bugundys would be broached on set occasions only and in the most discerning circle of friends drawn from his masonic lodge, rather as the old man might have done himself. There was a sufficient number of brothers who shared Paul's tastes and talked his talk. It was small wonder that he had been a successful suitor for the hand of Giles Malet's favourite child. So a Burgundy Night became an established event in Paul's calendar and was treated with due masonic solemnity.

The company was to meet twice a year only, a night in February and another in November. Conviviality was expected of the brothers; there was to be no nonsense about merely tasting the wine and spitting it out. Whatever it did for the palette it had to warm the tripes as well. Yvette served up a meal and usually joined them for it after the serious work of the evening had been done, which was the tasting and airing of opinions about the wine. Paul decided that it would be fitting to open proceedings by raising a glass to the memory of Giles Malet so this became an established part of the ceremony to be performed at the uncorking of the first bottle.

There were three dozen cases to be worked through and since the Malet Club, as they soon rather ironically dubbed themselves, met only twice a year it was some time before the end of the consignment was in sight. As that time approached, Paul, who by now was well into middle age and getting set in his ways, was finding the masonic type of bond ever more congenial. So he put his mind to what was to come next. It was agreed by all present that the club must confine itself to the consumption and discussion of only the very best that the Burgundian vineyards had to offer. There could be no relaxation of that rule and of course it went without saying that the honouring of Giles Malet's memory was to remain the lynchpin of the occasion.

Yvette, meanwhile, viewed her husband's ponderous ritual with a rather wry detachment. She could not be quite sure whether the apotheosis of her own father was meant to be a joke of some kind or not. Could the whole thing not simply be a silly schoolboys' game which none of them took very seriously? That would be a very British way of carrying on, after all. Yvette viewed it as all a bit childish - like her husband's lodge - but in the same way perfectly harmless, boys having to be boys, that sort of thing, and anyway coming round only twice a year it was no great burden.

With the broaching of the final case of Malet Burgundy, Paul indicated that the time for initiating his eldest, eighteen year old Gavin, into the rite had at last arrived. It was to be an occasion for bringing on the next generation. He took it for granted that his son, who was an inoffensive young man, would be interested. But while the lad did his best to avoid quarrelling with his nearest kin, he nevertheless had a streak of his Uncle Diccon's obstinacy in him and liked to keep a safe amount of space between himself and his parent. On this occasion he was able to contrive a prior engagement with his girlfriend, Rosie , who happened to have her birthday on that very same night, so he tactfully declined the invitation to join the Malet Club for the Broaching of the Final Case, as Paul had grandiloquently described the occasion on the embossed card he sent out to summon the brothers. But come next February he might indeed be ready to come on board, or so he informed his parent.

The Friday evening in late November arrived and the brothers assembled round the table in Paul's dining room in the usual manner. It was of course a black tie event. Their number included a couple of partners in Paul's firm of solicitors, Eddie Challoner and Ben Wyatt, who were fellow masons.

Paul lead off with the toast to the memory of his father-in-law while the circle listened with the customary show of solemnity, their glasses at the ready. He spoke more expansively than he normally did, and with greater feeling. Since this was the last of the Malet wine, he addressed the future and his hopes for it. Certain practicalities were touched on, for instance the selection and laying up of fresh stocks of wine. This he wrapped up first; he and Brothers Chaloner and Wyatt-they were punctilious about using the proper masonic form of address when in session together - had already embarked upon the renewal of supplies, it was hoped, of the right quality, but he assured the company in general that the selection of the finest Burgundys was to be a matter for the Club as a whole, where any brother's opinion would be given full weight. After all, were they not peers, a true band of brothers indeed, gathered about a round table in solemn and mutual appreciation of each other's palettes?

The last three bottles stood before them on the board: a Romanee-Conte, a Corton-Charlemagne and a Chassagne-Montrachet. The laughter grew louder as the evening advanced, almost too loud, indeed, and the observations less portentous, which of course was the direction things usually took. The Platonic element of the occasion, when clever ·comments were bandied about, invariably gave way to pawkier forms of male bonding, even outright bawdiness, a more robust, Hogarthian spirit.

The final bottle was reached, the Corton Charlemagne, and Paul rapped the table with a spoon, calling upon the company to raise its glasses to drink one more time to the memory of Giles Malet, their patron, but now he also embraced the future in the form of the old fellow's grandson, his own son, Gavin, who, alas, could not be present on this occasion as he had hoped, young men being what they are hem, hem. Knowing nods, nudges and buffers' chuckles duly did their round of the table. But like the Seige Perilous, the place kept empty and waiting for Galahad at the Round Table in Camelot, a place had been set for the absent and awaited Gavin. Then, in a single movement the company swept to its feet, glasses were raised, glances exchanged and the toast drunk, with the steadiness of a company of Guards.

*****

Gavin left Rosie at her flat and got home shortly after midnight. The lights were still on and before he was through the door his distraught mother flung her arms round his neck.

'Thank God you've come at last, darling! I never thought you were! Had you switched your mobile off?'

'I didn't take it with me. But what's the matter Mum? I was only leaving Rosie back at her place.'

His mother responded by hugging him frantically and with a torrent of weeping. 'Thank God you're here! Oh thank God!'

'What's the matter Mum?' repeated the bewildered boy.

By way of answering she dragged him into the house. 'Oh thank God you went out instead of joining your father!' she sobbed. 'Thank God for that at least!'

Gavin had no time to press any more questions. His mother had thrust him into the dining room. Round the table ten dead men lay slumped, some across the table, others on the floor, including his own father, all in different attitudes. Glasses were scattered about, while standing on its own in the middle of the table was a single empty bottle that had held the Corton Charlemagne.

*****

On the crematorium steps in the cold November drizzle, Diccon took Yvette's hand and pressed it firmly.

'You know, Lesser Sister, there's one thing I simply don't understand.'

Yvette glanced at him. 'Oh?'

'About Pa, I mean.'

She gave a short, mocking laugh.

'I don't understand why he gave that wine to me.'

'Oh God, it's bloody obvious isn't it?'

'What I mean is he surely didn't expect me to drink it, did he? He must have known me well enough to realize that I was more likely to sell it on... Wouldn't you have thought?'

Yvette merely shrugged her shoulders. She had no answer to that.

The Tutenkhamun Touch

Lionel Burridge died young, leaving behind him a mounting fortune and a handsome Jacobian manor house looking out onto the English Channel, not far from Lyme Regis. Yet his wife, Phyllis, in spite of the care she had lavished on the creation of a knot garden and the restoration of the great hall, while raising a family at the same time, sold up immediately and retreated with the two boys to Languedoc.

A few days before his death, her husband had suddenly become depressed, but his violent end came as a bolt out of the blue. If he had died by his own hand it would not have been altogether surprising, given his state of mind just at that time, but this was no suicide: Phyllis arrived home very late from London one November night to find him lying on the floor at the foot of the great staircase. The ugly gash on his head left no room for doubt as to the manner of his death: he had been struck by a heavy, edged object, possibly an axe, Her sister, Annabel, who was staying in the house at the time, and the children had heard nothing.

And the motive seemed clear enough too, for the prime piece in the collection of Central American pre-Columbian art, that Lionel had been

193

building up, was missing; a Mayan jade and obsidian mask, which, judging by the materials and the quality of its craftsmanship had once belonged to a powerful chief or some such royal person. Such an act of violence seemed at odds with the theft of works of art, a comparatively civilized type of crime not normally associated with the cruder forms of skulduggery. So obviously the thief or thieves had been disturbed in their dirty business by Lionel when he had descended in a splendid silk dressing-gown from his bedroom at the top of the stairs and had panicked. That was where it seemed to end. Lionel's fame as a writer notwithstanding, no perpetrator of the crime could be traced. The police drew a complete blank. no fingerprints, no DNA traces, nothing, and, it went without saying, that the stolen piece was never recovered.

The case caused a stir of course; the murder of a recently-famous writer in his own home and the speculation about what lay behind it grew more fanciful the more it was aired. Indeed, in an uncanny sort of way it seemed to mirror some of the darkness of the very tale which had brought Lionel Burridge his fame and fortune in the first place.

And that was the puzzling thing about Lionel Burridge's literary success. He had written only one book and in the four years since its publication had showed no inclination to follow it up with another, despite the pleas of his publisher. But then he could afford to rest on his laurels, because the book had turned out to be a bestseller and was rapidly on its way to becoming a cult. Film rights had followed with a potential blockbuster in the offing at the time of his death. Yet with all this in prospect Lionel Burridge, after an initial flurry, seemed more than ready to follow Voltaire's advice and to retreat from the world to cultivate his own garden. The occasional television interview was all he would concede, but he soon gave those up as well. His publisher was not too bothered, however, because the whiff of mystery surrounding the author served to sustain a growing legend that could only be good for his sales. And then came the sensational, Agatha Christie style murder, a cliché almost, a rising star slain in a silk dressing-gown at the foot of a grand Jacobean staircase in an English country house.

To the aficionados of the genre the colourful and mysterious circumstances of Lionel's death neatly underpinned the legend that was springing up around him and which he had helped to nurture by his retreat behind the walls of his Jacobean home; the mystery of the man who had written one sensationally successful book, gaining fame and fortune almost at a stroke, and the end to all to material cares. Then the manner of his death, that too amounted to a literary cliché. All in all, what need of anything more? He had been struck down, like the poet Rupert Brooke, in his prime with his youthful charisma still perfectly intact. The tale was complete.

Lionel hadn't been born to the purple, but into a moderately well-off upper-middle class family, his father being a general practitioner in the north of England. At university he had rubbed shoulders with a rich bohemian crowd - Old Etonians and Harrovians mostly, a pretty louche set, some of whom had pretensions to being artistically creative. And it was in that general direction Lionel felt that his own talents probably lay too.

His eventual degree was a meagre lower second, but as things turned out it mattered not a jot. Among the friends that he carried over from Cambridge was one Sam Ockleton-Brewster who enrolled in the Middle Temple with a view to a career at the Bar, while Lionel, on the other hand, having acquired a certificate of education, took a post as a history master in a north London prep school.

He still saw a quite lot of Sam who, though busy with his pupillage, nevertheless was working at what he confided to his friend

195

was his first novel - for he had aspirations beyond the Bar - regardless of how lucrative that might turn out to be. He talked about it readily enough to his friend, making no secret of what he was trying to do.

Lionel could not quite get to the bottom of Sam, who combined a nimble lawyer's mind with a penchant for tracing things back to obscure and unlikely sources. He had no time for inanities like conspiracy theories himself - and he suspected that Sam hadn't much either - yet, especially after the recent runaway success of a young American author writing in that vein, he thought he could see what was driving him.

'You surely don't seriously believe any of that guff about secret codes lurking in pictures and Holy Grails being handed down via the Knights Templar to the Freemasons, do you, Sam?'

Sam laughed. 'Enough people do,' he replied. 'And if that's the case, there's a pot of money to be made out of it - if you pitch it right.'

'But will it last?' pursued Lionel. 'The bottom is bound to fall out of that market one of these days, isn't it? It can't go on for ever.'

'You'd be surprised how tenacious things like that can be,' Sam explained. 'After all, look how long the Kennedy conspiracy theory has hung on - ever since the Sixties and it's still going strong. And then there's the murder of Princess Di. They'll never get enough of that one, will they? People get hooked on conspiracies - all that secret code crap – it's a drug - and they don't give a toss for what might really have happened, the boring old truth in other words, which would wreck the story. And often they're people who are perfectly rational in every other aspect of their lives. I'm far enough into the Law by now to see that they believe the things they are determined to believe, despite any evidence to the contrary - evidence which is perfectly plain, needless to say. They insist on going for the dotty explanation with its coded message instead of the obvious one that's staring them in the face.'

'But what you're writing now, Sam, isn't it - frankly - well - a bit beneath you, I mean?'

'Should I be trying to write a kind of sequel to Joyce's Ulysses instead? Is that what you're telling me?'

'Heaven forbid. I could never finish the bloody thing myself. But something more on the lines of Trollope, say. A career at the Bar should give you plenty of scope for that kind of a book.'

Sam laughed. 'But we're hardly living in Trollope's world anymore, are we?'

Lionel sighed his assent. 'More's the pity, perhaps.'

The Da Vinci Code was all the rage at the time and Lionel regarded the sheep-like adulation it had aroused with disdain, especially when he heard about the pilgrimages being organised for its devotees to view Leonardo's Last Supper in Milan so that they could witness the coded message locked inside the painting for themselves. So he was inclined to be scornful of Sam when he attempted to justify his own efforts in the same line.

'Sam, you do realise, don't you, there must be hundreds, probably thousands, of wannabes just the same as you, all trying to strike it rich in that kind of a way? I expect the publishing houses are swamped with their outpourings.'

But Sam only smiled rather complacently, his friend felt, 'When it's a bit further on I'll read you some of it. And see what you make of it then.'

'I think I know that already. It's a crashing bore. You're worthy of better things, Sam.'

But his friend smiled, more enigmatically this time, and shrugged his shoulders. 'Let's just wait and see, shall we?'

Nothing more was said about the novel for several weeks. In fact Lionel saw very little of Sam in that time as both were busy in their different ways. Then came the long summer holidays when Lionel took himself off to Central America to look at Mayan temples, a fancy of his from boyhood when he had discovered them in an encyclopedia, while his friend retreated to a family bolt hole in Burgundy. Sam's eyes lit up when Lionel told him where he was going.

'I never knew you were interested in the Mayas,' he said.

'Didn't I tell you? New World civilizations have always been a bit of a hobby of mine.'

'You never did. But that's great, Lionel, really great!' He patted him on the shoulder enthusiastically. 'You know, you could be very useful to me! I think the Mayas may be better for my purpose than the Egyptians.'

'Oh really? By giving you the key to the ultimate secret of the universe, something along those lines? The Last Secret concealed in a temple lost in the depths of the Honduran jungle? Is that what you're looking for? Is that the object of your quest?' Lionel laughed and shook his head.

'I'm being perfectly serious, Lionel. You think about it,' said his friend, who was managing to both look and sound serious at the same time.

Lionel spent five weeks of his summer holiday in Central America, on a journey that took him from Belize into Yucatan, back into Belize again, and finally into Guatemala. Time ran out before he could complete the Honduran leg, but he had a wealth of photographs to show for it - a lot of them taken at the well-known temple sites like Tikal, but also on a river journey he made in a motor boat to look at an unexcavated site in the Guatemalan rain forest. Back at school, needless to say, he was expected to give an account of his adventures to the boys. But it all had to be repeated for the benefit of Sam, who looked at the slides and questioned Lionel very closely about the temples; how they had functioned, the meaning of their artwork, hieroglyphs, the Mayan cosmology and so on.

'You really ought to go out there and see it for yourself if you're so interested,' Lionel suggested.

'Maybe I will one day,' said the other absently, 'but I don't know when I'll get the time. There are some good sources I can read up in the meantime, I daresay?'

'Loads of them. But start with Maudslay. A retired civil servant who devoted the last part of his life to studying the Maya, and Stephens, an American. Very reliable, both - there's no mystical mumbo-jumbo about either of them, just sober, scientifically-inclined men of the nineteenth century.'

'I wouldn't have it any other way,' laughed Sam. 'Leave the occult crap to me. I can handle that side of it' He recharged Lionel's glass with a generous measure of an excellent single malt, one somewhat beyond the pocket of his friend whose recent Central American jaunt had left him rather broke.

For a while Sam clammed up on the subject of his novel and, despite his friend's probing, gave very little away. Lionel began to wonder if it was beginning to die a quiet death as other, more pressing matters, took its place. Sam, he recalled from his university days, was less of a dabbler than some of the other members of his circle - he had gone down with a First after all - but he could not help thinking that the conspiracy novel or whatever it was going to be - rehashed Ryder Haggard crossed his mind - was a bit of a caprice and that once his nose was set firmly to the grindstone of a career it would soon be ditched.

Then one Sunday afternoon when Lionel dropped in he found

Sam immersed in what looked like a cheap paperback, which he handed to him. That indeed was what it was, a pulp novel, published in the Fifties by the look of its cover, with a lurid illustration, showing a party of explorers, kitted out in solar topees and gazing across a jungle clearing at a creeper-draped temple of the Mayan type. The author was one Arthur Cummings and the price of the book was two and sixpence or half a crown in the old money.

'Someone got there before you, have they, Sam?' said Lionel. 'Or do you think it's due for a fresh outing under a new title perhaps?' He noted the publication date which was 1953. 'The year of the Coronation and the first ascent of Everest.' And 'The Curse of the Maya' too, by the look of it,' he added, glancing at the title.

Sam laughed. 'It's pretty close to what I'm trying to do myself, except for the curse bit - I hadn't got round to that.'

'What? You mean to say you haven't got a curse?' expostulated Lionel. 'For God's sake, man, you must have a curse! - the Tutenkhamun touch. It's absolutely hopeless without a curse! I insist on it. In fact I'm amazed you hadn't come up with one already.'

'Well, anyway I hadn't,' his friend admitted, 'so I'm nicking his right away.'

'Good for you, Sam. That's the way that leads to fame and fortune. Never be afraid of nicking anything you might need.' It was an unusually cynical thought for Lionel - something he could not help noting in himself.

But that was the last time that Sam and Lionel spoke to one another, because Sam died in the most unexpected manner less than a month later. He was leaving the Old Bailey on an overcast November afternoon where he had been sitting in on an assault case with his pupil master and stepped in front of a prison van which was driving off at speed. There was a big Islamist terror trial going on in the court next to the one which he had just left, and the police were wasting no time in shipping the accused back to prison. But whoever was at fault, a rather nervous driver putting his foot down too hard or a jaded and abstracted pupil barrister, the outcome was the same.

Lionel attended the funeral of course. Sam was buried in a family plot in Cumberland, an agreeably old-fashioned touch, his friend could not help thinking. It was understandably a very sombre occasion, as everyone was deeply shocked by the sudden death of such a bright young hope, although Lionel could not but be impressed by the stoical way in which the Okleton-Brewster clan bore themselves. The stiff upper lip, he concluded, still had plenty going for it.

At the reception that followed the funeral, Lionel was approached by Sam's younger brother, Charles, whom he knew only slightly.

'Very decent of you to come,' Charles said.

'It's the least I could do. Your brother was a very good friend.'

Charles was holding a brown jiffy bag, which he handed to Lionel. 'This is for you,' he said.

It had Lionel's name on it but no address.

'For me?' Lionel took the bag. He had an idea of what was inside, but for some reason he did not feel that it was quite the moment to talk about it.

'I'm not sure what it is exactly,' said Charles. 'A disc - something Sam was working on - he always seemed to be working on something - but I must confess that I haven't got round to reading it. There's a note inside addressed to you - Lionel. I did read that much.'

'It's a novel - of sorts, anyway,' said Lionel, 'At least I think that's what it might be. He did mention it to me - and about having a look at it.'

'Really?' said Charles, who did not sound particularly curious about his late brother's literary activities. 'Sam always was a dreamy sort of bugger, so I suppose he had to be writing a novel, hadn't he?' He turned away and Lionel placed a sympathetic hand on his shoulder.

The circumstances, especially the manner of death of such a privileged and promising young man, attracted some attention in the popular press. A great deal was made of Sam's background - landed Cumberland family, Eton, Cambridge and so on - but also of his first class degree and the promising career that lay ahead of him at the Bar. Nothing, of course, was said about his ambitions as a novelist.

The note inside the jiffy bag had been written only a few days before Sam's demise and was a routine affair asking his chum to look at the disc and give his opinion. It was couched in terms which seemed mildly dismissive of the work itself. And of course there was no premonition in it of his fate. He merely stated that not having seen Lionel for a while he was posting him a copy and would pester him in a couple of weeks time for an opinion. But he had only got as far as writing Lionel's name on the bag which was still on his desk when he died.

Lionel put it on one side. It was, after all, not his sort of thing. But then his conscience pricked him in an almost superstitious fashion. Somehow he owed it to his dead friend to read his work at least, rather than consign it to immediate oblivion or merely return it to the family. It was almost certain to be junk, of course, but that was hardly the point.

Lionel was not familiar with his friend's style, but while he felt that he was writing a kind of pastiche - of Ryder Haggard or John Buchan - he found it oddly compelling and soon was racing along as if possessed. When he paused he was surprised to find how long he had stuck with it without a break in his concentration.

Yet it was a very conventional tale, a pastiche, a contrived period piece even, and the idea of his friend writing it with his tongue in cheek never quite left him. It was a thundering good read, nevertheless, and Lionel was forced to admit that in its own way it had real quality. It was all very well being highbrow and sniffy about it - and this was the point surely - it was the sort of thing that a lot of people enjoyed and even a literary snob like Lionel Burridge found himself being trapped in its spell. In fact he had the same guilty feeling as he had when he caught himself enjoying a piece of reality television which his judgement told him was unworthy of his attention.

'By God, Sam,' he said to himself. 'You've got a page-turner here.' And he felt a pang of envy - something that he had never felt for his old chum before.

It needed tidying up of course, it was pretty rough in places and the ending which had barely been sketched in, wanted pulling together. So what about it? Should he try to do the job himself for the sake of his lost friend? And then what? Publication? It might be worth a shot, but he would need to talk to the Ockleton-Brewsters about it first, surely. He thought back to the funeral, Charles had seemed scarcely interested, even dismissive. Other things must have been weighing more heavily on his mind just then, no doubt. But did he have to consult them even? So why not simply tidy it up and send it to a publisher and see what happened first? He could add a touching editor's tribute to the late author and the Ockleton-Brewsters, would, no doubt, appreciate that. Nothing could be lost, certainly, if he put out a few feelers himself.

Lionel sat for a long time in the living room of his small rented flat, thinking about what he had read, ignoring a pile of unmarked exam papers. It seemed to have the vital ingredient needed in a bestseller, a pace that drove it forward, dragging the reader along with it, willy-nilly. He knew that if he tried to do the same thing himself he could not -

not in a month of Sundays. But then Sam had got a first, hadn't he? and Lionel a mere 2:2. That was the difference between them, surely. It was not quite as simple as that of course, but was something less tangible. He couldn't put a finger on it. Not genius, that was altogether too pretentious a term for it. This sort of thing wasn't in that league - his friend had not written War and Peace or Vanity Fair - it was no great work of literature, yet was bloody good all the same, for what it set out to be.

Lionel needed to know if there were any other copies of the story in existence anywhere, on a laptop, for instance. He had to find out though he preferred not to ask himself why. Charles would be the one to consult, but he would leave it a week or two to give the family time to settle Sam's affairs. Something also was telling him not to reveal the contents of Sam's tale to anyone, least of all his family. If it came to the crunch he could make up an excuse to cover himself and quietly misplace the manuscript should anyone enquire after it. A plot was hatching in Lionel's mind, almost before he knew it, that his friend's work - if his impression was correct - should indeed see the light of day, not under his own name, but under Lionel's, It would still be Sam's work of course, nothing could alter that fact, but then did anyone really need to know? At the end of the day it was a detail as long as the book was published. The nom-de-plume of Sam Ockleton-Brewster would be Lionel Burridge which was much less of a mouthful.

He rang Charles to ask him if any other jottings - that was how he put it- on Sam's part had come to light since they last met, speaking in a tactfully dismissive way about the manuscript already in his possession. He did not divulge its contents and Charles, who seemed as incurious as before about it did not trouble to ask, He told Lionel what he wanted to hear; no copy of his brother's disc existed that he was aware of. Lionel decided to take the plunge.

It was about this time that he met Phyllis, the daughter of the headmaster and his wife at the school where he still taught History. She was just rounding off a degree in Botany and was mad keen on conservation, which fitted in quite neatly with Lionel's own outlook on the world. He fretted about such things and enjoyed talking about what he would do if only he had the means. They soon hit it off, while at the same time Lionel was getting a measure of satisfaction from his job. They were, after all, well-motivated children from educated backgrounds that he taught, and were inclined to be interested in a world beyond their own. They lapped up his yarns about his travels in Central America and wanted to know all about the Mayas and the Aztecs which was flattering. Of course they loved the gory details which their History master laid on with a trowel, the human sacrifices and so on.

And it seemed to come together so naturally, the traveller in the jungles of Central America with his tales and the audience of young boys who hung onto his words and wanted more of the same. Would not a stirring tale of exploration, a pastiche, written perhaps in the manner of Ryder Haggard, not be the appropriate next step for Lionel to take? After all, what was his career leading to? Agreeable in some ways as it was, it offered no real advancement in itself, not of the kind he thought about, though admittedly in the vaguest of terms, and it paid badly. But to be the successful author of an adventure story, that offered a serious career trajectory if he could find a publisher.

Lionel made his mind up and even fibbed to Phyllis about it, telling her that he had cooked up an adventure story as a result of his trip to Central America and was thinking about chancing his arm with a publisher.

'Go ahead,' she assured him, though only half-seriously. 'You've nothing to lose, have you? At worst you may have wasted a bit of time you could have spent doing something else.' It was enough for Lionel. He returned to the disc and set about making the necessary revisions, including working out a good ending. That eased his conscience somewhat, such as it was. By drafting a better ending the book to that extent became his own. Then he dispatched it directly to a leading London publishing house. Lionel did not even consider approaching an agent.

He waited eight weeks. And the thing that practically never happens to wishful first time authors happened to him; a letter came back with a report by a publisher's reader, expressing interest. Judging by its tone, Sam's manuscript had produced on the reader an effect similar to the one it had on Lionel himself. He felt vindicated: Sam had produced a winner. And because he had had the nous to send it to a publisher, Lionel told himself that he could with justice lay claim to the work, as its midwife, so to speak, especially as he had sorted out the ending. And another thing, the Ockleton-Brewsters hardly needed the cash while he, Lionel Burridge most certainly did, especially as he and Phyllis had decided to get married.

Phyllis presented a problem that niggled however. What should he tell her? Was he to lie to his own wife about his authorship at the very outset of their marriage? Lionel swallowed that by reminding himself of what he could do for her if he happened to strike gold, as an inner voice was already prompting him that he might. It was odd the way that this inner voice kept prompting him, in spite of the fact that he thought of himself as a sceptic about such things.

And it all worked like a dream: the book was reviewed in several leading periodicals and the supplements of the leading Sunday papers, a rare accolade indeed for a new author. And favourably too: the critics seeing it for what it was, a work that was making no extravagant literary claims for itself, but was a gripping yarn. Perhaps more importantly, it was taken up by the popular papers and covered in the racy manner that was likely to attract the kind of readership for whom such a book was really intended. And there was soon talk about turning it into a film: The Raiders of the Lost Ark was mentioned as a possible prototype. It was too good to be true. Television reviews and interviews followed and Lionel went with the swim, never giving the slightest hint that all was not what it appeared to be. He dilated, of course, on his own travels in Central America, especially on his visit to the Mayan temple in the Guatemalan jungle. And he certainly knew his subject well enough to sound plausible, while being sufficiently careful not to imply that he was a professional archaeologist, just a plain storyteller who had done his homework. Lionel came across as engagingly modest and rather bemused, if anything, by his success.

The curse placed on those who disturbed the Mayan prince's tomb was the central idea. It was hardly a very original one, but the menace hung like a dark cloud over all the hero's endeavours, while a nonstop succession of crises, including the closest of brushes with death alongside a subordinate love interest kept up the tension admirably. The villains were a gang of tomb robbers with highly sinister, but not clearly specified international backing and they were prepared to stop at nothing - the most sadistic forms of torture were all part of their remit - and here Lionel was able to fill out Sam's text with a little research of his own into such practises in the Pre-Columbian New World. Yes, he had assured himself, his own input was not insignificant and, after all, hadn't he urged Sam to include the curse?- something that he had curiously overlooked - that brooding menace from the ancient Mayan past, the thing that cast its shadow over everything that happened - an implacable force that had somehow to be neutralized or at least diverted from the hero and his party. This was what Lionel had worked on at the end of the story and he thought that his manner of diverting nemesis onto the sinister international organisation of tomb robbers was particularly neat, since he managed to keep the suspense up until the very last paragraph at the same time. It was an ending which, in Lionel's eyes, fully justified the mere technicality of a fib about the book's authorship.

And reassuring to Lionel was that no one attempted to dispute his authorship. He had had a twinge of unease when the book came out to such acclaim that Charles Ockleton-Brewster might have smelled a rat, knowing that his late brother had been working on something at the time of his death which he had wanted Lionel to read. But all that came from that quarter was a short letter congratulating Lionel on his success. There was, however, a wistful reference in it to what his brother might also have achieved in that line had he been spared. Lionel winced at that, but then sat down and wrote Charles a warm-hearted reply. He had, of course, dedicated the book to the memory of his friend which had pleased the brother and the rest of his family.

Things moved swiftly: his marriage to Phyllis, the massive royalties, the purchase of a Jacobean manor near Lyme Regis, and the birth of their first child, Roland. Oliver followed eighteen months later. Then the contract signed to film the book- a high point. It was a happy time with so much money to play with. Phyllis threw herself into the business of creating an authentic knot garden, the sort the house might once have had, and to restoring its hall while bringing up two toddlers all at the same time, Lionel was still giving interviews, but being very guarded in what he said about any future books. What he particularly enjoyed, now that he had plenty of money, was collecting Pre-Columbian art from Central America. Quite apart from the runaway success of the book and a need to keep up a suitable appearance, he was developing a genuine interest in the subject, an interest, after all, which had its roots in his childhood discoveries in the pages of an encyclopedia. And as he looked at works in museums at home and in the New World all the while reading more books on the subject, his knowledge increased substantially.

The finest piece was one he had acquired in an auction on the Internet. It had belonged to a private collector and was rumoured to have been brought home by one of the early nineteenth century explorers of Guatemala and Honduras. Of course it was not cheap as there was some heavy rival bidding, but Lionel stood his ground and secured his piece.

The piece was a jade mask of fine craftsmanship and had apparently come from the tomb of a Mayan prince. Archaeologists had dated it to sometime in the late seventh century A.D. The eyes were in dark blue obsidian, in contrast to the green of the jade and were very delicately rendered. It was in excellent condition, though the wooden backing had been restored since its discovery. Clearly it had been part of the grave goods of a powerful prince, placed with him at death and strictly speaking intended for the eyes of the afterworld only. The name of the prince was not known and there was no record of its place of discovery either, though it bore a close resemblance to another mask from Palenque in Yucatan which was found in the tomb of the so-called Lord of Pacal. But that it was genuine no scholar who had examined it was in the least doubt. It became the centre piece, the pride and joy of Lionel's collection.

And it had vanished when Lionel was murdered, showing up nowhere, not even on the Internet. Its disappearance was mentioned of course and was considered an integral part of the mystery surrounding the death of Lionel Burridge. Inevitably it gave rise to all sorts of speculation on the part of the aficionados of the cult, speculation which echoed the plot of his own tale, to the extent of involving an international ring of art smugglers. And then there was the curse... and his journey into the jungle of Central America. They were taken up in a big way and even featured in a popular Sunday tabloid. So the legend of Lionel Burridge went on growing, defying all rational explanation.

Of all people it was Charles, Sam's brother, who finally put his finger on something that had escaped the notice of the dabblers in the mystery surrounding the death of Lionel Burridge: he came across another work by Arthur Cummings, the author of the story that had provided his brother with the ingredient that his own efforts had lacked: the curse laid upon the despoiler of the Mayan prince's tomb - the Tuthenkhamun touch. It was also a paperback copy of a work by him in a similar vein and was in a box of old books which had been left in an attic, which Charles, who was still unmarried, was clearing out in the process of making a bachelor retreat for himself under the family roof. He showed it along with the other contents of the box to his mother, but did not draw particular attention to it. After all, the name of Cummings did not mean anything to either of them, Then it did ring the vaguest kind of a bell in Charles's head; he recalled finding the same name on the cover of an equally elderly paperback among his brother's things, though he had scarcely glanced at it, but sent it off in a job lot to a secondhand dealer along with other books that had belonged to Sam.

This fresh discovery had been published in 1955, posthumously. It was an adventure story set this time in a lost valley in Tibet and the few pages he read reminded Charles of Lionel's book. But the potted biography of the author on the back was possibly more intriguing to those who might have troubled to follow the thread from Cummings to Ockleton-Brewster to Burridge. Arthur Cummings was still a young man when he had died, the same age as Lionel in fact, and he had passed away unexpectedly in a hotel in Verona of all places, for some reason that last detail had been included in the biographical sketch on the back of the book. Nothing more than that, though no doubt it had aroused some interest in the papers back in 1955.. if not the same level as in the case of Lionel's death. Charles noticed the coincidence, but did not give it a second thought...

******

...and now, having committed the story of three young authors and an ancient Mayan curse to paper something disturbing has come my way - an envelope from Guatemala City. It is addressed to me personally, care of the periodical which recently published my story, and written in black ink, in a fussily neat hand, Inside the envelope there is a colour photograph - of a jade mask with delicately rendered obsidian eyes of Mayan type... a handsome thing in its way but nothing else, no message of any kind....

Antichrist

Luke had taken his degree and was ready to start his doctorate. It had gone surprisingly well, considering how he had blotted his copybook at the outset. Before he was even out of High School he had tried to steal a picture. And if it had not been for his accomplice's loose tongue, he would have got away with it too. It was the kind of mistake he was determined not to repeat. He had served eighteen months, but shortly after that he was involved in something even more serious. It was while he was on vacation in the United Kingdom and it had also resulted in failure, but to do Luke justice, this time it was not his fault. Instead it could be put down to his victim's lousy physical condition and untimely death. Obesity was something that Luke viewed with scorn. The man in question was his grandfather's mortal enemy from back in the Nineteen Thirties when he was selling ice-cream on the beach at Scarborough before he had crossed the Atlantic and made a fortune. And the grease ball had expired just as Luke was about to deliver the blow that would have settled Grandpa's score once arid for all.

It was his grandfather's fortune that had helped to see Luke through university despite his conviction for theft, which, indeed, because it had involved a significant work of art, had struck a number of his fellow students as pretty cool. A liberally-inclined university arts faculty had waived the matter, impressed by his knowledge and enthusiasm, as well as by the odd coincidence of his surname, so Luke had gone through his undergraduate days with relative ease and was accepted to try for a doctorate. His chosen field was the Italian Renaissance, in the period preceding what is generally termed the High Renaissance. Luke by chance happened to bear the name of one of its leading figures, Luca Signorelli, no less, the painter of the strangely disturbing frescoes of the Antichrist in the Cathedral at Orvieto, which he had finally got to see after finding his way barred by restoration work at the first attempt. And they had set his mind running in a fresh channel, or rather had directed it back into an old one.

On the former occasion his grandfather, who had always got on well with young people, had put him up to the business of settling the score that had been festering ever since his days in Scarborough. In the free-for-all world of the English seaside resort in the inter-war years skulduggery had been commonplace, for it was the time when fixed fairgrounds and amusement parlours were the coming thing and competition for the best pitches was often cutthroat. And it was Rinaldo Belotti's fellow Italian, Lorenzo Arnolfini, who had hounded him from his prime pitch on the town's beach where he was selling ice-creams from a van. But the thing for which Lorenzo could never be forgiven was his threat to kill Rinaldo's little Concetta, the apple of his eye, who was to grow up to become Luke's mother.

But having followed to the letter his grandfather's detailed instructions, meticulously updated over a lifetime passed mostly in the United States, with his victim finally ready for dispatch, at that very moment, Lorenzo had given up the ghost, almost certainly from a massive heart attack and Luke had been obliged to slip away, innocent of murder, but burdened instead with the guilt of having failed to carry out his grandfather's dying wish.

Then to cap his failure to kill Lorenzo, on the same European trip he had missed seeing the Signorelli frescoes in Orvieto which were undergoing restoration at the time. But, at last, after taking his degree, he had made it good and seen them in their newly restored state. He had examined them often enough in books, and seen them blown up in slide form, but it was only now, facing the Antichrist himself, in the flesh as it were, with Satan whispering in his ear, that the work addressed him directly, or rather the Antichrist did - with his eyes. What Satan was telling him, Luke could only guess at, but it was the eyes of the False Messiah that drew his own. He resembled the true Christ in his general appearance, a ploy which was necessary to maintain his deception and at the same time seemed to project a charm not unlike Luke's own, for the latter, with his Italian good looks, rather fancied himself to be in the Quattrocento style, a similarity that he was careful to nurture. He was softly spoken and wore a dreamy, mildly quizzical expression that people found appealing. Along with the name he bore, it had served him well with his tutors.

But looking at those eyes, with their questioning gaze, while their owner listened to the instructions being poured into his ear and the scenes of civil mayhem in the background, presumably the result of Satanic prompting, set the wheels of Luke's mind in motion, and once they had started to turn one thing led inexorably to another. He began to think up a game of chance, for the thrill of a gamble was in Luke's blood. It was to be one which would limit him to a randomly selected choice of one of two lines of action. In other words, he set about devising a progressive game, each stage of which presented him with

215

two lines of action only, but the one he was compelled to take was to be settled by the toss of a coin. That was an absolute condition of play. But one line of action was to be more dangerous and drastic than the other. The operation of chance would leave him with a single course only, which would lead him on to the next stage where he would once more be presented with a pair of possibilities, one of which was to be selected by the fall of the coin and so on to the close of the game.

Luke had brought home with him a portfolio of his namesake's frescoes which he consulted and the Antichrist's eyes, looking at him from the page, held him to his resolve. They did not pass on any direct instructions, of course, but empowered his own inventive mind to do the work, building its own edifice. Whether the inspiration came initially from Satan's prompting he could not say. Certainly the Devil had none of the pleasing qualities of his agent, the Antichrist, but was a typical medieval grotesque. No, it was the False Messiah himself, whose gentle eyes, reminded Luke of his grandfather's. And, he was forced to admit, of the ones that gazed back at him from his own bathroom mirror.

'Yes,' Luke murmured to that same mirror, 'I think something will come of this.' When he was alone he often addressed his reflection in this manner. 'It's got me thinking. Ever since I missed out on Amolfini I've remained a sort of virgin.'

It was a curious way to think of himself because he had failed to kill a man on the one occasion when he had set out to do it. He wondered if there was anyone else who had ever felt the same. Luke was keen to empathise. After all, it was important for him to be able to do so if he was to be a successful art historian.

But the element of uncertainty was imperative to any scheme of Luke's. It may have seemed paradoxical in one such as Luke, who liked to plan so methodically, deliberately to run the risk of a crash. But then, like many of his kind who took the law into their own hands, a big part of it was the compulsive pull of danger, the need to walk a tightrope. That's what he was in it for. Though in this instance it did not have to be all or nothing. It was to be a matter of alternatives. If a particular, more exacting, course was ruled out by the operation of chance, then there was always the alternative, offering its own intriguing possibilities - lesser ones perhaps - but presenting a challenge all the same. And in a way Luke felt that he was in control whatever way it turned out, because he was the one who had devised the rules which gave chance its crucial part. It was as if God had created the Universe in which He envisaged certain possible stages in its evolution being reached, at which points he would put His own omnipotence on hold, and leave the path to be taken to chance. For example conscious life might indeed emerge in His universe, to lead onwards and upwards to the appearance of the human species, but equally it might not and another way be taken instead. God playing with dice, in other words - very un-Einsteinian. Luke approved of the idea.

But of course he was not God, he was only playing the part, or rather that of the Antichrist, in the performance of a criminal act whose precise nature had still to be worked out.

Luke had to devise alternatives for each fall of the coin. For he had decided that a tossed coin would be his arbitrator. It was simple to operate and whatever way it fell would open up a line of action which would lead to a further opportunity for the working of chance.

But what kind of crime should Luke commit? This would have to be settled by the first throw and then its exact nature, the way to achieve it and the alternatives routes leading up to it, would be determined by subsequent throws. But it really came down to just two, both of which he could claim to have already had a little experience..... Art theft and murder.

And to make the exercise intellectually complete, as well as to protect himself, the deed would need to be as foolproof as he could make it. At this point in his life Luke did not want to have to make a clean breast of anything. Risk, of course, was crucial to his game, but he did not relish spending a lifetime in gaol - or perhaps suffering something even worse - if he could possibly help it. Notoriety might come as a bonus later in life, when he came to write his memoirs. Meanwhile he had a tricky crag to ascend, where a slip could prove fatal - depending partly on how the coin fell of course.

'An art theft or a murder?' he asked the reflection in the bathroom mirror. 'Both very risky, it goes without saying, in their different ways. But one more serious than the other and carrying a much stiffer penalty - a lethal injection even, depending on where it's committed. But the art theft would be easier to pin on me with my record. They would have a good idea of where to start looking, but then that could be part of the challenge, couldn't it, covering my tracks sufficiently well.' After airing the different possibilities, he devoted a few minutes to admiring his reflection in the glass. His face reminded him not of a work by his namesake but of a portrait of a particularly handsome youth by Perugino. Luke gazed with rapture at his reflection and wanted to keep it all to himself, not to have to share it with anyone...

'Snap out of it,' he ordered the reflection sternly, transforming its wistful expression into a broody one instead, but he liked that just as much. The lips had an appealing pout, which made him press his own to the glass.

The coin tossing would involve no solemn ritual, but would be carefully noted nevertheless in the running account he would keep of the game. With the result recorded, he would proceed to the next stage.

Step by step.

So now in the small living room of his flat he took the British one pound coin from his desk drawer and flicked it so that it landed and rolled across the rug. Heads for murder. 'Heads!' he called out. The coin teetered on its rim and fell flat. Heads.

Luke felt relieved, It would be easier to cover the tracks of a murder than an art theft and his failure to carry out Grandpa's instructions still rankled. He needed to redeem himself. It was all so perfectly Italian, he concluded, this necessity for settling scores.

The next step he did not like so much, but now he was caught up in the logic of what he was attempting and could not escape it. Young or old? He hoped it would be old. Killing an overweight and ageing slob like Lorenzo Amolfini was nothing to lose sleep over, it was a blessing even, but a child..., was quite another matter... something young and fresh... There was no way he could bring himself to do that. If the coin turned up young it would have to be someone around the same age as himself. What counted as young? Luke thought of himself as young, after all. He wasn't going to murder a child - he loved kids, like his grandfather.

He tossed the coin, hoping that it would be heads and tell him to choose an old victim, but it turned up tails and told him that his victim had to be young... He felt unhappy about it, but he had already made up his mind that it was not to be a child.

Boy or girl? That didn't matter so much. The coin turned up a girl. Probably easier than a boy... Why are we doing any of this, he suddenly asked the image in the mirror. Why not just get down to writing a thesis? He could not answer that question. It was something that lay too deep within himself. And anyway there were limits to self-analysis. It got morbid.

219

'Stop,' he commanded the image. 'Stop asking such pointless questions. You've started this business, so you've got to go through with it. And that's all that needs to be said.'

Something told him that it was the logic of the madhouse, but wasn't the universe just that anyway? Devoid of meaning except what we felt inclined to give it? So if anyone made sense at all, Antichrist could be the one.

So he had to kill a young girl. That was plain enough. But where, when and how were the next questions. The last of these could wait until later. nearer the time.

And where? A city was the obvious place, one where he wasn't known and which he could disappear from with no one being any the wiser. That had been the case when he had made his attempt on Lorenzo in Scarborough, but there it still might have been possible to link him with the crime because of his Italian surname. Luke had written it in a hotel register. Nothing had come of it as far he was himself concerned of course, but a metropolis would be a safer bet. A choice, therefore, between two cities. London or New York. London would suit him better of the two because he could combine it with a visit to some of the places that he wanted to see in Europe. And he would round it off with a pilgrimage to Orvieto - for a debriefing with Antichrist, so to speak, when he had completed his task. So he hoped it would turn out be London.

With some trepidation he tossed the coin up high, uttering a brief prayer as he did so. Heads London. Tails New York. Heads it was.

'Thank you, God,' muttered Luke involuntarily, with his eyes turned towards the ceiling, realising at the same time that he was making a gesture of doubtful taste.

So London it had to be. To find a girl of about his own age there and to dispatch her before moving on to Italy should not be beyond his powers of contrivance. After all, he had tested them pretty thoroughly in his attempt to kill Lorenzo and had not found them wanting then. There was nothing he could have done about that bastard's heart attack. It was bad luck, that was all - like the coin landing the wrong way up. So the next question: when?

Did he really need to toss a coin to establish that? The long summer vacation was the only realistic time. There was no other which was nearly so convenient. No, let that one pass. And how was he to do it? He'd postpone that until nearer the time when he would make a choice between two practical possibilities. The circumstances on the ground would provide him with a reasonable choice...

So in the summer he would go to London, find a girl and kill her. That much was clear.

He had a couple of months in hand during which he started to lay the groundwork for his thesis and to think out the Italian leg of his trip. He would not spend longer in London than he could help. A couple of weeks set aside to accomplish what needed to be done should be ample. It was good to have a deadline, and to make sure that he was clean away before anything could be laid at his door. It should not be too difficult, he informed the image in the bathroom mirror, which was stripped down to display a superbly proportioned torso, tightly muscled without a hint of exaggeration. Despite the stylistic link between Signorelli and Michelangelo, Luke was no fan of the latter. For him Mannerism went too far. He preferred things to be kept to their true proportion - like his own body. Mountains of straining muscles seemed tacky - like a hectic wallpaper.

So the time passed quietly without Luke giving too much thought to what lay in front of him. It would require circumspection and a cool head when he was on the ground, needless to say, but he knew now from his previous experience that such things were not beyond him, though this time he would have to select his own victim and not have one offered to him on a plate as Lorenzo had been. The Quattrocento face looking back at him from the mirror assured him that it should not be too difficult. My God... that perfect body with its broody beauty! Luke pouted and pressed his lips to the glass. He was every bit as good as anything the Quattrocento had to offer - even Donatello's David which was the one he most resembled. As he contemplated his own reflection, a tremor ran down Luke's spine.

And yet... and yet he was puzzled by the perversity of it. With all that he had and treasured, why was it necessary for him to commit murder? He knew that what he was planning the world abhorred. That, of course, was part of the reason he was doing it. So did it come down to the old Nietzschean saw about the superman rising above the constraints that inhibited the botched and bungled mass of lower humanity? But Luke had no lofty theories to justify what he felt impelled to do. It was a simply necessity embedded in his psyche, beyond the reach of any attempt at rational explanation. It seemed a manly thing to do, to take the gamble, and cowardice to refuse it. After all, he was putting his future with all its aspirations on the line, wasn't he? It was a perilous knife edge that he was walking along. One small slip and he was a gonner. And yet, life or death, what did they amount to anyway? Despite his sense of affinity with Quattracento's Italy, he had none of its piety. This thing was a game, with the intellectual fascination of planning a campaign and seeing how it worked out in practice. And to play it properly he had to enter a dangerous no man's land where the usual constraints did not count, If he had to choose a label, Luke might have called himself a humanist. He thought of Iago, whom of all of Shakespeare's characters, he admired the most - of the ones he knew anyway. That was something his fellow Italian, Machiavelli, could have understood - he'd been reading him recently- because he had no illusions about what people were really like.

So Luke booked his flight to London for the beginning of July. It was the height of the tourist season, but when was it not the tourist season in London these days? Though he was generously endowed- his grandfather's will had seen to that, creature comforts were not one of Luke's priorities, especially now, considering what he was intending to do. He took the Underground from the airport to King's Cross and went to one of the small hotels in the neighbourhood of the railway station. It was staffed by Lithuanians and the one or two guests he observed in its cramped little bar spoke with North American accents like his own. He did not feel obliged to join them. Instead he returned to the station where he bought a street map of London at the bookstall. Then he wandered round the King's Cross area. It had obvious possibilities, but then it was perhaps not a good idea to carry out his plan too close to where he was staying. On the other hand there were plenty of prostitutes plying their trade and he had reached the conclusion that his best bet would be to murder a prostitute - it was less complicated - prostitutes were murdered all the time, after all - so it would hardly cause much of a stir if one more came to grief in a city like London. But then, he reflected, there was also the style of the thing to be considered. Would it not look just a little cheap?

'Is it worthy?' he asked the reflection in the bathroom mirror back in his hotel. Indeed, what was worthy about a murder? Why try to sound pious about it? To dignify it and put it in a better light? But all the same, was this not, perhaps, a little too easy? Should he not be attempting something that tested his ingenuity more? Something with a bit more style to it - whatever that amounted to?

It was a niggling question, but then of course the toss of the coin would enter into it - deciding the manner of dispatching his victim. Could that involve some scope for imagination at least? At least it might give the police something to think about... Luke decided to sleep on it.

Luke slept on it soundly. Indeed, it was nearly half past eight when he surfaced and he did not like to miss his breakfast. So, having located the dining room and an empty table slightly apart from the other guests, he eavesdropped on their conversations about their plans for the day. He recalled that he had been rather like that himself on his first visit to London, a tourist knocking off the obvious places like Madame Tussauds and the Tower - oh and Big Ben and the Houses of Parliament, of course. They can't possibly miss those. He felt tempted to let himself be drawn into a conversation and to offer some patronising advice, but decided that he might attract unnecessary attention if he did so.

After breakfast he returned to his room for the toss of the coin. The means of murder... a firearm possibly? But could he acquire one in the time he had allowed himself? He believed it was possible to hire them - but then what a hassle! and, anyway, he had never used one in his life before. Luke had not the slightest interest in guns There were big risk attached to them too, such as making a successful getaway afterwards No, Luke decided that the choice would have to lie between a knife and a garotte. The latter had been the intended method of dispatching Lorenzo Arnolfini and in a way it might be appropriate if he made good his failure on that occasion by having another crack at it this time. But Chance was paramount and had to make the decision. Heads for a garotte, tails for a knife. Luke threw the coin up in the air and it rolled under the bed. Lifting up the rumpled counterpane he saw how it was lying.. tails.

'Shit,' said Luke. 'But never mind.' After all, when he thought about it, there was a greater aesthetic appeal about a dagger: a dagger, not an ordinary knife. He wanted to have that distinction clear in his mind. Renaissance bravos wielded daggers, not machetes. Rampaging African tribesmen did that. A gentleman carried a dagger.

He decided to take the Piccadilly Line to Earl's Court and look at the lie of the land there. He could go down in daylight and if it seemed promising return in the evening. After that he took himself to Brixton, the kind district where he felt like a fish out of water, but he needed a weapon and he knew that he was most likely to find what he wanted in a place where many of its inhabitants carried a blade as a matter of course. It did not take him long and he acquired something that matched his sensibility almost perfectly - the kind of weapon that Benvenuto Cellini would not have been ashamed to have worn on his belt; a stiletto with a slender, tapering blade; a weapon made for thrusting, not for slicing. Luke liked that idea, the neat thrust into a vital organ, such as the heart, rather than a squalid piece of butchery.

He included the National Gallery on his trip and returned to his hotel in the late afternoon, then took a walk down Euston Road. It was still early, but he felt that King's Cross might be his best bet after all. There seemed to be plenty of quiet byways at a safe distance from his hotel. Later, when it was beginning to get dark, he went out again.

The streets were full of life now, restaurants and cafes, Internet and otherwise, all doing business, the shops open and everywhere the seedy-looking cosmopolitan population that is typical of a district like King's Cross in the modern metropolis. It looked tawdry and drugs no doubt could be obtained easily enough when you knew where to look for them... and prostitutes too. The two things generally went together.

It would be easier to do the job in the privacy of a bedroom,

225

assuming that the neighbouring rooms were unoccupied. And that was the problem. The privacy had to be total, with no chance of being heard or spotted, either on the way in or out of the premises.. Speed and silence were essential. Maybe a street pick-up would be best and to accomplish his mission in a secluded side street... if the two things could be brought together. It need not take long. Wandering down Pentonville Road Luke noted a few possible locations, but then a professional prostitute would have her own ideas about that anyway. It might be better to leave it to her. It was part of her trade to handle such details, wasn't it? That probably was the way to go about it. Leave it to the hooker. Luke retraced his steps to the hotel in Crestfield Street where he booked in for another couple of nights. If nothing came of it in that time he could shift his base or at least do what had to be done well away from where he was staying. Somewhere in the vicinity of Victoria might be a good hunting ground.

Luke spent a pleasant afternoon at the Tate Britain where there was an exhibition of British landscape painting which was an area he had not really considered before. He admired the technique of painting in watercolour, which seemed a particularly English thing. It was disciplined and had to be right the first time. There was no room for mistakes, no scraping off of pigment and starting again. It fascinated him what X-rays sometimes revealed underlying the works in oil by some of Europe's greatest masters. But there was none of that ambiguity about a watercolour... And the landscapes themselves, many of them drawing their inspiration from his beloved Italy and European masters such as Claude Lorraine, were so English... If he hadn't had Italian roots Luke would have liked to have had English ones. And then he told himself something else: the girl he was to kill mustn't be English: Albanian or Ukrainian or Caribbean, anything would do, as long as she wasn't English...

Luke had a leisurely coffee and flapjack - he had a sweet tooth - in the gallery cafe and decided to walk back towards Trafalgar Square. He wondered about taking in a movie before returning to Crestfield Road, but chose to extend his walk instead. He always did his most useful thinking while he was walking.

He wandered up to Bloomsbury, by way of the Covent Garden market where he succumbed to an impulse purchase. Something he didn't very often do. He bought himself a black leather jacket. Inspecting himself in the mirror at the back of the stall he felt it suited him to perfection. Black was so clearly his colour. With his thick, slightly curling dark hair and the trace of stubble on his cheeks and chin, the effect was spot on. So, instead of having the jacket wrapped, he left wearing it, having first removed the label Then he walked up past the British Museum and eventually into Holborn. It took him past the Old Bailey. He had read in a paper about a terrorist trial that was currently going on there. That kind of fanaticism was a puzzle him. Eventually his steps took him back in the direction of the Underground. It was a warm evening, rather close in fact, and the streets were filling up. Smokers were spilling onto the pavements having been driven from the bars and cafes by recent legislation. Luke had mixed feelings about the smoking ban. It was not something he did himself, but then people should be left to go to Hell in their own ways, shouldn't they? Luke believed in liberty. It seemed to tally with his own notion of self-discipline. You could not have real liberty without self-discipline. He despised the loss of self-control which was such a rampant feature of the times he was compelled to live in, and wasn't self-control the key to the very thing that he was trying to do?

Still sporting his new leather jacket he went out later in the evening and found a small Italian restaurant not far from his hotel where he had a pasta and a red Tuscan wine, which he followed with an ice-cream, insisting on plain vanilla without any of the trimmings, except a sweet biscuit. An Espesso generously laced with dark sugar followed. It was a straightforward Italian meal, nothing special, but which left him with a clear head for what he was about to do.

He paid his bill and went out into Euston Road. There were plenty of people enjoying the summer warmth - the ethnically mixed bag of the King's Cross neighbourhood. Now it was a matter of finding the sort of prey that he had in mind - which was a new experience for Luke, because he had never picked up a prostitute before. But he knew roughly the kind of thing he was looking for. And once he had indicated his need the rest should follow easily enough. If it didn't for any reason, an unsafe location, for instance, he could always break it off. He fingered the knife that he was carrying in the top of his jeans. It seemed very suitable for his purpose: a single thrust to the heart or some vital artery was all that was required.

He walked slowly down Pentonville Road and then, hovering near the door of an internet cafe, he saw the thing he might be after. The light from the open doorway fell on the girl and revealed her clearly. From where he was Luke could see that she was not English. At a glance she appeared to combine African and Chinese features - which were melded very agreeably.

He sidled up to her. She was standing in the doorway, looking down the street rather than into the café.

Luke placed himself in front of her and made the sound of clearing his throat. Now that he was close to her he was able to inspect her features more closely. She was a very pretty girl, with a warm golden skin, not in the least bit sluttish. It struck Luke that she was much too pretty for the game she was playing. A girl with her kind of beauty

228

surely did not have to do it, but then if there was a lot of money in it...
But it was hardly the moment to be thinking about the economics of
the sex trade.

'Are you...?' he asked hesitantly. He did not feel confident
playing this game and wondered if the girl would see through him
straight away.

But then hookers were supposed to be used to diffident-sounding
men, weren't they? It was surely a part of their brief. After all, that was
the reason a lot of them took up with prostitutes instead of forming
more stable sexual relationships, wasn't it?

'Am I what, Pretty Boy?' the girl smiled and fluttered the lids over
her big dark oval eyes.

'Are you free?'

'Am I free? If you mean am I not doing anything right now, well
then, guess I'm free. That kind of free.'

Luke felt unusually tongue-tied. This was a way of talking he was
not used to. He wondered if he ought to begin by negotiating the price.

The girl, who looked to be in her early twenties, stroked his cheek
and glanced around. 'You really are a very pretty boy, aren't you?'

Luke agreed with her and felt flattered. 'Thank you. It's nice of
you to say so.'

'You're not English, are you? You sound American.' She studied
him with a kind of mock thoughtfulness. 'You sound like an American,
but you may not be. Italian?'

'Well done,' said Luke. 'Italian/American to be precise.'

'It's the Italian bit I'd rather have - not the American.' She stroked
his cheek again - tenderly with the point of a finger. Then she stepped
out of the doorway. 'Can you pay?'

229

'Of course I can pay. I wouldn't have asked you it I couldn't, would I?'

'You mustn't mind me asking, but you look so young. A little boy. You see, its mostly the older men that I work with. That's the part of my job I don't care for. I prefer your kind. So maybe I won't ask you for quite so much.' She looked round as she spoke. 'Don't let my boss catch me saying things like that, mind. He'd have the skin off my back. But you really are a very pretty boy. We can make an exception for you. What's your name? And don't pretend you haven't got one.'

'Gino,' lied Luke. 'Its an Italian name.'

'Gino? An Italian name! Oh I like that.'

'Do you really? I'm pleased you do. Shall we?' Luke indicated that they should move with a gesture of his head.

'Find somewhere you mean?'

'Sort of.'

'Sort of? What do you mean sort of?' The girl laughed.

But it was done in a kindly fashion. God, thought Luke, its one hell of a pity I've got to kill her.

'Come with me, then, Gino - or Pretty Boy. Do you mind if I still call you that? Somehow it suits you best,' said the girl. 'I think I know a place where we won't be disturbed. Have you got your money with you?'

'Of course.' Luke tapped the wallet in his hip pocket.

'Come along then - my little Gino.' She linked her arm in his own.

Luke liked little Gino. This was really very trying. Why did she have to be such a nice kid? Not a bit like what he thought a hooker should be. Moreover she seemed to have sussed his sexual naivity straight away and he didn't feel the slightest bit humiliated that she had. I should have done something like this before, he reflected, I mean gone with a nice sympathetic prostitute who considered it her vocation to take a virgin boy in hand... But I mustn't think that way now... The die is cast - fuck it.

'What's your name?' Luke asked her as she steered him along.

'Diana.'

'Diana! You don't really mean it, do you?'

'Yes I do. That's my given name, but you can call me Di if you like.'

Di wasted no time. They went rapidly down Pentonville Road. She seemed to have him completely under her control and, despite what he had in mind, Luke felt that she was the one who was calling the tunes. She seemed to fancy him and her behaviour was more than merely professional. But then you just had to think of the disgusting old men she was usually forced to lie with... Like Lorenzo Arnolfini, for instance. She obviously knew where she was going. They turned down a side street and took several more turnings. Luke found himself losing count. Meanwhile it had fallen suddenly silent after the noise of the busy streets.

'This way, Little One,' whispered Di.

'Are we alone?'

'Of course we are. You've got to trust me.' She made it sound as if he'd asked a dumb kind of question. 'No one will disturb us here. It's as quiet as the grave.'

Her saying that startled Luke. Could she possibly...? 'I'm not going to like doing what I have to do one little bit,' he told himself. 'I never dreamed it was going to be as difficult as this.'

The place was dark, except for a street lamp casting its soft orange glow from over the top of a boundary fence. They were on a grassy patch as far as he could make out and the girl drew him to what looked like a decrepit park bench where they sat down.

Luke had told Di his name, though a false one, and he had learned hers. It would have been better if they had remained nameless. Anonymity would have made it easier. A nameless woman of the streets…and her nameless killer.

Anyway I'd better get it over with, he told himself with an inward sigh. He slid his hand into the top of his jeans. And then he felt his wrist being grasped in a tight grip and twisted painfully.

The knife dropped into the grass. A hard-faced man, young and looking like he was North African or Middle Eastern in the light of the street lamp, possibly a Moroccan or a Tunisian, held him fast, pinning him to the bench. Di was no longer leaning against him. She had disappeared. The man, meanwhile, held Luke down and clamped a hand over his mouth as a companion emerged from the darkness. It seemed unnaturally quiet away from the streets faintly humming in the background. They were alone. Deftly the newcomer slipped a twisted handkerchief round Luke's neck. Even in this desperate situation he was forced to admire the man's technique, the very thing he had hoped to do to Lorenzo Arnolfini…

Wasting no time, the first man picked the knife up from the grass, then rapidly went through Luke's pockets and removed his wallet. His head seemed to explode and… oblivion.

When Luke eventually came round, he found himself lying with his face in an oily puddle, the place where a motor car had been standing. Probably it was that which brought him to his senses. His head throbbed horribly and there was a hot, burning sensation in both his cheeks. Painfully he dragged himself onto his knees. He realised that he was no longer wearing his jacket, that had been taken, but it was his face… it felt as if it was on fire. It was difficult to make anything

out in the dark. Crawling on all fours towards a street lamp he was able
to see a sticky substance on his fingers. The pain in his head was bad
enough, but frantically Luke ran his fingers over his face. It had been
lacerated on each cheek, carved with what felt like a cross - something
he confirmed later when he was able to confront his ravaged features
in a mirror. The incisions ran from top to bottom, side to side, cut deep
into the flesh, requiring many stitches and despite the passage of time,
the scars remained impossible to eradicate. The Pretty Boy had been
scarred for life. And either way he still hadn't scored.

Panama Jack

'There's been a terrible accident!' Debbie was running along the passage clad only in a bath towel.

Dan stuck his head out of the utility room where he was just about to bed down with Rachel. What's the matter? What sort of an accident?'

'It's the Doc,' Debbie gasped. 'I think he might be dead!'

'The Doc? Where is he?' Dan meanwhile had been joined by Rachel dressed in just her knickers.

'In... in the bathroom.'

They looked at Debbie in her towel and at her dripping hair.

'I thought that's where you were,' said Rachel, glancing at Dan.

'I was,' Debbie gasped. 'I think he must be dead.'

Dan and Rachel exchanged another glance which registered not so much surprise but that the situation might be awkward.

'Mind you,' mused Dan, 'he's had it coming to him - for a long time.'

'But we have to something about him now, don't we, you idiot?' Rachel said. We can hardly leave him where he is, dead or alive.' She looked again at Debbie. 'You were in the bath when he appeared?'

Debbie nodded and her jaw wobbled. 'It was so horrible,' she mumbled in a small voice which sounded suspiciously like a stage whisper. 'Horrible!'

'Leave this one to me,' answered Dan, sounding masculine and assertive. 'I'll have a look. Just a second.' He retreated into the room to put on a pair of trousers. 'I'm not at all surprised - not the way he carried on,' he declared as he emerged.

'Don't talk like that. Please! We're supposed to be guests in his house, aren't we?' Debbie's jaw wobbled once more.

He gave a contemptuous snort. 'You leave this to me.'

Doctor Ravenshaw was lying face down on the bathroom floor, stark naked.

'Not a very pretty sight,' observed Dan. 'But then you'd hardly expect it to be, would you?' He turned to Debbie. 'How did it happen? Did he hit his head?'

'He slipped and hit it on the tap. At least I think he did,' she said. 'It was all so quick.'

Dan squatted down beside the Doctor and turned him half over onto his side. Then he put his ear to the man's mouth. 'Nothing going on there,' he said.

The Doctor's eyes were wide open and his puffy face wore a baffled, rather reproachful, expression.

Dan prodded the man's paunch. 'Not exactly in top condition,' he pointed out. Dan was inclined to be smug about his own trim twenty-four year old figure. 'I wonder, could it have been a heart attack?'

Debbie meanwhile stood on the threshold of the bathroom, gazing down at the corpse, a fist pressed against her lips and looked as if she was going to burst into tears at any minute.

236

Dan was priding himself on sounding coolly forensic, as if dealing with corpses was all in a day's work. He noticed the bump on the Doctor's forehead.

'Aha! He's hit his head,' he declared authoritatively, stating what he had already been told as if he was a great detective about to make a significant discovery.

'I told you, he hit it on one of the taps,' explained Debbie.

'Hm. No sign of any blood though. Did you see it happen? Presumably you were in the bath at the time.'

'It was all over so quickly.'

'How did he get in? Didn't you lock the door?'

'Of course I locked the door, but the other one... it doesn't lock.' Debbie went back into the passage.

'That figures,' Dan said, eying a second door, which was standing ajar. He peered through into an untidy bedroom, with a duvet lying half off a low divan bed.

Debbie said nothing and Dan could hear a sob coming from outside the bathroom. 'Run along and have a good blub on Rachel's shoulder,' he called in a patronizing tone. 'If you ask me, you've had a lucky escape.'

The bathroom was shabby with the paint flaking off the walls above the pale blue tiles which in several places had shed their grout. The bath itself had a dark stain running round it, the result of infrequent and very perfunctory cleaning. There were a few bottles, lotions of one sort or another, on the undusted window shelf between the bath itself and the lavatory. On the wooden rack across the bath were a loofah, a ragged sponge and a large bottle of shampoo, while the glass basin shelf was host to shaving kit, a tub of skin cream, a toothbrush and toothpaste in a plastic mug.

One thing which appeared to have fallen off the window ledge and was lying on the rumpled bathmat beside the corpse caught Dan's eye. It was a yellow plastic bottle, with a face on it, a sun-blackened face under a wide-brimmed straw hat, with a monocle screwed into one eye and a bristling moustache of a kind that had been fashionable at the beginning of the twentieth century. It glowered fiercely from a bottle of sun lotion and a scroll above it proclaimed 'The Original Panama Jack' while second one below read 'dark tanning lotion'.

Dan looked at the dead man. He had a florid complexion - livid still in death - a northerner's fair skin burnished a blotchy crimson by the ravages of alcohol. There was no way a dark sun lotion could have repaired that complexion. It looked like another instance of the Doctor's wishfulness.

I bet you could tell a tale or two, thought Dan, mentally addressing Panama Jack, about quite a lot more than tonight's little episode, I'll be bound.

But meanwhile something had to be done. He and the two girls, Rachel and Debbie, had stopped over in Doctor Ravenshaw's flat for the night, where the seminar had degenerated, as so often happened, into a drinking bout and the Doctor had insisted that they stay until the morning which, again, was quite usual. Rachel had hesitated at first, but not for long because she felt safe enough with Dan there. While Debbie, who was the more vulnerable of the two girls, had seemed to embrace the offer, which was rather odd because she knew perfectly well the kind of tricks that Doctor Ravenshaw got up to.

*****

'She's probably after a First,' Dan had suggested once he and Rachel were ensconced in the utility room.

'Quite possibly,' agreed Rachel who was feeling very sleepy.

Dan had a point. It did indeed lie within Dr Ravenshaw's remit to influence directly the level of degrees that were handed out by his department.

They could hear a bath running.

Debbie bolted the door into the passage, but there was no bolt on a second one. It was shut and she put an ear to it. She could hear nothing on the other side.

'What the hell,' she told herself, Her wits were sluggish with the gin punch she had consumed a reckless amount of, and she felt in need of a bath after the session in Dr Ravenshaw's foetid living room - which was a typical bachelor's mess, but of one a good deal younger than the Doctor, who by now was in his late fifties. People at his time of life had normally found someone to do for them and on his salary he could easily have afforded it, but then it appeared to suit him to live like a student still, though he seemed to have moved beyond the stage of plastering his walls with images of pop stars at least.

Dr Ravenshaw taught English Literature, specialising in the post-war period from the Fifties onwards. In his youth he had been something of a political firebrand, cutting his teeth on anti - Vietnam War demonstrations - he had marched to Grosvenor Square with Tariq Ali's cohorts - and the latter stages of the student rebellions of that time. Inevitably, perhaps, he had adopted a Marxist viewpoint which stood him in good stead when gaining a foothold on the bottom rung of the academic ladder in a new university. Now, in his late fifties, while he had never achieved a chair, he had nevertheless clung to his particular niche while at the same time coming to be something of an icon of an age that had passed. His wispy, greying hair was still swept forward Beatles fashion, he seldom wore a tie, his drainpipe jeans were suitably washed out and he continued to wear his old CND badge. Not that he worked at it. There was nothing manufactured about his style of life. It was just dishevelled and sybaritic. For, despite his political virtue, Dr Ravenshaw had the appetites of a satyr. Indeed, in a flabby kind of way he resembled one with his double chins and heavy, sensuous lips. Not that it did him much harm. There was the allure of forbidden fruit about the Doctor and a kind of romance, even, of re-living the heady days of libertarian struggle in the late Sixties and early Seventies before the onset of Thatcher. A tumble with the Doctor , who himself fancied that he bore a passing resemblance to the late Dylan Thomas, was a brush with vintage hippydom and of course worth it when it might deliver an academic dividend, like an Upper Second or even a first class degree, which, to the girls under his supervision, was more important in the long run than the exotic experience of coupling with the man himself. For his male students to win the Doctor's favours required a more oblique approach, which on occasions amounted to a form of pimping.

Yet in spite of his efforts to play down his status and to be at one with his students - for instance he tried to get them to call him Mick - he could not quite pull it off. He was always referred to as the Doc or the Doctor in the deliberately distancing fashion that young people have of avoiding being patronised by an oldie, who seems a bit too keen to climb on board their bandwagon. But he did wield real power in the English faculty and with his legendary supplies of gin and reputation as a pioneering fighter in youth's struggle for emancipation, he was a figure of curiosity, while at the same time in a subtle, and indeed mildly contemptuous, way his students were unwilling to enroll him as one of their own.

*****

For the moment Dan was at a loss what to do with Dr Ravenshaw's body now that his death was established. Whatever he did with it was not going to bring the man back to life again, so he left it lying where it was and returned to the utility room to find Debbie in a huddle with Rachel. Any desire for sleep had vanished.

'Tell me, Deb, did he arrive like that? I mean completely starkers?'

Debbie nodded.

'And then what? Take your time.'

Rachel gave her a reassuring hug.

'Did he... did he try to rape you?'

'For Christ's sake, Dan, what a bloody awful thing to ask now of all times!' Rachel sounded cross and Dan could see that the girlish ranks looked set to close against him.

'I'm sorry, but we must know. He did attack you, didn't he?' he asked Debbie. 'I mean when he burst out of his bedroom like that, in his birthday suit? It must have been pretty horrendous, unless...'

'Unless what?' Debbie's voice sounded hard for the first time and she looked back steadily at Dan.

'You were expecting him. We've discussed the good Doctor's proclivities often enough, haven't we?'

'What are you suggesting Dan?' Debbie spoke very deliberately.

'Without putting too fine a point upon it. An upper rather than a lower second?'

'Fuck off, Dan,' said Rachel.

'But we have to know,' he insisted. 'After all it might be the difference between a rape and what? A more gentlemanly way of proceeding?'

'I've already told you... fuck off.' Rachel gave Debbie an extra hard cuddle.

'Whatever it was he wanted I wasn't going to let him have it in the bath,' declared Debbie roundly.

'So you did figure he might rape you? It would be entirely understandable if you did, in the circumstances. After all, you weren't given much time to think about it, were you?'

'Dan,' said Rachel, 'stop trying to play at being a policeman. You sound so fucking pompous.'

Dan sighed. 'You can say that,' he said, 'but the cops are going to want some answers. The real ones I mean.'

'So can't we just leave the Doctor where he is and let them ask the questions?' Rachel's tone sounded more reasonable.

'I guess we'll have to. There's not much else we can do, is there?'

'I suppose you're right. You usually are,' she appended as a gratuitous piece of sarcasm.

'Please, you two, don't start a fight. Not now,' pleaded Debbie.

Dan wandered back to the bathroom, eyed the Doctor's corpse and prodded it with his toe.

'A fitting end, you old goat, to a grubby career, if you ask me. All very right and proper,' he told the dead man.

Panama Jack was still lying face up on the floor. Dan picked the bottle up and addressed the sun-blasted visage.

242

'God, I bet you could tell us a thing or two,' he said to it out aloud. 'Was the bathroom the doctor's favourite stamping ground? You could tell us all about that, I'm sure.'

It fitted - the connecting boltless door leading from his own bedroom. To burst in upon his victim in the bath, clad in the battle armour of his nudity, so to speak, and to have his way with her then and there. It fitted, but it was a bloody risky way to go about things all the same. The bait of an Upper Second, or even a First, would have to have been a powerful one, aided, of course, by a preparatory supply of gin punch. Dan went back to the utility room.

'That bottle of sun lotion,' he said, 'The one lying on the floor. Did you happen to notice it?' he asked Debbie.

She shrugged.

'It's nothing much really,' went on Dan. 'It just caught my eye, that's all. I expect the Doc knocked it off the windowsill when he fell.'

'What about it?'

'It's a rather striking thing in its way.'

The two girls said nothing, but looked at him, perplexed, not quite sure what he was getting at or if it was just a another instance of Dan trying to play the cool detective.

'So what?' retorted Rachel. 'What's that got to do with it?'

'Nothing at all really,' Dan said. 'It just caught my eye, that's all. I mean that if he could talk Panama Jack, the guy on the bottle, that is, might be able to tell us a thing or two about the Doctor's bathing habits.'

'Hang on a minute,' cut in Debbie. 'A bottle of sun lotion from the windowsill, you say? I grabbed something from there and jabbed the Doctor in the balls with it.'

'There you are,' exclaimed Dan. 'So Panama Jack played an

243

active part in the drama of Dr Ravenshaw's death as well. He's certainly a pretty dark horse is our Panama Jack! In more ways than one. And because he struck him in the balls, the Doctor slipped and bashed his head on the tap. Fell so hard that he killed himself.'

'For Christ's sake Dan, why do you have to sound such an old fart?' interjected Rachel. 'Stop being so hammy. You're not Hercule Poirot.'

'That's about it,' said Debbie, 'but as I told you, it all happened so quickly.'

'Well done, Deb,' declared Rachel. 'You did the just right thing. It was good thinking - to do that, on the spur of the moment. I mean to hit the Doctor in the nuts.'

'Good thinking,' repeated Dan, 'and deadly as it turned out.'

'Why do you keep harping on it?' Rachel protested. 'Are you saying that she killed him on purpose?'

'No, of course I'm not.'

'Well stop sounding as if you are, then.'

For a moment none of them spoke.

'Hadn't we better ring the police?' Rachel suggested at length.

'I suppose we should.' Dan sounded reluctant as if he would be surrendering something he wanted to keep for himself.

'Well, you've played Sherlock Holmes enough for one night, haven't you?' sneered Rachel. 'Or perhaps you haven't?'

'Please, Rachel,' pleaded Debbie. 'Just drop it.'

'As long as we know what were going to tell them,' said Dan, pretending to ignore Rachel's tone.

'Just tell them what we know,' said Rachel. 'Why should we tell them anything else? I would have though hitting the old goat in the nuts was an entirely justified piece of self-defence. And any way he died by bashing his head on the tap, didn't he? That's one for the coroner, isn't it?'

The other two did not speak.

'Well, isn't it?'

'I think we should sleep on it,' said Dan.

'What on earth do you mean? Do you think any of us feel like sleeping now?'

'I mean ring the cops first thing in the morning. After all, it's not going to make any difference to Ravenshaw, is it?'

'What's the point of waiting?' Rachel demanded to know.

'I just think we need to be careful how we approach this one. There may be a bit more at stake than you think. We need to think it through a bit.'

'Why exactly?' said Rachel. 'It looks straightforward enough to me.'

'I mean all this shit about motives for things - us being here... and stopping over.'

'Oh?' challenged Rachel, while Debbie bit her lip and said nothing.

'I'm talking about the possibility of Upper Seconds,' explained Dan.

'Is that why you're here?' said Rachel, 'to act as my pimp? In case I took the Doctor's fancy?'

'Rachel, how could you? That's pretty unfair!' protested Debbie. 'Say what you like about Dan, but I don't think he'd sink as low as that!'

'I'm not so sure. You could use a first, couldn't you Dan?'

Dan chose not to reply and went out into the passage again. He felt rather pleased with himself for not rising to Rachel's bait. At the same time he knew that whatever had existed between them was over.

Dr Ravenshaw's demise had laid that to rest - once and for all.

He went into the bathroom and picked up the bottle with Panama Jack's portrait. It occurred to him that he oughtn't to be touching anything in case the police wanted to take fingerprints, but he had handled it already and didn't much care. In fact he was beginning to get sick of the affair and the sheer bitchiness it was giving rise to. In a word, Dan was doing what he was good at doing, which was feeling self-righteous.

'What really happened here?' he said out loud to the sun-blackened face on the bottle. 'Did you hit the Doctor in the nuts like she said?'

Panama Jack glared back at him through his monocle.

'I believe you might well have done,' mused Dan. 'In the circumstances it was the deed of a gentleman - even if it was below the belt. But who cares a shit about that when a damsel's in distress?'

'That's me you're talking about Dan, isn't it?'

He turned round to see Debbie who had followed him into the bathroom.

'I must say I've never thought of myself as that before a damsel in distress.'

'It's just a way of speaking,' replied Dan, 'And I was thinking out loud.'

'About what might have actually happened?'

'Possibly. Was it different from what you told us?'

'What I said did happen. The Doctor burst in upon me, all right, in his birthday suit and took hold of my hair. So 1 grabbed the first thing that came to hand and jabbed him in the balls with it. He let out a big groan, doubled up slipped on the bathmat and cracked his head on the tap...'

'Hard enough to kill himself?'

Debbie looked at Dan steadily. 'You don't like that bit, do you? I mean you don't think that was all there was to it, do you?'

'No Deb, quite frankly I don't. To kill himself he'd have to have fallen really bloody hard.'

'The ace detective.' Debbie sounded almost as sarcastic as Rachel.

'What actually happened, Deb? The next bit, I mean - after he cracked his head? I can see how he did that. It's no problem.'

Debbie drew breath and looked him steadily. 'O.K., then.' She paused before going on. 'I finished him off.'

She paused and Dan said nothing.

'Does that shock you?'

'It does a bit, but then he was trying to rape you, wasn't he?'

'Certainly he was.., before he hit his head...'

'So what did you do, Deb?'

'The fall stunned him... and I simply helped things along a bit... by holding his head under the water. He didn't object.' Debbie shrugged her shoulders and looked at Dan to measure his reaction. She seemed to have complete control of herself and even smiled. 'Does it shock you?' she said again.

'On second thoughts, I don't think it does.'

She gave an exasperated little snort. 'Really Dan... it should, shouldn't it? I mean, why do you have to behave as if you've seen it all before? You're only...what? Twenty-three? Twenty-four? What have you seen?'

'You're beginning to sound like Rachel.'

'So what if I am? Well anyway, you've seen it now. And I don't feel all that sorry. At least now I don't. Maybe I will later on. As you said yourself, he had it coming to him and anyway it was a painless end. He just went off to sleep. Lucky old Dr Ravenshaw I'd say.'

'I hope this won't become a habit of yours, Deb.'

'You really are a pompous old fart, Dan. Rachel's dead right. You're forgetting that he did try to rape me.'

'He probably calculated that you wanted an Upper Second badly enough for him to get away with it.'

Well in that case he calculated wrong.' Debbie glared back at Dan defiantly.

'Good for you Deb.'

'Good for you Deb,' she repeated in a hoity-toity tone.

'But we've got to tell the cops something. Something they'll believe.'

'It was self-defence, wasn't it?'

'Probably, but it could be more than that.'

'Why should it be? he fell, stunned himself and then drowned in the bathwater. In a way that's exactly what did happen.'

'And you made no attempt to save him? In fact helped him on his way by holding his head under the water?'

'He'd just tried to rape me, hadn't he? Never forget that.'

'I wonder what our friend Panama Jack might say about all this? He looks as if he's seen, a bit of life. He might come up with a few good ideas.'

'I suppose I should be grateful to him, shouldn't I? I mean for him being at hand in my hour of need,' said Debbie.

Dan fixed his gaze on the bottle of lotion. 'Well then. The Doctor appeared suddenly... stark naked... grabbed the girl by her hair and showed every sign of wanting to rape her...she seized the first thing that came to hand... a bottle of tanning lotion from the windowsill, namely your good self, sir, and jabbed her attacker in the goolies... he slipped.., bashed his head on the tap and accidently drowned in the bathwater after she had fled the scene in a very understandable state of fright...' Dan put the bottle to his ear, as if it was a telephone. 'Yes... yes... quite... you reckon that'll do?... sufficiently plausible? Good.. if you can think of anything more, you'll let us know?... Goody-good... it's not the first time he's tried it on?... But at least it'll be the last... we don't need to know about all of that now, do we?... Quite... You reckon we're covered?... With the cops, mean? And the coroner? Goody-good.. bow to your experience. You've seen it all before? Things like it anyway? You've seen a thing or two in your lifetime, I'll bet... Whereabouts? in Central America?... In Panama? I like that hat by the way... It's pretty cool. The genuine article eh?.I must get one like it...'

'Dan,' said Debbie. 'You don't have to be such an arsehole. But we'll settle for that. It sounds pretty watertight to me.'

'As long as you don't try to be too cool about it. That's the only thing that worries me about you, Deb, The cops need to be convinced that you really are shaken... traumatized, in fact. But I know you well enough. You can pull it off. Ill ring them now, shall I? Where's the Doc's phone? And a pity about the 2:1, by the way. It would have been pushing it to have given you a First, mind you... a way over the top, but a 2:1 sounded like a fair price...'

But strangely enough that was what Debbie did get - a 2:1. And Dan got one too - he missed the First that he had felt was his due, while Rachel had to settle for a lower second. 'Serves the bitch right,' gloated Dan. He could at least take some satisfaction from that.

Beau Geste

'Thank you. Peggy, I'll be perfectly all right'

'Are you quite sure now?'

'Perfectly sure. Now you run home. Your husband'll be wondering where you've got to.'

'I doubt it, Lady Portia. There once was a time maybe.'

Lady Portia Meynell smiled from the pillow and started to sip her hot milky drink. She was in her eighty-third year and lived by herself in Raikswood, the ancestral home of the Meynells, an old North Riding family. Usually every second weekend her older son, Sir Julian, descended from London with his wife Maryon to play the part of lord of the manor, which, being a successful banker, he could afford to do. It was a role he found congenial and he looked forward to the time when he could devote himself to it more fully. There was an occasional visit from a grand-daughter as well, Emily, who was recently married and living near Appleby. Then there was her favourite grand-child, Robbie, just down from Cambridge with a good degree in Fine Arts. He liked to stick his head round the door into what he called the granny flat, usually without warning. Lady Portia enjoyed his banter.

Otherwise she relied on Peggy Chambers, whose husband, Roger, was styled head gardener with a lad to help him. Between them they kept the externals of Raikswood in good shape while Peggy came in daily from the gatehouse where she and Roger lived with their grown-up daughter, Elsie, who had been deaf from birth. Peggy cooked and generally did for Lady Portia, often bringing Elsie with her to assist with the washing and heavier housework - of which there was no shortage in a house the size of Raikswood.

It had been the family seat of the Meynells since the late seventeenth century, receiving its Palladian makeover in the eighteenth. The Meynells had been prominent Whigs and a couple of them, Sir Montagu and his cousin Titus, had served in Sir Robert Walpole's government. In the enlightened spirit of the age they had farmed efficiently too and their Wensleydale estate had prospered. Several astute legal and financial brains in the family, such as that possessed by Sir Montagu himself, had assisted them on their way as well. So at the beginning of the twenty - first century the Meynells were still on their feet and thinking up new schemes. For instance, Robbie had ideas of restoring the famous Arcadian garden to its former glory and opening it as an attraction for visitors - something his grandmother had mixed feelings about, but then, she told herself, she was a lot nearer the end than the beginning and had not been born a Meynell.

But Meynell or not, Portia had always belonged to their kind of world, coming from a landed family herself across the Pennines, so playing chatelaine of Raikswood at the side of Sir Andrew, her baronet husband, had been quite natural to her.

But he had passed away five years previously, leaving Portia, who remained in fairly robust health, by herself in a house from which her children had set out into the wider world.

Her son Julian, the new baronet, took his duties seriously in the time that he could spare for them and his own son, Robbie, an art historian, also had a keen sense of commitment to the place, though of a rather different kind. Both were eager to see Raikswood remain in the hands of the family.

All of which was gratifying to Portia, who passed much of her time now in the small sitting room which adjoined her bedroom, where she was surrounded by a number of the smaller pictures which had been transferred from other parts of the house because they had come to mean something to her. It was also a good vantage point, commanding a view across the farmland in the bottom of the dale up onto the moorland beyond - a fine sweep of northern countryside: gentle in the foreground, but running off into a backdrop of bleakness to make it the kind of English landscape she loved best of all.

'I'm a drystone wall sort of person rather than a hedgerow one, she liked to tell people. 'Not that I don't love the English hedgerows too, of course, with all their plants and wildlife, but it is our own dry stone walls that I feel most at home with.'

Since the end of the seventeenth century the Meynell star had risen with the part they had played in the Glorious Revolution which had brought William and Mary to the throne. The family had consolidated its position after the Hanoverian succession with the patronage of Sir Robert Walpole and the Meynells had come to exemplify Whig ideals and aesthetic values. For instance, their sons had assiduously performed the Grand Tour while the family had had themselves painted by the leading portraitists of their day. In a couple of cases these two things had come together: there was a fine Battoni of young Sir Maynard in Rome and one of his siblings done shortly afterwards by Gavin Hamilton who specialized in the same kind of thing - both rather supercilious-looking young men posed in front of works of antiquity.

Sir Montague Meynell, who had served as a treasury minister under Walpole, graced the great dining room along with his spouse, Isobel and their two daughters. All were rendered in a grand rococo manner with Sir Montague in bag wig, holding a brief in his left hand with the right resting on an ormolu occasional table where there lay a quill pen, inkwell and a bundle of papers tied with red tape. A purposeful working image. On an adjacent wall was his youngest son, Henry, who, alas, had died in his early thirties, a penetrating likeness by the Scottish painter, Alan Ramsay. It was an alert, mildly saturnine, intelligent face - a face full of promise sadly cut short, whose eyes confronted the viewer squarely. The Grand Tour portraits of his two older brothers graced the drawing room wall. Portia could not help reflecting that Henry looked a more suitable beneficiary of such an educational excursion and wondered if he had made it as well. Sir Godfrey Meynell, in the guise of ageing Regency buck, was there also, painted by Sir Thomas Lawrence, no less. Various portraits of beguiling children - boys in grey flannel breeches and wielding curiously curved cricket bats and small girls in silk dresses scampering after puppies and butterflies lined the staircase walls while a miscellany of similar, but smaller works by more minor artists, mostly of collateral kin, occupied part of the landing space.

But one of the works which Portia had removed from the relative obscurity of the landing passage was of a younger son of the family, painted, by the look of it, shortly before or after the First World War. It was of Raymond Meynell, the uncle of her late husband, and for some reason had been hung at the end of a row of childish portraits of second cousins and the like.

He was a handsome young man, sporting a heavy moustache of the kind that was popular at the beginning of the twentieth century, but was to go out of fashion after the Great War. In this picture of him he struck a debonair pose in opera cape and hat. He appeared to be standing on the steps of a theatre or opera house under a gaslight. His banishment to the darkest end of the landing passage struck Portia as odd. For apart from his own striking good looks the painting was of high quality.

'Uncle Raymond,' the late Sir Andrew had explained to his bride. 'Pa's younger brother and a bit of a goer. I never knew him - not properly at least. Rather a dark horse, they said. He went abroad to Africa - according to the family legend- and never returned. He seems to have wandered off the map. Easy thing to do in Africa then, I suppose.'

'Hes a good-looking young man, so why has he been banished to this dark corner with these second cousins and the rest?' Portia wanted to know. 'Is he in some kind of disgrace?'

'Standing in the corner, you mean?' Sir Andrew had laughed. 'It could well be. He was a bit of a bad lad - a goer as they say. Stuck his neck out a little too far.'

'What that means I'm left to guess, I suppose. But I rather like the sound of your uncle Raymond. Every family should have its skeleton in the cupboard, shouldn't it? - the one they don't like to talk about. They are much the most interesting. I suppose it depends what he got up to, doesn't it? If its something shameful and in the fairly recent past they'd naturally want to bury it.'

'No one was ever quite sure about Uncle Raymond. But people like my mother wouldn't talk about him, except in the most general sort of way. He made a life for himself abroad for a time - before vanishing into the Heart of Darkness.'

'Packed off to the Colonies, was he? On the run from something grubby - like messing about with small boys?'

Her husband, who tried to think of himself as a tolerant man in the Whig tradition looked shocked at such an outspoken suggestion.

'I'm sorry,' said Portia. 'I shouldn't have said that, should I? But if I'm not told anything, Im going to imagine the worst, aren't 1? It was a silly idea of mine. He doesn't look that sort of a man at all.'

Nevertheless Portia remembered hearing such rumours about Lord Kitchener himself and he sported the same type of moustache. And then the scandal of Oscar Wilde's downfall was still a living memory.

No, Portia decided, if anything he looks like a ladykiller. So for the time being the mystery of Uncle Raymond was passed over and he was left skulking penitentially in the shadows of the landing passage.

But when Sir Andrew died and Portia withdrew to the citadel of her bedroom and sittingroom - her granny flat- she decided to take some of the smaller pictures with her. As a result her walls were very crowded; she was reluctant to dispense with what was already there but among other items she adopted a little girl in a shimmery sea-green silk frock with a puppy in her lap and a sturdy lad in grey flannel breeches carrying an old-fashioned cricket bat over his shoulder like a war club. Pictures of children were always agreeable at close quarters and she was happy to include these strangers alongside pictures of her own. She had never understood the Meynell habit of confining them to the gloomier corners of the house.

And as well as the children she took Raymond, whom she felt had done penance in outer darkness for long enough, whatever his offence might have been.

'You're out of detention now, young man,' she told the picture severely. 'So whatever you've been up to you can enjoy a bit of daylight for a change.'

And when she looked at the picture more closely in the good light she could see that it did indeed have quality. She could not identify the painter, but it looked suspiciously like a Sargent - in his latter days - and possibly commissioned by its subject himself.

'There are a number of questions I'd like to ask you in due course, young man,' said Portia still addressing the picture sternly once it was hanging on her sitting-room wall. 'And don't think you can hide anything from me.'

Her son the new baronet, Sir Julian, of course raised no objection to his mother moving some of the smaller pictures around, for, if the truth be known he had little eye for such things himself, while his wife preferred horses. The only one to express an opinion was Robbie.

'It's great what you've done for these pictures, Granny,' he told her as he looked round the room after they had been hung. 'They're really rather good and you could never see them before. You have set them free.'

'Thank you, Robbie, you're the first person to say that to me.'

'But at the same time they do give rise to some radical thoughts,' he went on.

'Oh dear, do they really? Do we have to be political about a thing like this? '

'I'm afraid everything is political in this world of ours, Granny. It's something we can't avoid. '

Portia sighed but said nothing. She had hoped he was going to be flippant instead of moralizing. But then you never quite knew with Robbie.

'What I mean is that some people have so much that they can't

257

possibly enjoy the half of it.'

'For Heaven's sake, Robbie, we've been over that ground enough times already, haven't we?'

'These pictures provide a perfect example. Each one of them a thing of beauty and worth a tidy sum too, I don't doubt. But where have they been all this time? Skulking in a dark corner of a country house where no one could be bothered to look at them. Unless, of course, they happened on them by accident. It's not right, somehow.'

'The flower that blooms in the forest unseen. Is that what you're saying? But aren't you being a little unfair? If people like us didn't hide our treasures in dark corners they might vanish completely. At least we're keeping them safe that way and it's better than locking them up in the bank. Think of it- the day they're re-discovered! Stumbling across a forgotten or long-lost Rembrandt or whatever! Like that Raphael in Alnwick Castle, belonging to the Duke of Northumberland. Half-forgotten for years at the end of a passage and now the whole world can enjoy it in the National Gallery.' Portia had almost become passionate.

'Well anyway, Granny, you're doing a great job, bringing these ones to the surface at last. But there is a downside.'

'Oh? Not a political one, I hope?'

'No, not a political one. They need a bloody good clean. Now they're in broad daylight you can see how filthy they are.' Robbie licked a finger and rubbed it over the surface of Uncle Raymond.

'Well that's one for you to think about - or whoever gets them after I've shed my mortal coil.'

Robbie looked closely at Uncle Raymond. 'You know, I've never really taken a proper look at him before. It's a bloody good little picture. It's a shame it's so grubby.'

'It could be by Sargent, but I'm only guessing. It's his style.

Painted around the time of the Great War.'

'You could well be right, Granny. That's something we need to find out.'

Robbie scanned the other newcomers who now kept company with his grandmother's private collection before returning to Uncle Raymond. It seemed, almost, as if a mute dialogue was opening up between them. Uncle Raymond seemed eager to talk, having been kept in the shadows for so long. Since when? Probably the nineteen-twenties. Eighty or so years.

'This guy is trying to say something to me, Granny.'

Portia gave a small snort. 'Don't start reading into it what isn't there, young man.' She scrutinized the picture closely herself. 'But come to think of it, there is a bit of a family likeness. The moustache makes it a little difficult to spot, but once you've penetrated that thicket, you can see it, I think. Don't you ever grow one like that, by the way.'

'It hadn't crossed my mind, Granny, but perhaps I'll give it some thought one of these days.'

'Don't you dare do such a thing.' She looked critically at the picture. 'They're tiny, but those eyes really do sparkle.'

Robbie went right up to the picture and examined it closely. 'I like to look at a picture as the artist sees it when he's applying the paint,' he explained. Then he took a rapid step backwards. 'My God, Granny, you're quite right about the eyes. The fellow's just winked at me!'

His grandmother laughed. 'I think you might possibly be reading a bit more into Uncle Raymond than is really there,' she said. 'He's a dark horse, certainly - or even a black sheep?

'Probably the two of them rolled into one. But his eyes really do sparkle. When you think about it, it's quite uncanny what can be done

259

with a dab of a brush. I'd dearly like to know what he did to be banished to outer darkness. I'd always assumed that we Meynells were a pretty open-minded lot - the kind who could have carried off the occasional scandal - even welcomed it, for adding a dash of colour to a pretty grey-looking picture. In Walpole's day they were supposed to be good book keepers, like a bunch of tradesmen. I mean the aristocracy was expected to cut loose once in a while, wasn't it?'

'As the heir apparent, that's one for you to think about. Now, you can tell me what you make of these children.'

Robbie eyed the girl in the sea-green frock holding the puppy and the boy in grey flannel breeches with his bat.

'Sadly this one never reached thirty,' said Portia, shaking her head at the little girl. 'Poor little Jenny! But better in a way to go before the flower begins to fade. Look at me, after all.'

'Stop fishing, Granny.'

She laughed because she liked him telling her things like that. 'But this little fellow, Godfrey rather makes my point. You can go downstairs and see what the loveable scamp grew up into.'

It was hard to reconcile the scruffy little boy with his breeches undone at the knees and his shirt tail half hanging out, with the purple-cheeked old rake painted by Lawrence and hanging in the dining room.

It was a little odd, Robbie reflected, to imagine Godfrey being packed off to do the Grand Tour, when the turf and the port bottle were probably his true element.

'I think that pictures of children are the most poignant,' he said, 'for the reason you mention.' He turned back to the picture of Uncle Raymond, 'The wastrel younger son, the blot on the escutcheon, even. Sorry to pile on the clichés, Granny, but he's the one who interests me most. If indeed there was a family cover-up how did he blot his copybook? Moreover I could swear that the fellow winked at me just now. Maybe he'd like to tell me.'

'And what about me?' his grandmother complained. 'I was the one who brought him back into the light of day, wasn't ?'

'Of course you were, Granny. But - how do I put this? - It could be a bloke's thing. The way he winked at me, I mean. Has he ever winked at you?'

'Not yet, but I'm waiting for it. He looks as if he might have the sauce.'

'To make a pass at you?'

'Don't be such a bloody fool!

That was the way it usually ran between grandmother and grandson. None of the other members of the family seemed to have a share in it. For the most part they took the things that surrounded them for granted, though Sir Julian was keen on the practical business of running his estate. Robbie wondered about his forebears; Jenny who had died so young, for instance? And what about the mysterious Uncle Raymond? He had gone to a good painter to have his portrait done, at least. Was it Sargent? It certainly looked in his league.

The bugger dropped an eyelid when I looked at him, mused Robbie. I could have sworn he did. Which says something for the painter, I suppose…

*****

Robbie had taken his supper on a tray with his grandmother in her sitting room before bidding her good night and retreating to his den at the far end of the main landing. Peggy in the meantime had brought up her milky drink and seen her into bed. With just her reading light on, Portia settled back on her pillow to read her book. She was revisiting something she had not looked at since she was a much younger woman. Indeed, it was the very same copy that she had read then which she had discovered on her late husband's study shelves. It was The Big Sleep by Raymond Chandler. She had forgotten the plot and though she tended to lose the thread - she was constantly having to turn back to pick it up again - she enjoyed its ambience, so different from the one she inhabited herself. Moreover, its idiom seemed as fresh as when she had first read it.

But a chapter was generally enough to bring on sleep and she was nodding off before the final paragraph, Chandler's Los Angeles already starting to merge into her dream world. However she roused herself sufficiently to be able to turn off the light.

As she did so and was about to sink back into a comatose state, she heard a man's cough.

Startled she sat up and fumbled for the light switch. 'Robbie? Is that you?'

The light went on and there was no sign of her grandson in the room. She was by herself. The door into her sitting room was ajar and the sound could have come from there.

'Is that you, Robbie?' she called a little more loudly this time.

There was no reply. Clearly no one was in the other room. Or at least they were keeping very quiet if they were.

It occurred to Portia that if there was an intruder in the house, hearing that she was awake might be enough to warn them off. Better that, perhaps, than confronting him directly.

She listened hard for a couple of minutes, but heard nothing more, no movement, nothing. Eventually she decided to switch off the light.

But no sooner had she done so and plunged the room into darkness, than the sound was repeated: a deliberate, attention-seeking cough.

On went the light once more and revealed what it had done a minute earlier. Portia decided to take the bull by the horns, so she got out of bed, went through to her sitting room and to the outer door onto the landing.

'Robbie! Are you awake?' she called in the direction of the young man's room. There was a light under his door which opened and her grandson appeared.

'You're still awake. I'm so glad,' Portia said. The relief in her voice was palpable.

'Is something the matter? her grandson asked. 'And oughtn't you to have your dressing gown on instead of wandering around in your nightie?' He sounded authoritative and Portia felt reassured.

'I thought I heard someone in my room. I wondered if it might be you.'

'Not guilty,' replied Robbie' I've stayed put since I left you.'

'I heard somebody cough. It was a man's cough.'

'Well I didn't hear anything, Granny, and I've been awake all the time. Shall I take a look downstairs? We may have a visitor.'

'All the more reason for not going downstairs,' his grandmother admonished him firmly. 'We don't want the heir to Raikswood, of all people, having his brains knocked out!'

Robbie put on the landing light and leaning over the balustrade, peered down into the dark hall well. He could hear nothing, not a creak nor the rustle of a draught, nothing.

'You get back into bed, Granny,' he ordered her, 'and I'll keep my door open. I'll hear anything that moves.'

Portia returned to her bed, partly reassured by her grandson's gruff manner. She climbed back into bed, but was reluctant to switch off the light. Eventually sleep got the better of her and having taken the plunge into darkness, was snoring lightly a moment later.

Robbie was up early in the morning and looking in on his grandmother. He could hear Peggy downstairs putting the breakfast tray together.

'No more nocturnal visitors?' he said.

'None that I was aware of, I slept like a log after I spoke to you, which is rather unusual for me.'

'Maybe it was Uncle Raymond, coming to make his pass at you.'

'It certainly sounded like a man's cough.'

'There you are then. But are you sure it wasn't a mouse running about behind the skirting board, or even a rat? There must be plenty in a house like this.'

'Nothing like that. It was definitely a man's cough. As if he was trying to draw attention to himself.'

'Then it can only have been Uncle Raymond, the dirty old man!'

He went back into the sitting room and addressed the picture in a loud voice.

'You're a fine one, aren't you? Putting the wind up an old woman in the dark!'

'Don't be ridiculous, Robbie.'

Peggy meanwhile arrived with the breakfast: a pot of tea, a boiled egg, two slices of toast and a small bowl of marmalade.

Robbie came back into the room. 'I'm taking the matter in hand, Granny. I'm going to get these pictures cleaned for you. I expect the fellow is dying for a bath. That was what he was trying to tell you - as nicely as possible. And the two kids could certainly do with one as well - especially that little boy. He positively stinks. '

When his grandmother opened her mouth to protest, having put down her cup, he raised his hand.

'Not a word from you, Granny,' he commanded her. 'The decision has been made. I know someone who can do it at a very reasonable cost and you won't miss them for long. Alastair is a good friend of mine. So don't argue about it, because I'm not listening to you. Think of it as your Christmas present, if you prefer it that way.'

He leaned over her tray and scooped up a generous dollop of marmalade on his finger and she slapped the back of his wrist.

'The truth is I want to see them looking their best, as they did in their piping days - especially Uncle Raymond.'

With a shrug and a sigh Portia surrendered to her grandson's command the way she usually did.

*****

Robbie wasted no time. Before the week was out Alastair Oakshott had arrived from London, and the pictures were off to the capital in his four by four before Sir Julian had made his weekend descent on Raikswood. Not that he was likely to have caviled over the cost of cleaning three small pictures, for he generally ignored such trifles, preferring to leave the arty-farty stuff to his son, which suited Robbie admirably.

It was a week later that Robbie received a phone call from Alastair. It concerned Uncle Raymond. Behind the picture was a small wooden panel tacked over it which he had removed to take the picture from its frame. Inside he had found a sealed envelope, very yellow and clearly old, dating most likely from the time the picture was painted. However he was reluctant to break into it on his own, considering it a family matter, so he would bring it with the cleaned pictures for Robbie to open. He believed it could be important, saying something about the pictures provinence.

'The plot surrounding Uncle Raymond thickens,' Robbie informed his grandmother. 'Alastair has found a sealed envelope at the back of the picture. It might even contain a clue to the artist himself. It's pretty exciting, don't you think? Like an old-fashioned mystery story.'

After another three weeks Alastair made his next trip to Yorkshire, having cleaned all three pictures. And there was no doubt that he had made a good job of it.

'These children are a sheer delight,' exclaimed Portia. 'They have come to life!'

And Uncle Raymond, too, had acquired an added lustre. The glint in his eye on which Robbie had already remarked was sharper than ever.

'He really does seem to want to say something,' Robbie declared. 'To get something off his chest that he feels we ought to know.'

The three of them were sitting around his grandmother's little walnut table in her sitting room. Robbie put his hand in his jacket pocket and took out an ancient yellowing envelope which he flourished dramatically.

'The moment has arrived, Granny. I hope you're ready for it!' He winked at Alastair.

There was nothing written on the outside of the envelope, but it looked fairly bulky.

'Stop being so mysterious. Just open it. We're all dying to find out what's inside,' ordered his grandmother.

'Knife?' Robbie looked round for a paperknife. Having found what he wanted, he flourished it like a pompous pater familias about to carve the Christmas turkey and inserted it carefully into the edge of the envelope.

He sliced it cleanly and drew out a piece of card. Turning it over, he saw that it was the mount for an oval photograph contained within an embossed gilt floral wreath. The picture was of a young girl - she looked to be in her mid teens - mildly mischievous, a repoussé nose and hair bobbed in the style of the Nineteen-twenties. A fetching creature, Robbie decided on the first glance. Written below the picture was the single word Marie and a date December 1925.

Which is helpful up to a point, thought Robbie. He passed the picture to his grandmother who put on her spectacles and inspected it closely. He then took it back from her and passed it to Alastair.

'1925,' he said. 'If I'm not mistaken two years after Sargent's death.'

'You are not mistaken,' replied his friend, 'but it doesn't tell us when the picture was painted.'

'True. But who on earth was Marie and what is she doing stuck behind a picture of Uncle Raymond?'

'She's certainly a sweet creature,' Alastair observed.

'On the contrary, she looks wanton,' retorted Portia.

'That's a little strong, isn't it?' said Robbie.

'Not in the least. I know the type.' His grandmother set her lips tightly to preclude any further discussion about it.

Robbie examined the card and discovered a name printed in the bottom left-hand corner with an address: He read M. Valentin, 22 the Rue Clichy, Montmatre. The photographer presumably. A rather seedy district and a jampot for tourists.

'A Parisienne,' he said, 'but what does that tell us about Uncle Raymond? Probably that he wasn't gay.'

'Which was a perfectly useful word before it got pinched,' his grandmother pointed out. 'He was a bit of a goer, as the family liked to say in its sporty kind of way. But what's she doing at the back of a picture of him?' said Robbie. 'They do seem to be creatures of the night, don't they, the pair of them? I mean there's Raymond confined to the darkest corner of the landing for all these years with this sweet creature hiding behind his back. And then he vanishes - in Darkest Africa. Where else? What takes him there? Had it anything to do with the girl? It all looks a bit lurid, if you ask me.'

For a moment none of them spoke.

'Can we pin down the painter?' Robbie asked Alastair. 'It still could be Sargent.'

'It could be, but doesn't have to be. But it's certainly no mean amateur.'

'Definitely not Sickert anyway,' said Robbie. 'I always think of him as Sargent's antithesis since they were working at about the same time.'

'Definitely not Sickert, it's not remotely his style,' Alastair replied.

Robbie picked up the photograph of the girl and frowned. An unsettling thought had crossed his mind. 'What do you think, Granny?'

'I'm leaving it in the hands of the experts,' she said. 'But she's a wanton little hussy!'

'That's pretty harsh. What makes you so sure of that? '

'She's a little flirt.'

'That's not quite the same thing. I find her rather to my taste. And anyway, you must have flirted in your time too, Granny.'

Lady Portia smiled. She was pleased when her grandson told her things like that.

But the mention of Walter Sickert, the contemporary and antithesis of Sargent, had set Robbie thinking. Walter Sickert...

Sargent was the fashionable portrait painter of his day while Sickert was the painter of low life, using appropriately dingy subfusc tones. They were two sides of an early twentieth century coin, and sat uneasily side by side in their different representative roles. Robbie thought of those sombre Sickert paintings of women done to death in drab lodging houses. Indeed such was Sickert's fascination with the theme that his name had even been put forward as a possible Jack the Ripper. It was the underside of the world represented by the works of Sargent. And Uncle Raymond? Who seems to have vanished, rather romantically in the Heart of Darkness? How did he fit into this early twentieth century English world, if indeed he did at all? He had had his portrait painted, if not by Sargent himself, then by someone in his class. And literally behind the picture was this girl - Marie - photographed in a studio in the Montmatre district of Paris. Were his disappearance and the cloud which hung over his family's memory of him somehow linked to her? Lady Portia had looked at the picture of Marie and without hesitation dismissed her as wanton, meaning that she was a tart - which struck her grandson as unfair. But what kind of a girl was she really? And what did she mean to Raymond? It was easy enough to hazard a few guesses. Dark or light, whatever it was, the riddle of Uncle Raymond was beginning to take over Robbie's life. In fact it was something that he felt he might put to good use one day. Apart from his aspirations as a landscape gardener and restorer of Raikswood, Robbie had literary dreams too, ones that combined his interest in art with the mysterious, possibly of a disturbing kind. The dashing Uncle Raymond and the smell of scandal he gave off was a gift horse not to be looked in the mouth...

He was going to have to follow up different lines of enquiry: the records of what was then the Colonial Office for any mention of Raymond Mcynell in the decade following the Great War and, a longer shot perhaps, Paris for any sign of him there in the same decade. Would there be any Embassy records, for instance? The boulevadier of the portrait and the Montmatre photograph of the flirtatious Marie hinted at a playboy past the first flush of youth.

The Foreign and Commonwealth Office came up with nothing. There was no record of a Raymond Meynell on its files covering Africa or anywhere else. But that still did not rule out the possibility of an adventure and his eventual demise in the Dark Continent.

Robbie needed little excuse for a trip over the Channel, so he thought he would descend on his chum Caspar, who was living in Paris and see if there was any anything he could find about Marie. The Montmatre photographic studio and indeed the girl's attitude in the picture suggested a theatrical demi-monde - which matched the image he was starting to form of Uncle Raymond. He might draw a blank, but it was worth a shot.

Caspar, who had a French mother, was an art historian like Robbie and they had been contemporaries at Cambridge though in different colleges. Robbie had been a Magdalene man while Caspar had been at Jesus. Caspar was now working on behalf of a London dealer in the French capital, though Robbie had never formed a clear idea of exactly what he did. He had a flat overlooking the Seine with a fine view of Notre Dame and spoke French fluently. Cynical with an already world-weary manner, he was prepared to take on the French bureaucracy - in its own tongue, needless to say - whenever he felt it necessary. So as well as enjoying the pleasures of Paris in his agreeable company, Robbie thought that his friend might be able to open a few doors for him.

By now the idea of writing a book about Uncle Raymond was taking a firm hold. The more he thought about it, the more he liked the Sargent-Sickert dichotomy. It might provide a skeleton on which to flesh the tale he hoped to tell. But I mustn't get too carried away by it. I could be barking up completely the wrong tree, he warned himself.

Most of this he explained to his grandmother and she dipped generously into her own kitty to help the Paris visit along. It was something she had done ever since he was a small boy. Indeed she was becoming almost as caught up in the quest for Uncle Raymond as her grandson.

*****

'You've certainly landed on your feet here!' Robbie told Caspar as he admired the view across the Seine towards Notre Dame from his top floor flat on the Quai Henri IV.

His friend smiled and shrugged his shoulders. 'It's the silver spoon I was born with, and I don't feel the least bit guilty about it,' he said. 'Anyway, cheers!' He raised his glass.

Robbie of course had been absolutely open with him regarding his quest. Caspar was the last person to conceal anything like a family

271

scandal from, especially if it was eighty or more years old. In fact the more outrageous it was the better. His friend, too, was intrigued, by its art - historical angle: the possibility of Sargent being the painter of Uncle Raymond and the Sickertlike aspect of it as well. He knew all about Sickert's interest in dark themes, of murders committed in dingy rooms in London's drearier streets. Yes, he told Robbie, it would be an interesting idea to bundle them up together - if he could uncover enough about his relative to make it plausible.

But pursuing Uncle Raymond on the strength of one photograph of a girl with a very commonplace French Christian name like Marie was a tall order. Nevertheless Robbie felt that if anyone could open doors for him it might be his friend.

If the name Raymond Meynell had ever cropped up in French police records, Caspar was the one to find out. And the mysterious Marie, probably more elusive, like a woodland sprite, as well perhaps, though it might be like looking for a needle in a haystack.

In the meantime Robbie was going to enjoy himself. Paris in the spring was a good time to be there, before it got too crowded. He had a number of his own contacts, like a curator at the Quai d'Orsay, and revisiting old favourites in the different galleries was a pleasure that never cloyed. And to sit and daydream in a street cafe or bistro was bliss too. He liked to think that it was a good time to jot down a few ideas for his projected book; the barest outline, of course, but hopeful of what might emerge from his friend's research. His own imagination, he felt, might manage the rest, recreating, for instance, the kind of lodging house scenes that Sickett had suggested so vividly with his brush.

And Caspar soon came up with something, so that Robbie felt that his enterprise was blessed. It was from the police archives for the earlier part of the twentieth century: a register of missing persons for the city of Paris, a list of those who had never been traced which in most cases included a photograph. He had acted on a hunch: as Raymond Meynell had disappeared from the map so possibly the girl associated with him had too. But there she was: Marie Boulanger, a cabaret artist with an address in Montmatre. The picture of her in the police file was more brazen - there could be less doubt about the nature of her profession, but Robbie when he looked at the photocopy could still see a trace of that more subtle brand of coquetry that was apparent in the version secreted behind Uncle Raymond's portrait.

'You've been fantastically quick,' Robbie congratulated his friend. 'But little too quick for my liking. I was looking forward to spinning things out here for a bit longer.'

'You're welcome to stay for as long as you like,' Caspar assured him. 'It's no skin off my nose. You never know, there might still be more.'

But what more? The girl had vanished and never been found, which in her line was probably not such a rare thing. She was registered missing in 1926, so the possibility of a chance discovery of her remains was very unlikely. But if Uncle Raymond had tried to make a new life for himself in Africa, could she have played a part in his adventure?

It was good to have identified Marie Boulanger so quickly, but Robbie realised that the next step lay with his own kin and any light that could possibly be thrown on Raymond's movements during the mid nineteen-twenties.

The disappearance of the cabaret artist gave rise to some disagreeable speculation about the possible proclivities of Raymond Meynell: that he might have had murderous tendencies towards young women, for instance.

'A kind of Gilles de Rais,' suggested Caspar. 'except that in his case he preferred to kill children, not young women. If that's so it is not much wonder your family didn't want to talk about him.'

'Which slots in rather neatly with my Sickert theme,' mused Robbie, who was becoming more concerned about the shape of his book to come with each passing day.

Robbie understood that if the trail was not to go cold he would have to ferret around in his own family's records: among the contemporaries of Raymond, for instance, for the faintest trace of him, because he could hardly have vanished so completely that there was not the occasional reference to him, however oblique, apart from the ponderous sporting euphemisms like 'he was a bit of a goer'. Reluctantly he would have to leave his agreeable life in Paris and return to England, for the time being at least.

His great-grandfather, Sir Andrew's father, was a possible place to begin. He was, after all, the man's older brother, so could have arranged things for his tiresome sibling. And then there was his sister Adelaide.

Aunt Adelaide was an interesting possibility. She had never married and had spent a large part of her life abroad. A highly enterprising traveller in the Mary Kingsley tradition, she had reached the far North-West of Canada and even the Kamchatka peninsular on the extremity of Siberia. As well as that she had been a very competent painter - mostly of landscapes of the places she visited with some rather good studies of their native peoples. But for some reason, apart from being a copious letter writer and the author of the occasional article in a periodical she had never put any of her experiences into book form. Her last years had been spent living the life of a semi-recluse in Burgundy. There were even innuendoes made about her, not unlike the sort of things that so-called liberated intellectuals were inclined to say about the founder of the Boy Scouts Movement. She might well be worth a book in her own right too, Robbie reflected.

And she had been living in France, at the same sort of time as Raymond seems to have been on the loose there. That, surely, bore looking into. Most of her papers, were stashed away in a trunk in the attic at Raikswood, awaiting the attention of a biographer or historian. Robbie had riffled through them once, reading the occasional one here and there, but could recall no mention of her younger brother in anything he had looked at.

It was possible that any indiscretion on the subject had been purged by her other brother of course. But before chasing up Aunt Adelaide in France, where she had lived with a companion, Robbie needed to check out the material in the attic again.

Ancient trunks and suitcases, discarded pieces of furniture, mostly of a kind only suitable for servants' bedrooms, was the stuff of attics in houses like Raikswood. But with the summer before him, Robbie did not feel under any great pressure. He was enjoying his quest for uncle Raymond, despite it not having turned up and dramatic results so far. And when he was not ferreting among Aunt Adelaide's papers he went on elaborating the theme of his book about Uncle Raymond, some of which he discussed with his grandmother, though he left out his creepier speculations.

But in one of the trunks he found a second likeness of Raymond: a photograph of him as a subaltern in a local regiment of Yeomanry and his grandmother was able to confirm that he had served on the Western Front in the final battles of the Great War, in Haigh's push leading up to the Armistice of November 1918. So he had been a warrior and the picture of him in his uniform stood well beside the more rakish image of him as Paris boulevardier.

The rest of the trunk's contents were directly to do with Aunt Adelaide and her travels, as well as her later years living near Beaune in Burgundy. Apart from a few garments and some notebooks, there were letters she had written home to her family from different corners of the world and a number of curious objects collected at the same time. It struck Robbie as odd that the family should have considered them unfit for the light of day, but then, as he knew already, they had some pretty strange ideas about which of their possessions to condemn to obscurity.

For instance, there was a curious wooden object, painted in still-bright colours and seeming to represent a whale. It was clearly the work of one of the coastal tribes of North-West Canada, possibly the Kwakiutl or the Nootka, who were the carvers of the famous totem poles, though these days such artifacts are manufactured largely for tourists. Deeper inside the trunk Robbie came across pieces of wampum and what looked like a tobacco pipe, a calmulet. None of these things had been arranged in any kind of order or were labelled, but his grandmother made a home for them among her own things.

However Lady Portia could not say anything useful about Aunt Adelaide since she had only met her once, so it was on the letters that Robbie focused his attention.

He glanced at the postage stamps: some of them Canadian or French of the late nineteenth century, with the occasional Russian one as well. All the letters were addressed to Sir Cecil Maynell, Adelaide's brother. They were written in a loose, rather masculine hand, with something of an aristocratic nonchalance about it, as if to say a clear hand is for counting house clerks and other lesser mortals not for the likes of ourselves. Aunt Adelaide had never married and the photographs of her in the house showed firm, masculine features.

The letters addressed to her brother were perfunctory and appeared to have been written more from a sense of duty than anything

276

else. For one who wrote so vividly in her notebooks they were oddly stilted - rather like a child's Sunday offerings to parents from school. Robbie noted considerable time lapses between them which perhaps indicated a reluctance to get down to a disagreeable chore.

It seemed as if, like her younger brother, Aunt Adelaide was semi-detached from the rest of her family, who nevertheless looked on her with a certain pride because of her cleverness and eccentricity - an adventurous and creative lady of the late Victorian and Edwardian periods. It fitted their Whiggish ideals rather well. Raymond, on the other hand, had been virtually airbrushed from the record like an enemy of the people in Stalin's Russia, but for the survival of one wartime photograph and a small portrait of high quality.

Robbie as a matter of course showed his grandmother the letters, for whom they confirmed what she had been told about Aunt Adelaide: that she was a tough-minded lady from a time when women had to be very assertive if they were to be heard at all.

Yet Robbie felt that the key to Uncle Raymond lay somehow with his sister, Adelaide. He was a lot younger than her, very much an afterthought, a small boy when she was already a grown woman. Aunt Adelaide had settled in France, near Beaune, in the heart of the Burgundy country, which was an added incentive for pursuing the enquiry in France. Caspar, it went without saying, could be roped in to assist him.

Mention was made in a number of the letters of a French companion, called Brigitte, who was considerably younger than Adelaide. The nature of their relationship of course gave rise to some post-Freudian speculation on Robbie's part, though they did seem to have shared an interest in travel and the arts. One of the letters described a journey they had made together to Marrakesh. In this one Adelaide had let herself go more than in the others. She painted a vivid word picture of the Atlas Mountains, the Berber villages and the Marrakesh bazaars. It seemed almost a throwback to her youthful travels in her Edwardian heyday and Brigitte emerged in high relief- in particular her rapture at her exposure to the splendour and the havoc of the Muslim world for the first time. There was mention also of her twenty-fifth birthday, celebrated with a camel ride to a desert oasis.

Robbie had never been to Beaune before, but he had good reports of it. There was of course the Hospice with the famous Van de Weyden wall painting of the Last Judgement as well as all that wine, so Caspar's presence there was imperative. If we can pin Aunt Adelaide down and also get a lead on Uncle Raymond, the time will have been well spent, he decided.

Caspar, needless to say, made the time available.

'But first things first,' Robbie announced to him rather piously. 'We must make sure that the work is done before we succumb to the douceur de vivre.'

'We can run the two of them side by side, can't we?' his friend said. 'I manage it most of the time. I don't exactly spend my days in a state of eremitic austerity until my labours are completed.'

'All I'm saying is that we mustn't lose sight of the main purpose of our visit which is to address certain disturbing ambiguities with regard to former members of my family.'

Lady Portia would have liked to come along too. She had read about the Hospice at Beaune and had seen a television programme that featured it, but had never been there. Robbie told her that he would take her one day.

'Soft soap,' she retorted.

On reflection, however, he decided that a painting of the Last

Judgement was hardly the ideal thing to be showing a grandmother in her eighty-third year.

So the first week in July saw Robbie and his friend comfortably installed in a hotel, La Cloche, in the Place de la Madeleine in Beaune. The house where Aunt Adelaide had lived was not hard to locate: it was a modest-sized villa, built in the nineteenth century by the look of it, outside the city walls on the southwest side of the town. It stood in its own grounds with a handsome Mansard roof showing above the trees that curtained it. It was apart, but not too far, from the centre of things.

Robbie decided to take the bull by the horns and to approach its present occupants to see if they could tell him anything at all about their predecessors. And to the middle-aged couple now living in the house, Monsieur and Madame Aubigny, the name Brigitte did indeed mean something. A single lady, one Brigitte Dessalines, had lived there on her own since shortly before the Second World War until her death in 1970. It seemed that the house had been bequeathed to her by an elderly English lady, for whom she had acted as a sort of companion, but whose name they could not recall. There was one owner since then before the Aubignys took it over in 1985.

'And the English lady? Did she die here? ' Robbie asked.

Monsieur Aubigny said that he did not know the answer to that, but that the town cemetery might provide it if he knew her name.

Aunt Adelaide was there all right - in a neglected corner which few people seemed to visit. Her death was recorded as occurring in 1938 on her headstone with a further inscription written in French.

It meant a return to the Aubignys with a more delicate request that they might have a look at the house, because the Adelaide Meynell was indeed the person that Robbie had thought she was, namely a member of his own family. He even offered to show Monsieur Aubigny his passport to allay any suspicions he might have, but the Frenchman waved it aside.

Robbie cast an eye over the garden which had been prettily maintained in the French manner. There was a small parterre and a weeping willow with a backing of a well-trimmed box hedge and shrubs. The house itself had been furnished in a homely, unpretentious fashion without any claims to taste or style. It was the kind of furniture that looked as though it might have passed through three or four generations. Naturally Robbie and his friend looked over the pictures, but saw nothing that stood out until Robbie happened to notice a watercolour by the empty fireplace in the living room.

'Hullo?' he said. 'I think I can guess who painted that.'

The plaster frame was flaking and there were several foxing spots on the paper.

'Marrakesh I think.'

It was a view across the town towards the Atlas Mountains under a cloudless somewhat faded gouache sky.

The Aubignys had nothing to say about it except that that it appeared to have been overlooked by the previous owners or their executors and as they had liked it, they had brought it down from the upper reaches of the house where it appeared to have been forgotten. Robbie thought of his grandmother and the strange yet likely link with another picture that she had rescued from obscurity.

He was sorely tempted to make an offer for it then and there, but decided that it would be pushing the boat out too far at this stage. It was clearly Aunt Adelaide's work, similar to a pair of paintings of hers back at Raikswood. Nevertheless he did let drop that his friend was a dealer in fine art, a statement supported by Caspar in his perfectly accented French, implying that he was always on the look-out for anything interesting and was ready most of the time to negotiate a reasonable price for it.

Monsieur Aubigny merely shrugged and said that they had little of interest to a dealer in fine art.

'Mais non, Phillipe,' his wife cut in. There was one picture that was interesting, but of course she would never think of selling it.

Neither of her visitors said anything.

'La petite fille,' Madame Aubigny told her husband. 'Ma petite Parisienne.'

Yes, he conceded, there was her petite Parisienne. But of course selling it was out of the question. He knew how attached to it she was. It was another picture that had come to them with the house. Robbie and Caspar each marvelled that someone could have been so offhand in making the inventory of possessions in the house to have overlooked two such items.

But despite her unwillingness to part with the picture, Madame was happy to show it to them and if possible learn something about it. They might, for instance, know who painted it? She went up to her bedroom to fetch it. Robbie was not surprised by what he saw, yet highly gratified. It was one of a pair, the other member of which hung on his grandmother's wall at Raikswood. And it was indeed of Marie - the wanton little showgirl, as Lady Meynell had expressed it in her dated fashion. She appeared to be standing under the very same gaslight as Raymond, a fur muffler drawn up around her neck against the night air, and a smile hovering on her lips. It lacked the cheek of the photograph and could have been any young girl of the decade following the Great War, It occurred to Robbie that while Uncle Raymond struck a distinctly backward-looking, Edwardian note - due probably to his moustache - this girl seemed to be very much of her time.

'Jolie, n'est-ce pas?' Madame said.

'Enchanting,' declared Robbie while his friend gave a perfunctory nod without committing himself too rapidly, as behoved a serious art dealer.

Sargent had died in 1925, which looked about right for the time the picture had been painted, so if he was not the artist, who was? Someone pretty damned good, by any account. Of course the two pictures needed to be re-united, but that was not the immediate matter. What had become of their subjects and what part, if any, had Aunt Adelaide played in their fate? But for the time being at least Robbie decided to talk about the garden.

He rattled away in very passable French about gardens in general and the importance of figures like Le Notre in particular, observing that Madame Aubigny had laid out a parterre in his manner, its beds divided by neatly clipped box, Caspar chipped in to say that it reminded him of a Turkey rug - which of course was the idea, especially when viewed from an upper floor window. A spirited discussion ensued about the comparative merits of the French formal garden and the English informal one.

Beyond the parterre and behind the shrubbery, Madame revealed a small concession to a later, more romantic style of gardening. It was a grotto, but too small for a fully-grown adult to enter comfortably. Immediately Robbie was down on his hams looking inside. He peered closely at the pieces of quartz and water-worn limestone which made up the feature.

'Where is the hermit?' he asked. He stuck his head inside once more. 'Hullo? Anyone at home?'

On a flat stone in the middle of the space he noticed something which he removed and offered to Madame Aubigny.

'Here's your hermit,' he said. 'Or what remains of him.'

'Oui. The remains of our hermit,' she replied.

It was a human jawbone, complete with a perfect set of teeth. It had a delicacy which suggested a that it had belonged to a child or at least a young, probably female, adult.

'Has this always been here?' enquired Robbie.

Madame shrugged. 'Who can say? We found it there when we first came, but by then the grotto was grown over. We had to dig it out to restore it.'

'What do you make of it?' Robbie handed the jawbone to his friend.

I'm no anatomist,' said Caspar, 'but boy or girl? I'll go for a girl.'

Madame Aubigny took it back, stroked it tenderly and replaced it in the cave. There was something maternal, about the way she did it.

Monsieur Aubigny then produced a very good bottle of Burgundy from his cellar and they drank and chatted on the terrace. Robbie dilated on the subject of Aunt Adelaide - he even produced a photograph of her - and his intention of writing a book about his own family, which naturally had to include her, and asked if he might return just to look over the house, to establish the geography as he expressed it. Both of them also congratulated Monsieur on his wine - which was genuinely felt.

'Are you thinking what I'm thinking?' Robbie said to his friend as they strolled back into the middle of town.

'How do I know what you're thinking?' Caspar replied, 'But it's possible.'

'That jawbone. It probably belonged to a young female.'

'Very likely. They were nice teeth, weren't they? In perfect condition.'

'And then there's the picture - putting two and two together.'

'And Madame's affection for them both? Aren't we hastening on a bit?'

Robbie shrugged. 'Maybe we are.'

They settled in a cafe from which they could admire the Burgundian patterned rooftiles on the opposite side of the street.

'The jawbone possibly of a young girl turns up in an ornamental grotto in the garden of a house where a mysterious portrait of just such a creature still hangs on its walls and no one can explain the presence of either of them,' he mused after a pause during which he admired the steeply-pitched roof opposite.

'It's beginning to get Gothic, isn't it?' said his friend, no doubt feeling the affect of the fine old Burgundian ambience.

'I suppose the house has got a cellar,' said Robbie. 'A house like that is bound to have one.'

'Now we really are entering the realm of Edgar Allen Poe.'

Robbie said nothing more for a minute, but sipped his coffee.

'Do you know that old Neapolitan tradition?' he said.

'Which one? There must be plenty.'

'The one where they helped themselves to human skulls. Under the city there were crypts, or ossuaries, stuffed with human bones- generations of them and the people were in the habit of breaking through from the basements of their own houses and helping themselves to a skull-which became - how do I put it? - a kind of talisman, or a guardian spirit to bring the house good fortune. A weird idea, but there might have been the same kind of thing going on here.'

'And involving your great - however many greats - Aunt

Adelaide?'

Who knows?'

'A skull was sometimes kept as a kind of memento mori. You know all about that tradition in European art. Wasn't Dutch dead nature once supposed to be your thing?

'We can always ask a bit more about it - in the name of Art, of course. And have a look at the house at the same time.'

It sounded perfectly feasible and they were determined to pay the Aubignys a further visit. Aunt Adelaide was the ostensible reason, of course, but Caspar felt that they might put out a very tentative feeler about La Petite Parisienne at the same time. Especially, as he pointed out, the picture had come down to the Aubignys inadvertently and was likely to be the property once of Robbie's own forebears. Not that they should not offer a fair price for it, it went without saying. Flowers for Madame would be a good sweetener in the meantime, but they decided that to take her husband a bottle of wine would be like carrying coals to Newcastle.

Meanwhile they thought they would take a good look at Van de Weyden's great masterpiece on the wall of the Grande Salle des Malades in the Hospice - a memento mori if ever there was one. Both of them had seen illustrations of it plenty of times, so it held no surprises for them. But the scale of it and its naturalistic Flemish style gave it great dramatic impact, which they felt, especially in the depiction of the Damned being dragged down into Hell. There was nothing sentimental about the way death was confronted then. It was taken head-on. No comforting evasion, it was to be followed by further life, it went without saying, and if this worldly one had been misspent, it could mean damnation forever in the next, a stark reminder for the sick and aged who were approaching the end of their earthly span in

Christopher Arthur

full view of the painting. Robbie and his friend both preferred it to the muscular excess of Michelangelo's version in the Sistine Chapel.

And when they returned the next day Madame was delighted with her flowers and was happy to let them look over her house, flattered, if anything, that her home should feature in such a way. They only wanted a quick look and, of course, to see her pictures.

The survey was swift and uneventful. The rooms were not large, though several of them had rather interesting moulded ceilings in the Second Empire style. There were no pictures of interest apart from the watercolour of Marrakesh and Ma Petite Parisienne as Madame insisted on calling her.

'Is that everything?' said Robbie after a quick inspection of the roof space.

'Just my husband's cellar. Where he keeps his wine,' replied Madame. 'I think he is expecting to show you that himself.'

'I like the sound of that,' said Caspar.

They trooped down to the cellar where Monsieur Aubigny was waiting for them He went to work immediately, taking a dusty bottle down from one of the capacious racks, which lined three sides of the chamber.

It turned out not to be a wine tasting in the true sense, because the wine was swallowed and the bottles recorked. Robbie and Caspar liked it better this way, though they felt the need to be careful to keep their wits about them. It was Robbie's private opinion that there was a lot of bullshit talked about wine, though he was ready to concede his own ignorance of the subject and felt that it might simply be beyond the power of words to do justice to its subtlety.

While Monsieur launched into an account of the regional wines and poured out generous glassfuls, Caspar kept up a convincing show

286

of interest. In fact with his fluent French he did it splendidly well, managing to flatter their host with his apparent enthusiasm and expertise. Listening to him Robbie began to wonder if there might not be something in this wine guff after all.

Meanwhile he cast an eye round the cellar which was lit by a single naked bulb. The pointing in the brickwork was very even, except, he noticed, for where it retreated under one of the racks. Here the cement between the floor bricks was ragged, as if they had been taken up and relaid in rather a hurry. It seemed significant, but he felt in no position to ask Monsieur Aubigny about it. The man was well into his stride, discoursing on the subject of Burgundian vineyards in an increasingly rhetorical manner, but, like a good host, keeping his eye on the glasses of his guests at the same time. Caspar was nodding manfully and interjecting the occasional comment.

Whoever patched the floor was a bit clumsy about it, but was clearly confident of not getting caught.... the wine was getting to Robbie's tripes by now.

Monsieur Aubigny stopped to draw breath and to recharge the glasses.

'Tell me something, Monsieur,' Robbie blurted out. 'Is that where the body's buried?' He indicated the untidy cement line running under the rack with his toe.

For a second the man seemed bewildered, as if he had been put off his stroke, and Caspar frowned at his friend who smiled back at him archly.

'I'm thinking of the rest of it,' he said. 'The jawbone having turned up in the grotto.'

Monsieur laughed heartily. 'Who knows?' he chortled. 'You may be right. But it was long before our time! Ha! Ha!'

The others joined in the joke too.

It seemed the right moment to end the episode and to surface once more. Robbie and Caspar thanked Monsieur effusively both for the generous helpings from his truly excellent cellar and his highly informative talk on the subject.

Upstairs once more, Caspar wasted no time in asking Madame if he could come back again to examine her Petite Parisienne more closely. He assured her that she had an interesting picture and that for insurance purposes she should have a proper evaluation.

Like her husband in the cellar, she felt flattered by the interest shown in her picture by one who was so clearly an expert from Paris. Robbie could not avoid feeling how pleasantly provincial she seemed to be and liked her the better for it.

'You were pushing it a bit about the floor of the cellar, weren't you?' Caspar said to his friend as they returned to town. 'I'm not sure he entirely appreciated the quip about the body.'

'But it could be true,' Robbie insisted. 'Uncle Raymond's dark secret may lie beneath Monsieur Aubigny's wine racks - or the best part of it at least. The bit that isn't in the grotto.'

'Let's keep our minds on the picture - for the time being, shall we?'

'Aren't they the same thing?'

Back at La Cloche the wine seemed insipid after Monsieur Aubigny's offerings, so they launched into Cognacs instead.

*****

288

'Now for La Petite Parisienne,' Robbie declared as they finished their breakfast croissants. 'I must confess I find that name cheesy, but we won't labour the point. It's one of a pair, the other being a portrait of Uncle Raymond, painted by the same hand. But whose hand? That is the question. And what can we learn from it that brings us closer to uncovering the fate of the vanishing lovers?' It was a portentous speech for Robbie to be making at breakfast.

'Aunt Adelaide?

Robbie mumbled something in reply.

'She might have done them - in the manner of Sargent. By the look of her watercolour she was good enough.'

'We've got some of her other landscapes at home - which are in the manner of Edward Lear - if anybody.'

Then, over the crumbs of their croissants, the pair of them devised the procedure to be followed in the matter of examining Ma Petite Parisienne under the protective eye of Madame Aubigny.

By the time they arrived at the house the picture was propped up waiting for them against a book on the dining room table. Madame had put out a plate of biscuits as well and offered them coffee.

As the senior surgeon Caspar took control of the operation. He requested a sharp kitchen knife, assuring Madame that no harm would come to her Petite Parisienne and laid it beside his own pocket one. A pair of pliers was his next request. It was necessary, he said, to take the picture out of its frame, but all would be made good, he assured her.

Madame went to fetch the pliers from her husband's tool box, while Caspar whispered urgently to his friend.

'I'll give you the wink when I'm ready.'

Robbie nodded.

'Ten seconds should be enough.'

When Madame returned with the pliers she found Caspar already probing the back of the picture with the kitchen knife.

To Robbie's eye the mounting looked the same as the one on the picture at Raikswood.

'Merci, Madame,' Caspar said as he took the pliers and began to address one of the tacks that held the back panel in place.

Madame Aubigny watched him intently as he worked, more from curiosity mingled with concern for her Petite Parisienne than any suspicion of his motive. He took his time, not only out of consideration for the work of art in his hands, but the longer he took the more likely she was to get bored.

Robbie sat opposite, making the occasional inconsequential remark in English, waiting for the signal from his friend.

Caspar paused in his work. All the tacks had been loosened, but were still in place. It was only a question of tweaking them out with the pliers. He glanced across at Robbie and dropped his right eyelid.

'Maintenant, Madame,' Robbie declared. 'Before I forget there is something I need you to explain to me.' He took a tourist map of central France out of his pocket. 'These famous Pälaeolithic caves I want to see very much - how would I get to this place from Beaune, for instance?' He pointed to Lascaux on the map, the site of the most famous prehistoric painted caves in France.

Madame Aubigny turned to look at the map and began a detailed explanation of how to get to Lascaux saying, first of all, that it was better to go by car, but that it was also possible by a combination of train and bus. It started to get complicated and all the time Robbie nodded and probed her with supplementary questions, without giving his friend a glance.

'See, Madame,' Caspar announced at length. 'Your picture outside its frame.' He presented her with the little wooden panel bearing the portrait of Ma Petite Parisienne, giving Robbie a long hard look and a rapid nod.

It was then a matter of going through the business of inspecting the picture outside its frame with his pocket magnifying glass and then returning it to its original state. All of which he carried out plausibly without getting carried away by his own virtuoso performance.

'The identity of the painter is still a mystery, Madame,' he said with a light sigh. 'It could be the English lady, Madame Meynell, or her friend Brigitte or even your Petite Parisienne herself - but the last seems unlikely. It may even by the hand of a well known portrait painter of that time - I will need to take a photograph. Demain?'

Of course, there was no problem. Madame Aubigny was clearly enjoying the protracted ritual.

Caspar said nothing to his friend until they were back in the street.

'My hunch was correct, but of course we still have to inspect the goods. Let's have a drink first, shall we?'

They settled at a table at what had become their regular watering hole in the Place Madeleine where Caspar fished inside his coat pocket. He produced an ancient and very yellow envelope.

Back at the hotel, behind a locked door with whiskies from the mini-bar, they set to work. Robbie slit open the envelope with his friend's pocket knife. It contained something that he half-expected: a photograph of Raymond mounted in the same manner as the one of Marie and, also like its counterpart, bearing the briefest of messages: pour mon amoure, Marie - Raymond. And that was all: laconically businesslike.

But in the envelope Robbie found another piece of paper which he had nearly missed. It was so brittle that he was afraid that it might come apart as he unfolded it. This time it was the title page torn from a book in English. It was the classic tale of an English gentleman's adventures in the French Foreign Legion, Beau Geste by P.C.Wren and published in 1924, just a year, before the photograph of Marie had been taken in the Montmatre studio.

He handed it to Caspar. 'It's not hard to guess. I think that just about wraps up Uncle Raymond, don't you? After all, the Legion didn't have to know a man's real name to take him on. But I'd still like to know who painted these bloody pictures.'